DASHIELL HAMMETT
and the
HEARST CASTLE MYSTERY

by Gregory Urbach

Dedicated to my mother,

Betty Nell Olson

Who may not have read detective stories,
but she loved trashy novels

Gregory Urbach

© 2020 All Rights Reserved

ISBN 978-0-9907294-6-4

Table of Contents

Acknowledgments
Matthew Bernstein, story editor
Cover by Kwei-lin Lum

Exhibits
The Maltese Falcon, Pocket Books Inc., 1944
Real Photo Postcard, Hearst Castle circa 1930, no attribution
Florsheim Shoes advertising blotter card circa 1930
Godfrey Phillips LTD 1934, Screen Stars #19 William Powell
Gallaher Ltd 1934 Famous Films #10 Tarzan and His Mate
Rothman's Pall Mall 1925, Cinema Stars #23 Marion Davies
Secret Agent X-9, David McKay Co., King Features, 1934
Four of Hearts by Ellery Queen, Pocket Books, 1943
Gallaher 1934 Famous Films #36 Barretts of Wimpole Street

References
The Builders Behind the Castles by Taylor Coffman, San Obispo Historical Society, 1990
Building for Hearst and Morgan by Taylor Coffman, Berkeley, 2003
Castle Cookbook by Collord & Miller Lopez, Central Coast, 2008
The Chief by David Nasaw, Mariner Books, 2000
Dashiell Hammett: A Life by Diane Johnson, Random House, 1983
The Golden Days of San Simeon by Ken Murray, Doubleday, 1971
Hammett: A Life on the Edge by William Nolan, Congdon, 1983
Hearst Castle: The Biography of a Country House by Victoria Kastner, Abrams, 2000
"The Pig" by Dashiell Hammett, Collier's, March 24, 1934
Shadow Man: The Life of Dashiell Hammett by Richard Layman, Harcourt, 1981
The Thin Man by Dashiell Hammett, Vintage Books, 1989
The Times We Had: Life with William Randolph Hearst by Marion Davies, Ballantine, 1975

"Oh that. We didn't exactly believe your story, Miss O'Shaughnessy. We believed your two hundred dollars."

Sam Spade
The Maltese Falcon

Chapter One

MIDNIGHT AT THE COCOANUT GROVE

The drunken brawl started just after midnight. I had come down from San Francisco to find work, so I wasn't looking for trouble as the Cocoanut Grove hurriedly emptied of movie stars, politicians, showgirls and gangsters. Some fled for their limousines. Others tried to find cabs. A few enterprising patrons had reserved rooms in the hotel. Before Prohibition had ended, they would have been afraid of the cops. Now they were afraid of the press.

But not me. As a mystery writer, I had the reputation of a crime solver, not a brawler. My latest book had just been turned into a movie, my articles were appearing in magazines, and I was a regular presence on the lot at Metro-Goldwyn-Mayer. William Randolph Hearst had even hired me to write a cartoon strip for his newspapers. Life was looking good for Dashiell Hammett—until that fateful weekend.

I don't know what started the fight. The Ambassador Hotel was usually quiet on Thursday nights. Gus Arnheim and his orchestra had been onstage playing when Bebe Daniels got up to reprise her song "You're Getting To Be A Habit With Me" from *42nd Street.* The waiters served colorful cocktails. The cloakroom girls stayed busy, for it was a cold April night. And then there was shouting from somewhere beyond the dance floor. Fists started flying. People began running. A Chinese lantern sailed across the room, followed by a champagne bottle. Several unfortunates with bloody noses were laid out on the floor.

I remained at the bar, choosing to mind my own business.

"Hell of a night, ain't it, Dash?" Maisie Walker said, sliding onto the tall leather stool next to me.

A busty brunette in her early forties, she liked the low-cut lavender gowns that had become popular among the Hollywood crowd. The silky dress was set off by a string of pearls, presumably fake, and a black slouch hat that nearly covered her dark brown eyes. She spoke with a husky New Orleans accent despite growing up in Cincinnati.

"Did you start the fight?" I casually asked, sipping my Manhattan.

"Not this time, lover," Maisie said with a charming laugh. She'd been drinking a little too much, which was nothing new. For either of us. "You can't stay over tonight. Expecting company. A real sugar daddy."

"Thanks just the same. Need to drive up the coast in the morning."

"Any place special?"

"I've heard it called Hearst's Castle."

"Some kind of palace, isn't it?"

"Yeah, a regular Shangri-La."

She glanced around the room, seeing only chaos.

"Last night was great," she whispered.

"Worth the trip," I agreed.

The brawl seemed to subside for a moment, and then a loud drunk decided to cause more havoc. It was just a matter of time until the cops showed up.

"Got to scoot. Don't want to end my night in the clink," Maisie apologized.

She gave me a quick peck on the cheek and ducked out through the kitchen, shaking her hips just enough to keep my attention.

Maisie didn't leave a moment too soon. I'd hardly taken a deep breath when the police broke in, swinging batons at anyone offering resistance. When the bartender wasn't looking, I snatched an unattended martini, adding an extra olive. Despite making more money than I could imagine, my pockets were always empty.

"Hey, Dash. Hanging out with Sam Spade?" a burly cop asked.

It was Carl Putnam, one of many officers who moonlighted as studio guards at MGM. We had shared a few beers together.

"Left him in San Francisco, Curly. Still looking for the black bird," I replied, stirring my stolen drink.

"I'm sure he doesn't mind a reasonable about of trouble," Carl said, paraphrasing a line from *The Maltese Falcon.* He shook my hand and moved on.

While the cops were rousting the miscreants and waitresses were tending to the wounded, a slimy character slipped onto the stool next to me. He had a furtive look in his beady eyes and a nervous twitch to his bony hands. He was dressed well, but not well enough by the Grove's classy standards. Even I, in my double-breasted tweed suit, was barely passing muster.

"Long time, Mr. Hammett," Skinny the Rat Hamilton said.

3

"Not long enough, Skinny. What do you need?"

We were old acquaintances from New York, down in the Bowery, where late-night pool and all-night poker had been my favorite pastimes. Skinny's reputation as a snitch caused him to move west.

"Got myself in a tight spot," he whispered.

Skinny put a dirty handkerchief on the bar and gently folded it open. Inside was a diamond necklace worthy of a duchess. If it was the real thing, which I doubted. Probably pilfered from a studio prop room.

"Where'd you steal it?" I asked.

"Didn't exactly steal it, but it's plenty hot."

"How so?"

"Belongs to a friend. She wanted me to hock it, but her boyfriend got wind that something was up, so she took it on the lam. Now he's looking for this, and he thinks I've got it."

"You *do* have it."

"But it ain't mine. Belongs to Rachael Macao. She's a stand-up gal. Pretty, too. Scrambles eggs down at Canter's on Fairfax. Rachel will need this when she gets back."

"How is this my problem?"

Skinny looked around as if sensing danger, and suddenly he was gone, the handkerchief still lying on the bar. I counted four white sparkling stones in what appeared to be a platinum setting, highlighted by a blue gemstone in the center. Even if it was just costume jewelry, the necklace could still be worth fifty bucks.

I slipped the bundle into my pocket and considered paying my tab. Breaking glass caught my attention. A table near the dance floor had been overturned, and underneath was an old friend.

Though reluctant to get involved, I really had no choice. A loud bully was shouting something while waving a chair. He was tall, better than six feet, but sloppily attired. His red cheeks were flushed, the tattered jacket unbuttoned, and he had a big belly hanging out over his belt. Not exactly Jack Dempsey. I strolled over, tapped the fellow on the shoulder, and gave him a quick right jab to the schnoz, hoping the cops wouldn't notice. The lout folded like a house of cards, crawling off into the mayhem.

"Bill, you okay?" I asked, helping Bill Powell to his feet.

"Dash?"

"Yeah. What are you doing in a bar fight?"

"I wasn't fighting anybody. Some idiot wanted a refund for my last movie."

"The Kennel Murder Case?"

"How did you guess?"

"It was a dog."

I led Bill back to the bar, stealing an abandoned martini for him. The cops were finally chasing out the riffraff, letting the band come back on stage.

"Good to see you again," Bill said, reaching to shake hands. "You disappeared after leaving Paramount."

Forty-two years old, tall and slender, with thinning black hair and dark eyes, the handsome movie star hardly needed an introduction. I noticed that, like myself, he was wearing a three-piece Brooks Brothers suit.

"Saw you on the lot once after Ladies Man, but you were busy," I said. "Glad you volunteered to make The Thin Man."

"Didn't volunteer. Got assigned by Mayer. The story makes no sense, but Myrna and I had a great time on the set."

"Wasn't my best book."

"I hear you're heading up to Hearst's Ranch tomorrow."

"A last-minute invitation," I confessed.

"I'm heading up that way, too."

"Is Miss Harlow coming with you?"

"No, Jean's shooting a film with Gable. It's okay. Sometimes the guys just want to let loose."

"I hear Hearst doesn't allow drinking on his mountain."

"That's not exactly true. Is this your first time?"

"My first adventure since returning from Florida. Hearst hired me to write a cartoon strip for his newspapers."

"Watch out for the old crook. He didn't become the richest man in America through his generosity."

"Hearst isn't the richest man in America," I disagreed, finding the subject of such fabulous wealth filled with objectionable connotations. But I generally sought to suppress my socialist leanings when on the West Coast.

"With all the newspapers and magazines he owns, he may as well be. Even the movie studios won't cross him."

"I'm just looking for writing assignments, not take down his empire."

"Mr. Hearst will appreciate that," Bill said, offering a toast. "How about we ride up together? Where are you staying?"

"The Roosevelt."

"I'll be out front at eight."

"Let's make it ten," I said.

Bill took off, and I decided it was time to leave. The bartender still hadn't returned, so I put two bucks on the bar and headed for the door, ignoring the aftermath of the evening's turmoil. Just as I handed my ticket to the hatcheck girl to retrieve my overcoat, another old acquaintance strolled in. Watching his back was a brutish bodyguard the size of a grand piano wearing a gray trench coat. But the man he was guarding attracted the real attention.

"Dash, what brings you here?" Bugsy Siegel said, reaching to shake hands. Though those who called him Bugsy to his face were looking for a beating.

Benjamin Bugsy Siegel was a young man, not yet thirty, just under six feet tall, with broad shoulders and piercing blue eyes. Known to be a Jewish member of the New York mob, he rarely seemed to get arrested. And despite his reputation as a gangland enforcer, Bugsy could be charming. We both enjoyed Broadway shows and the pastrami at Katz's Delicatessen.

"Hello, Benny. Script doctoring for MGM," I replied. "How about you?"

"Have some business to settle," Bugsy said. "Is your bookie treating you right? Getting a fair shake?"

"No complaints so far."

"Let me know next time you're out at the track. I may have a horse for you."

"Happy to buy you a drink at the clubhouse when I do," I replied, shaking his hand again to take my leave.

"Oh, have you seen Skinny the Rat tonight?" Bugsy off-handedly asked.

"He was at the bar a few minutes ago. Rushed off in a hurry."

Bugsy motioned to his muscle, who hustled toward the back door.

"Thanks, Dash. Maybe you can give me a tour of the studio," Bugsy said. "I've always been interested in Hollywood."

"Let me know. I'll get you a screen test," I said with a grin.

William Powell

Chapter Two

THE PALACE

Hardly twelve hours later I stepped out of Bill's midnight blue Chrysler Imperial, staring up at a tall brown mountain with a Spanish cathedral perched on its crest. Behind me was the Pacific Ocean. The gray sky was streaked with scattered clouds. It was my first visit to La Cuesta Encantada. The Enchanted Hill. Hollywood's most cherished destination.

It was a pleasant Friday afternoon. We found a dozen cars parked in the dirt field at the foot of a winding tar-covered road. Two were as fancy as Bill's. Three were reasonably fashionable. The rest were old V-8 Fords still painted in their original black. Probably owned by employees. It was clear the main road to the great house was being repaired, a dirty flatbed truck with two workers visible near one of the sharp turns.

"Sorry for the inconvenience, Mr. Hammett. My name is Tom. I be helpin' you. No cars up the hill today," an old black Joe said, rushing to take my leather overnight bag.

"Don't need to call me sir, Grandpa," I replied. "I'm nothing but another studio hack looking for new place to get drunk."

"Mr. Hearst don't allow no drunkenness at San Simeon, sur. Hardly no drinkin' at all," the butler warned. He was well-dressed in a dark purple jacket and string tie, the fabric covered in a light coat of dust.

"I won't be asking his permission," I said in the Baltimore accent of my youth.

"Hello, Tom. Good to see you again," Bill said, stepping forward to shake the butler's hand.

"You, too, Mister Powell. You always a welcome sight," Tom said. "We got you all a lift."

The yellow tram transporting us up the hill looked like something left over from the Chicago World's Fair. The passenger section was covered by gray canvas and loosely attached to a cab with small wheels. The contraption bounced back and forth, tossed the luggage up and down, and in every way sought to put on a show. Though the gravel road was disturbingly narrow in places, I gave it little thought, accustomed to the treacherous trolleys of San Francisco. Bill was not so complacent, gripping the handrail.

The pastures and gullies surrounding Hearst's mansion were not empty. I noticed herds of elk, buffalo, and even zebra. The Hearst zoo was legendary, though it was not visible from this side of the hill. I assumed it had cages, doubting lions and tigers would be allowed to stalk the hills slaughtering the cattle of local ranchers.

After a lengthy ride, we came around a steep bend to see the great house, a tall white stone edifice complete with twin bell towers and enough surrounding bungalows to fill a Mediterranean village. Said to be built during World War I on an old family campground, the castle had attracted the world's elite for the last fourteen years, including Charlie Chaplin, Charles Lindbergh, the Marx Brothers and Calvin Coolidge. And now Dashiell Hammett.

We stepped off the tram at the foot of several steep stone staircases. It led up to a large plaza, the main doors of the mansion to the right, several cottages to the left. Before me was some sort of ancient Egyptian statue, at least 3,000 years old, carved from black rock.

"That's the Goddess of Sekhmet, Mr. Hammett," Tom explained. "She was the daughter of Ra. He was an Egyptian sun-god."

"She looks bloodthirsty," I said.

"Rumor has it that's true, sur," Tom agreed.

Tom showed us around a little. The plaza was filled with a variety trees and flower gardens, marble benches, and cleverly designed tiled walls. Beyond the plaza, down the other side of the hill, was a pool worthy of Caligula, with ornate Greek columns and flowing water fountains. As Tom carried our bags, a young black maid rushed to help. I looked at my gold pocket watch.

"After lunchtime," I said to Bill, who took the hint.

"Nice to get a sandwich. Or maybe a steak," Bill said.

"No problem, sur. No problem at all," Tom said, bending forward with his head down.

"Do we have our own hotel, or do we sleep in Norte Dame?" I asked, ignoring the feigned groveling. My years as an investigator had taught me to see through such shams.

"Oh, no. Yous gots good rooms. Real good rooms. Rights over here in Casa del Sol," Tom said, leading us to a string of giant bungalows perched on the edge of the hill. "Not many folks here at the moment. We gettin' ready for Mr. Hearst's birthday at the end of the month."

Accessed through a garden, the middle of the three guest houses was large, probably holding half a dozen bedrooms. The lobby featured fancy vases and oil paintings.

It may as well have been a hotel. Our rooms were on the main floor, joined to a massive sitting room with a view of the ocean. Fireplaces would keep the rooms warm. There were painted wooden statues, most of them religious, and all sorts of European art works. The furniture looked hundreds of years old. There was no bar. I followed Tom to the right, finding a nice room with a view of the pool. Tom set my bag on the quilt-covered bed.

"Who lives downstairs," I asked. "The servants?"

"Ain't no servants here, Mr. Hammett. They is staff. Mr. Hearst is very particular about that. Best be on your good manners."

"I respect working people, sir. Why is the hotel so quiet?"

"Not many up 'ere this weekend," Tom said, showing me the closet and bath. The fixtures were brass and polished.

"Shower gots plenty a hot water. If you wants a bath, we kin gets you a room over in Casa del Mar," Tom offered.

"That won't be necessary. The shower is fine," I said, reaching into my pocket.

"Oh no, sur. No tippin' here. Mr. Hearst don't permit it," Tom protested. He was adamant, so I relented. Which was just as well. I didn't have much change.

After Tom left, I took a seat at the old wooden desk. *This sure is fancy*, I thought. Clean, wood-paneled, and giving the feel of a forest retreat. Except for the van Dyck hanging on the wall.

I dug into the leather overnight bag for my cigarettes and turned

11

back toward the main house, for I'd not eaten since the night before at Musso & Franks. Well before the party at the Cocoanut Grove began. I still remembered some studio flunky saying I should write another Sam Spade book, but gave the idea no mind. I had long since grown weary of detective stories and wanted to branch out.

"Dash, over here," Bill called out from the marble steps. He had changed into swimming trunks and a colorful short-sleeved shirt. Someone had found him a straw hat.

A few quick steps brought me to a balcony high above the crystal blue pool. Folding deck chairs looked fresh off the *Titanic*. Two beautiful young women were sitting at poolside. One I recognized instantly. It was Maureen O'Sullivan, who played Jane to Johnny Weissmuller's Tarzan. Their most recent film, *Tarzan and His Mate*, was rumored to be so daring that the Hays Office was looking for ways to censor it. The other beauty was not familiar, but still quite handsome.

We ran down the winding stairs, passing nymphs and Greek goddesses. Mountains and beaches could be seen in the distance.

"Dash, this is Maureen and Alice. You've seen Maureen's pictures. Alice works at Cosmopolitan where Marion's films are made," Bill explained. "Ladies, this is Dashiell Hammett, the foremost mystery writer in America."

I offered my most gallant nod, tipping my new fedora and then casting it aside. The ladies laughed. I found O'Sullivan, at age twenty-three, particularly striking. Born in Ireland, with short curly hair and high cheekbones, she'd had a series of supporting roles until Irving Thalberg cast her as Jane two years before.

Young Alice Fowler was a head turner, too. I guessed her at twenty-five, with long auburn hair, a lithe figure, and the gleam of a college education in her vivid green eyes. Alice's black one-piece swimming suit hugged her in all the right places.

"Hello, Mr. Hammett. I loved your last book," Alice said, climbing out of the water to greet me. I resisted a temptation to whistle.

"It's an honor to meet you both," I replied, kissing her hand.

"Maureen is in The Thin Man movie with Myrna and I," Bill explained. "Good actress. Better than those trashy jungle movies."

"Speaking of which," I said, seeing a new guest arrive.

Though wearing a brown suit instead of a loin cloth, it was easy to recognize Johnny Weissmuller. At 6'3" and 190 pounds, the thirty-year-old Olympic swimming champion looked like a giant.

"Hi, Bill. Who's your friend?" Johnny asked, reaching to shake my hand.

"Dash Hammett, the writer," Bill introduced.

Weissmuller had a grip like a truck driver, though I was no slouch. We both grinned.

"What brings you out of the jungle?" Bill asked.

"Just up for the weekend. Lupe's a little out of control again," Johnny explained.

I had heard stories of Weissmuller's tempestuous third nuptial, though my own broken marriage was no model.

"Who else are we expecting?" Johnny asked, stripping down to his swimming trunks in front of the ladies.

"I heard a rumor that Norma and Irving might be driving up," Bill said. "Maybe we can all get parts in The Barretts of Wimpole Street?"

Bill meant it as a joke, thinking little of a bi-op about a couple of 19th century English poets.

"I've been cast as Henrietta," Maureen said. "Katharine Cornell may play Elizabeth Barrett. Maybe Bill can play Robert Browning?"

"Miss Davies would be so much better as Elizabeth. I know Mr. Hearst wants her to do it," Alice said.

"It's Irving's film. MGM, not Cosmopolitan," Bill pointed out. "Any chance Irving might pick Norma for the role?"

"Marion's done lots of costume dramas. All Norma plays are ingénues," Alice protested.

"Norma has won an Academy Award," Bill said.

"That doesn't mean anything," Alice pouted. "What do you think, Dash?"

"I think they're both great," I answered.

One of the maids led me up to a nearby dressing room. Hearst provided everything a guest would need, but I decided to remain clothed, taking only a comfortable shirt with a pocket for my cigarettes. Almost forty now, I spent little time in the sun and rarely exercised. Appearing at the pool in a swimsuit next to Johnny Weissmuller would only be embarrassing.

I was eating a roast beef sandwich in a wicker chair under a red umbrella when Miss Marion Davies came down from the big house. Thirty-seven years old, 5'5", blonde-haired and blue-eyed, Marion had starred on Broadway, appeared in the *Ziegfeld Follies*, and made silent movies. Now she was the leading actress of Cosmopolitan Pictures. Her acting in historical epics was often criticized by everyone except the Hearst newspapers, but her comedic performances were delightful. Sadly, Marion's career was overshadowed by her role as Hearst's longtime mistress, one of Hollywood's worst kept secrets.

"How is everyone? Thank you so much for coming on such short notice," Marion said, greeting each guest with a hug.

"We noticed there was no train," Bill said.

I had heard that most visits to estate followed a well-established pattern. A train would pick up guests at Glendale Station north of Los Angeles on a Friday, arriving in San Luis Obispo. From there, a fleet of limousines ferried guests up to The Ranch. Festivities lasted through the weekend, and for some, even longer. Our small group had arrived separately, drifting in on a Friday morning in our own cars. It was a curious change of pace.

"This is more of a business gathering," Marion explained. "Pops wants to discuss another Thin Man movie with Bill. And he needs to speak with Mr. Hammett about writing the script."

I liked that. Living high off the hog between New York City, Los Angeles, and my cottage in Florida was expensive. I was tired of ducking out on my hotel bills.

"How about Johnny and me?" Maureen asked, her Irish accent delightful.

"Everyone is talking about your new movie," Marion said. "I was wondering. May I take photos of you in the zoo? In costume? Tarzan and Jane at San Simeon would generate wonderful publicity. In exchange, Cosmopolitan will donate ticket sales from your premiere to the children's clinic."

"Had to mention the kids, didn't you?" Johnny said.

"I knew you wouldn't let them down," Marion replied with a mischievous smile.

Maureen and Johnny traded a quick glance. *Tarzan and His Mate* was their second team-up, and more were sure to follow. Their on-screen chemistry was amazing, though I didn't sense anything romantic between them off-screen.

"Of course we'll do it," Maureen agreed, poking Johnny in the ribs with her elbow.

"Photos only. I'm not going to fight your lions," Johnny said.

"How about a rhinoceros?" Marion teased.

"You have a rhinoceros?" I asked.

"No, Mr. Hammett," Marion said. "But we can get one."

Johnny took the joke well. *Photoplay* had shown pictures of Tarzan riding a rhinoceros, mentioning that Johnny had declined to use a stuntman.

Marion waved to me. We left the pool area, climbing up the stairs to the wide courtyard in front of the towering mansion. Mexican gardeners were sweeping the grounds, trimming trees, and I noticed several ancient Greek sarcophagi being used as planters. Hearst was known to gather such treasures from all over Europe.

"Pops wants to meet with you later, Mr. Hammett," Marion said, taking a seat on a marble bench.

"Call me Dash," I said, sitting next to her.

"Our producers at Cosmopolitan think The Thin Man is going to be very successful, and King Features has high hopes for Secret Agent X-9. Pops is wondering if you're happy with the work?"

"I think the cartoon will give Dick Tracy a run for his money," I said, for that was why Hearst's syndicate recruited me. "And I have an idea for another Nick and Nora adventure."

"With more scandalous dialogue?"

"It's what the public wants. Even if Redbook did censor my first version."

Marion paused to look me over. She seemed well-informed, and I wondered if she knew I was having trouble meeting my deadlines. As much as I needed the money, sometimes drinking got in the way.

"Marion, I'm very pleased to be at Mr. Hearst's beck and call. Doctoring scripts for the studio suits me just fine."

"Be sure to tell him that," Marion said, giving me a look under bent brows. Her deep blue eyes were lovely. Her warning well-meant. And appreciated.

Alice came up from the pool wrapped in a white cotton robe, her long hair shimmering in the afternoon sunlight. Marion jumped up, whispered in her ear, and they disappeared into the smaller cottage. Bill joined me a moment later.

"Staying out of trouble?" Bill asked.

"Not sure," I said.

Dinner was scheduled for eight o'clock. Half an hour before, Bill, Maureen, Johnny and I gathered before the huge oak doors of Casa Grande where the two bell towers rose four or five stories. The evening was cool. We smoked cigarettes and swapped backstage stories from MGM. A gangster film Bill had made earlier in the year with Myrna Loy and Clark Gable, *Manhattan Melodrama*, was due to be released in May. Having finished playing Dorothy Wynant in *The Thin Man*, Maureen was about to star in *Hide-Out* with Robert Montgomery. Johnny was hoping to branch out from Tarzan but wasn't getting much encouragement.

The doors opened. Formally dressed in a tailed jacket with a high collar, Tom greeted us with a gracious bow. The main hall of the cathedral was gigantic, bigger than the lobby at the Waldorf. Filled with 17th century Dutch tapestries, paintings by old masters, Spanish Missionary furniture, and Persian carpets, it was a museum curator's dream and an interior decorator's nightmare.

"Cocktails?" Tom asked.

He didn't need to ask twice. I ordered a double Manhattan.

"Enjoy it," Bill said. "You only get one."

"One what?"

"One drink."

"You're kidding?"

He wasn't.

Bill and Johnny settled for Scotch on the rocks. Maureen tried a mint julip. A few minutes later, Marion and Alice arrived, smartly outfitted from shops on Rodeo Drive. Their make-up was subdued, maintaining a sense of informality. Marion gave a tour of the exhibits like she had done a thousand times. Bill had been there before, but Maureen, Johnny and I were new. The ancient curiosities reminded me of the Metropolitan Museum of Art.

Just before the clock struck eight, a secret door in the wall opened and William Randolph Hearst burst into the room like a thunderstorm. Having only seen him in newsreels, I was surprised how large he was. At 6'3", he was the same height as Weissmuller, with a broad chest, huge hands at the ends of long arms, a puffy face, and thinning snow-white hair. In three weeks, he would be seventy-one years old but seemed younger. Hearst wasn't just wealthy beyond belief. He had been a congressman, run for governor of New York, run for president, and owned the biggest newspaper chain in the world.

"Welcome, welcome," Hearst said, shaking hands with the men and hugging Maureen. His voice was slightly high-pitched, but not squeaky. "Sorry it's so quiet this weekend. Big plans coming up. Always big plans. Glad you could join us."

Then the Chief gave another tour of his treasures, more animated than Marion had been, sharing stories on where the artifacts had been acquired, the bargains he had found, and hinting that this collection only scratched the surface. Apparently, there were still entire warehouses waiting to be uncrated. I felt sorry for the hapless Europeans whose countries had become a rich man's bazaar.

It was close to dinner time when we had last-minute arrivals.

"Ladies and gentlemen, Mr. and Mrs. Irving Thalberg," Tom announced from the door.

I had seen Thalberg on the backlot several times. Only thirty-five, he was known as The Boy Wonder, having made MGM Hollywood's most successful studio. He was tall, nearly six feet, with black hair and a pale complexion. Heart trouble had made him thin, and he wasn't looking good now, using an ivory-handled cane for balance.

With Thalberg was his famous wife, Norma Shearer. She was in her early thirties, sleek and beautiful, though tiny. Hardly more than five feet tall, and weighing about a hundred pounds. Nevertheless, Norma's fine bone structure, piercing dark eyes, and spicy spunk had earned her three Oscar nominations and one gold statue.

There was an immediate tension as the Thalbergs entered. Hearst began to frown before catching himself. Marion looked embarrassed, nervously smoothing down her black velvet skirt. Bill Powell grinned like there was going to be a fight. I'd heard that Norma and Marion had been in competition for several parts but hadn't realized it was growing personal.

Another presence soon caused frowns all around. Following Thalberg into the room was Ambrose "Sharkey" McCann, a notorious fixer with a reputation for fast dealing. Rumor had it that Hearst wanted Marion to play Elizabeth Browning in the upcoming *Wimpole Street* movie, but Thalberg wanted Katharine Cornell, who had created the role on Broadway. McCann had just been to New York, apparently on a recruiting mission.

Not only did Hearst choose to ignore McCann, but Weissmuller did, too. I didn't know what the disagreement was. Bill was maliciously grinning again. If Maureen had a reaction, she didn't show it. Only Marion went forward, being the good hostess, offering McCann a cocktail. At 5'8", rather slender with a dark complexion, he did not cut a dynamic figure. There was something about the steel blue eyes, a craftiness that was unlikely to win him friends.

"Dinner is served," Tom said, opening a door into the interior.

Hearst led the way into a cavernous dining room filled with even

19

more tapestries, hanging banners, and old furniture. The wood ceiling towered above us. A long narrow table had twenty chairs, though we would only be using ten of them. More chairs lined the walls, looking like stalls pillaged from a medieval church. I noticed a slightly musty smell.

The Thalbergs took seats across from Hearst and Marion in the middle. Maureen sat to Marion's right, and Alice next to her. Johnny sat to Hearst's left. Bill had the seat next to Norma, me next to Bill, and Sharkey next to Thalberg. Having been placed at the end, Hearst made it clear where I stood in the pecking order.

"I've ordered something special for our new guests," Hearst said, standing for attention and clapping his hands. The sound echoed throughout the great hall.

"Anna Lee, we are ready," Hearst called out.

The Negro maid I'd seen earlier entered and placed a large bowl of bananas in front of Johnny. The Jungle Man took a look and snarled. Hearst roared with laughter and waved the bowl away.

We started with red caviar canapés and butterflake rolls, followed by a shrimp salad. The aroma was wonderful. The main meal consisted of oyster pepper roast, rissole potatoes, and string beans with shallots, all prepared in a most excellent fashion. The kitchen staff appeared small, only one cook, his assistant, and the waitress. Tom was helping out, which seemed unusual for him. I heard that, in anticipation of the big birthday bash in three weeks, Hearst was giving his large staff some time off.

Marion kept the conversation going, briefly inquiring about my cartoon strip. No one at the table took *Secret Agent X-9* seriously, but they liked the artwork that young Alex Raymond was doing. I personally preferred the other strip Raymond was drawing, a space adventure called *Flash Gordon*.

"I hear Mayer doubled the budget of this new jungle movie," Hearst said, finally speaking up.

"My movies deserve a big budget," Johnny said. "We made millions before, and this time we're going to make millions more."

"Becoming a bookkeeper?" Bill said.

"I do my homework," Johnny replied, grimly scrunching his thick eyebrows.

"Movies are quite a step up from modeling underwear, aren't they, Johnny?" McCann remarked with a Brooklyn accent. "Which do you prefer, a loin cloth or BVDs?"

By the scowl on his face, it looked like Johnny had something harsh to say, but in deference to our host, he held his tongue. Bill poked me with his elbow, hiding his grin with a napkin.

"Marion deserves to be Marie Antoinette," Hearst declared, leaning across the table to look Thalberg in the eye. "She's a queen. She *is* the queen. She's perfect for the role, and you know it."

"That hasn't been decided yet, and we're at least two years away from production," Thalberg replied.

"I know you're pushing your wife, and you're cutting Marion out of the Wimpole movie," Hearst complained. "Sorry, Norma, you're good in those silly girl roles, but Marion has the gravity for the big parts."

"I don't know why you say that, Mr. Hearst," McCann interjected. "Miss Davies just isn't suited for those stuffed shirt historicals. They're an embarrassment. Why not let her do the musicals she's so good at?"

Hearst stood up, knuckles on the table. For a moment, I thought he might pick up the bottle of Heinz Ketchup and throw it.

"Is this your opinion, Irv? Marion isn't good enough?" Hearst asked.

"Of course not. No, of course not. Calm down," Thalberg said, holding up his hands.

"Please, Pops, let's not do this here," Marion begged, pulling him down into his chair.

The room fell silent, and stayed that way through most of dessert. Boiled apple dumplings. Maureen began talking about walking red carpets, with all the flashbulbs going off, asking Marion what she should wear.

"We are having a premiere here, Miss O'Sullivan," Hearst said, his good humor slowly returning.

"What do you mean, Mr. Hearst?" Maureen asked.

"We will be showing Tarzan and His Mate in our theater tonight. The show starts in one hour," Hearst explained. "Best seats in the house."

"You know, Maureen and I haven't seen it yet," Johnny said. "We only finished the reshoots a week ago."

"Our copy is a little rough," Hearst admitted. "But Irving made sure to get us the best print available."

Everyone turned to Thalberg, who nodded. Given the stress on his relationship with Hearst, coming through on the movie was the least he could do. I was looking forward to it. If even half the stories they were telling were true, the nation was about to be shocked.

We adjourned for a break, Johnny, Bill, Alice and I slipping out the side door for a smoke. This portion of the garden was dimly lit with a few electric Japanese lanterns, and a fog was rolling in. All the workers were gone now, a few of their tools stacked near the worksites. I sat on a bench next to one of the big marble coffins, wondering if it had ever held the body of an ancient Greek or Babylonian. Alice landed next to me, the cigarette elegant in her long fingers.

"I hear you are married but not married, Mr. Hammett," she inquired.

"Separated," I admitted. "After the doctors diagnosed me with TB, they told Dolan that she and our daughters shouldn't live with me anymore. I got better, the marriage didn't. She lives in San Francisco with the girls now."

"So you consider yourself single?"

"In every way that matters," I said, sliding closer.

"What about Lillian Hellman?"

"Just friends," I replied.

"I am so glad to hear that," Alice whispered.

I reached in my pocket for another smoke and found the handkerchief containing Skinny the Rat's stolen necklace.

"What's that?" Alice asked, snatching it away from me.

"A string of fake ice I've been stuck with," I answered. "Probably heisted from a studio prop department."

Alice took out her compact, looking in the tiny mirror while holding the blue stone up to her neck. Her eyes glistened in the reflection of the lanterns.

"This is awful fancy, Dash. I've never seen one like it at MGM, and Mayer orders the best."

"They're just for show. From what I learned during my detective days, real stones like this would be worth forty or fifty grand. The guy I got it from doesn't have two bucks to his name," I said, slipping the troublesome trinket back in my pocket.

I noticed Hearst in the plaza. He waved me over.

"I suppose you know why you're here?" W.R. said, imposing in his white suit.

"You may be unhappy with me missing deadlines."

"And you may be right about that. I pay you a lot of money, the

23

least I expect in return is respect."

"I don't mean any disrespect, sir. And you are making plenty of money from my work. I hear you want another Nick and Nora script?"

"We can talk about that. After I talk to that rogue Bill Powell. I would like another novel, too. Something for Redbook. Spicy, but not vulgar."

"Novels have been difficult for me lately."

"I've heard why, but that's none of my affair. As long as you meet your obligations. You understand that making movies and publishing are businesses, don't you? Thousands of employees rely on us to provide jobs. The people rely on us to entertain them, and to tell them the truth. Not all of us have the luxury to get drunk and chase women."

"I won't let you down, sir."

"That's fine. And now that we have an understanding, welcome to La Cuesta Encantada," W.R. said, shaking my hand. He had a charismatic smile, and a strong grip. "You'll find plenty to entertain yourself. Enjoy the weekend."

He went back in the house. I wandered toward Bill and Alice. Maureen had joined them, laughing at someone's joke. Her smile was charming.

"Mr. Hammett, we must talk," Maureen said. She'd had more than one drink but wasn't drunk. No more than I was.

"Miss O'Sullivan, I am at your service," I said with a bow.

"You may call me Mo, and I want a book. A character. A female detective to rival Miss Marple."

"Miss Marple is an elderly spinster," I said.

"And I am not!" Maureen said, giggling.

"What do you have in mind?" I asked.

"Oh, I don't know. Maybe a curious girl. Someone like Nancy Drew, but more grownup. Like Nora Charles, only with a gun."

"What do you know about guns?" I asked.

"Everything I need to know," she replied, looking feisty.

I gave the idea a moment of serious consideration. A young female detective? Gorgeous? Spunky? Witty? No, I decided. America isn't ready for that.

"Let me give it some thought, Mo. Though from what I hear, you are very busy these days."

"It's been a whirlwind," she said. "Four years ago, I was living in Dublin, and now I've been in twenty movies."

"How old are you?" Alice asked.

"Over twenty-one," Maureen answered.

Tom summoned us to the movie theater. We walked through the gardens on the north side, the castle looming above us on the right, until reaching another wing of the building. The bottom floor was a movie theater, quite large, with fifty plush seats and a big screen. Carpets cushioned the floor. Hearst greeted us at the door, directing us where to sit. Maureen, Norma and I sat together, Johnny and Bill behind us, with Hearst and Marion behind them. I didn't see Thalberg or McCann. Alice was with us for a few minutes before disappearing. As Marion's assistant, she probably had work to do.

The lights went down and the movie started with steady war-like drumbeats. The first thing I noticed was the superior production values. The cinematography was crisp, the sound clear. After making a surprise two million dollars on *Tarzan the Ape Man*, MGM had decided to take their property seriously.

Like the first movie two years before, a pair of great white hunters set off into deepest darkest Africa in search of ivory, whipping their overburdened safari bearers. They were attacked by fearsome natives, and then fearsome apes, before being rescued by Tarzan's famous yodel. And then Jane appeared.

"Wow," I loudly whispered, taking her hand.

Maureen wasn't naked. Not quite. But her skimpy two-piece outfit left little to the imagination. The image was going to leave an ache in the loins of every red-blooded American male. I glanced back to see Johnny's reaction, but his seat was empty. Sitting alone, the film had Bill's full attention. Behind him, Hearst was frowning and Marion looked embarrassed.

Tarzan and Jane took over the movie, frolicking through the jungle like two uninhibited Bohemians. When Tarzan tore Jane's dress off and threw her nude into the river, everyone gasped. The bold sexuality was bound to drive the Hays Office crazy.

"That's not me swimming," Maureen said in a hushed tone. "It's one of John's Olympic friends. Josephine McKim."

"No one will know the difference," I remarked. "If you weren't famous before, you will be now."

"Maybe I'll finally get serious roles instead of always playing the daughter or younger sister," Maureen hoped.

When Jane emerged from the river, trying to retrieve her clothes from a teasing chimp, I looked back again for the audience reaction. Now Marion had disappeared. Was the nudity too much for her? Bill had moved back to sit with Hearst, who was slowly shaking his head in disbelief. I had the impression he wanted to stop the projector. Norma turned to see what I was looking at and suddenly got up.

"Excuse me," Norma said, going up the aisle and leaving the theater.

"Think she's jealous?" I whispered to Maureen.

About halfway through the film, Johnny returned, sitting alone in the back row. He looked unhappy, his hair was mussed, and I noticed his tie twisted to one side. I wondered if he had gone out for a forbidden drink, causing me some envy.

Toward the end of the movie, just as the great white hunters were being massacred by marauding lions, Marion and Norma quietly returned together, taking seats a few rows behind us. They were in conversation about something, but I couldn't hear what they were saying. I doubted it had anything to do with Tarzan and Jane. Hardly a moment later, Tom appeared at a side door, summoning Hearst outside. Bill moved down to sit with me and Maureen.

The movie concluded with Tarzan and an army of elephants defeating the lions just in time to save Jane. The pachyderms returned the stolen ivory to the elephant graveyard, and they all lived happily ever after. Until the next installment.

As the screen faded out, I saw Alice had arrived, sitting in the back row next to Johnny. She seemed tense.

"Great film, Maureen. Just great," Bill praised. "Makes me want to run naked through the woods."

"Let's hope the censors don't ruin it," I said. "There's still time for the studio to cut the more risqué scenes."

We went out the main door into a cool, damp evening. A fog had rolled up from the ocean. Bill did the honors of lighting cigarettes for me and Maureen before using his gold lighter to spark up a cigar. Hearst and Thalberg were briefly seen toward the front of the house, possibly having an argument, before going their separate ways.

"Anyone looking for a snort?" Bill asked, producing a silver flask from his coat pocket.

We snuck down a garden path toward the road, hiding under a drooping tree. On a more crowded weekend, it might have been harder to be discreet, but the grounds were empty. Bill took a swig and gave the flask to Maureen. I drank from the cap.

"Johnny's unhappy. Any idea what that's all about?" I inquired.

"He and Lupe are having trouble again," Maureen confided. "Mr. Thalberg told Sharkey to keep the gossip columns quiet while they work things out, but Sharkey hasn't been helpful. They're afraid of bad publicity."

"There's no such thing as bad publicity. Johnny should just let the story ride," Bill said.

"He's very private, and because of his stilted dialogue in our scripts, he's afraid no one respects his acting," Maureen explained.

"All actors are insecure," Bill said. "Mayer said I'm too old to play Nick Charles, and I'm a great Nick Charles. Isn't that right, Dash?"

"I was watching Myrna Loy. Were you in that movie, too? What do you think is going on with Hearst and Thalberg? That Wimpole movie?"

"It's a growing sore point. They've been friends for years, but W.R. doesn't tolerate any slights to Marion," Bill said.

"Mr. Thalberg isn't looking well," Maureen mentioned.

"Ten years of heart trouble. Works twenty hours a day. Carries MGM on his shoulders. Not a job I want," Bill said. "To Irving, may he survive the wrath of Hearst."

We toasted The Boy Wonder, hoping he wouldn't kill himself.

Though we weren't pickled, the three of us were a bit tipsy as we strolled back up to the big house. Bill didn't seem worried about incurring the great man's ire, but as newcomers, Maureen and I were fretful. We encountered Marion and Norma on the path, but Norma scampered off.

"Enjoying the night? What did you think of the movie?" Marion asked, being gracious.

"Everything is lovely, Marion," Maureen said.

"Wonderful night. Glad to be invited," I added.

"Pops is a bit tired. The rest of us will be meeting in the gallery for music and cards," Marion said. "Beer is available from the kitchen, unless you'd rather have coffee."

She gave us a look that spoke volumes, followed by a wink.

Returning to the big museum, Alice and I partnered to play bridge with Marion and Bill, penny a point. It was a casual game, on the surface, but each of us quietly displayed a competitive edge. In the rough and tumble world of movies, and publishing, no one likes to lose. Bill's expressions were easiest to read, always smiling even when he had no cards. Marion was more inscrutable, revealing little. Alice was the surprise, thrusting down her trump cards like they were daggers, then shyly leaning back to catch her breath.

As we played, Maureen and Johnny sat at the piano, belting out popular Broadway tunes. Johnny proved he could do more than yodel. Norma entered, minus Thalberg, and climbed up on the baby grand piano wearing a black satin gown, lounging on the smooth surface like a New Orleans Blues singer. She had a nice voice, too, with an ability to project despite her petite size. After the bridge game, the four of us joined in, singing and occasionally dancing. The party lasted until two.

"See you at breakfast," Marion said, hugging each guest as we returned to the cottages. She seemed in much better spirits than earlier in the evening. Norma lingered behind for a moment.

"Where is Mr. Thalberg?" I asked, pausing for a cigarette.

"Irving turned in early. It's been a long day," Norma said, her lilting accent a bit Scottish and a touch Canadian.

I'd not met Norma Shearer on the lot but heard good things about her. After struggling for several years on Broadway, presumably for being unattractive and untalented, Norma was signed by Thalberg. The career she'd built in the ten years since was due to her grit as much as anything. Now many were wondering how the heavy hand of the Hays Office was going to affect her, being one of Hollywood's most sensual actresses. If Norma began taking more costume dramas, it would trample the niche that Hearst had cut out for Marion.

"I appreciate the support Cosmopolitan has given my books, but I have projects MGM might like to take on," I suggested. "Do you think Mr. Thalberg might have some time this weekend?"

"You may discover that being friends with both Cosmopolitan and MGM is difficult at the moment, Mr. Hammett," Norma replied.

"Please, call me Dash."

"All right, Dash. Perhaps you can have a word with Irving over lunch tomorrow."

"Thank you so much," I said, nodding my appreciation.

As Norma went to find her husband, Bill walked up to offer me another snort.

"What was that all about?" he asked.

"Hedging my bets," I said.

Back in my room, I set my leather bag on an antique dresser to pull back the quilt. The mattress was firm, the sheets expensive. The lodge was cool but not cold, so I probably wouldn't need extra blankets. I'd brought a notebook in case I felt like writing but wasn't in the mood. Someone had left a stack of magazines for me, including one that was very familiar. I had just started to glance through it when there was a knock on my door.

"Hello, Dash," Alice said.

"Please enter, Miss Fowler," I offered with a gallant bow.

She wandered in slowly, taking in the scene. I wasn't sure where Marion's assistant usually stayed, possibly in the next bungalow over. Or a lower floor of the great house. She wore a light red coat, open down the front, and a frilly yellow dress underneath. Not the same dress she'd worn at dinner.

"Mr. Hearst provides every comfort for his guests," Alice said. "You'll find soap, toothpaste, and a toothbrush on the nightstand. And pajamas in the drawer. If you need them."

"Maybe I won't," I hopefully replied.

"What's that?" Alice asked, seeing me holding the magazine.

"A story Collier's ran. I called it This Little Pig."

"Good murder story?"

"Not a murder story at all. It's about Hollywood."

She sat on my bed and began reading, smiling at first. Then she frowned.

"Gosh, you don't have much respect for the movie business, do you?" she said. "Do you think actresses are all scheming bitches?"

"It's not about the actresses. It's a satire about a jaded script doctor hired to sex up a Western."

"The hell it is. I hope you don't feel all women are out to manipulate men."

"Of course not. It's just a story."

"Dash, everyone wants another detective novel. That's what you're good at. Mr. Hearst will make it into a movie."

"It may come to that," I agreed.

There was another knock on my door. Alice scooted back out of sight as I peeked into the hall.

"Sorry to bother you, Mr. Hammett. Mr. Hearst needs to see you. Needs to see you right now," Tom said, wrapped in a black cloak from the damp night.

"Why? What is it?" I asked.

"They's been a killin'," Tom whispered.

THE SHOE OF SUPERIOR QUALITY

C. R. BOONE
Raleigh

Chapter Three

A TYCOON'S REQUEST

"Just a minute, Tom," I said, closing the door.

I turned toward Alice, unsure if she'd heard what the manservant said. She showed no sign that she had.

"Mr. Hearst wants to see me. It might take a while."

"My room overlooks the courtyard. If I see you coming back at a reasonable hour, maybe we can continue our conversation," she suggested.

"I would like that. I would like that a lot," I said, pulling her close for a hug. I wanted to kiss her, but it was too soon.

Finding my hat and coat, I slipped out the door. If Tom knew I had company, he was discreet enough not to say anything.

"What's this all about?" I asked as we walked toward the mansion.

"Can't say, sur. Can't say a word," Tom answered.

The courtyard was dimly lit with electric globes. We bypassed the main doors, going around the south side to a smaller door accessing a steep spiral staircase. No one else was up, the house eerily quiet.

We went to the gothic study on the third floor, finding a vaulted gallery filled with couches, overstuffed chairs, a dozen lamps, hundreds of antiques, books, and stacks of newspapers. A meeting table had eight sturdy chairs. Beyond was an annex with wide windows. Persian carpets filled the floor.

Hearst was sitting in a large chair at the head of the great table. Behind was a portrait of himself as a young man. He waved Tom back and me forward.

"I appreciate you coming, Dashiell," Hearst said, indicating for me to sit.

He looked older than he had a few hours before, the fleshy face drooping and shoulders slumped.

"My privilege, sir," I replied, not saying too much.

"Do you know about Thomas Ince?"

"Movie producer. Mostly Westerns. Died about ten years ago."

Hearst looked at me, waiting.

"Something about a scandal. Some say he was murdered."

"He died of heart failure after celebrating his birthday on my yacht," Hearst explained. "But rumors started that I accidently shot him while trying to shoot Charlie Chaplin in a jealous rage. Everyone from the widow on down knows that didn't happen, but the stories have never gone away. Now I have another potential scandal. I need your help."

"Tom said there had been trouble."

"Sharkey McCann is dead. Maybe an accident. Maybe not. I've had the road closed and the switchboard shut down. No one is leaving this hill until I have this under control. Will you help me?"

I delayed answering. Just for a moment. Covering up a murder is serious business, but he hadn't actually asked me to do that. Just help, whatever that might mean. And having Hearst in my debt might solve some financial problems.

"Of course, sir. What do you know?"

"Next to nothing."

"Who else knows McCann is dead?"

"No one except Tom, as far as I know. And the fewer that do, the better."

"Have you considered taking the body down to the ocean?"

"I'm not a criminal, Dash," Hearst angrily replied. "I just want the situation controlled until we know what really happened."

"I understand, sir. You can count on me. I take it Tom found the body?"

"Yes. He'll show you. Let me know if you need anything."

I nodded and left the room, seeing it was now after three o'clock. Not an unusual hour for me, especially when in Los Angeles. Tom led me down another circular staircase. Apparently, the castle was pocked with them.

"People get lost in this maze a lot?" I asked.

"Not so hard to figure out, after a couple years."

"Do you always work so late?"

"Does what needs doin'."

"Even such odd duties?"

"Been with Mr. Hearst a long time. A long time. I do anything for him. Any of us would."

We went back out a different door to a smaller courtyard around the corner from the main entrance. The fog had grown thicker. Tom stopped before an ancient marble sarcophagus hidden in near darkness, the lid slightly ajar.

"Where are we?" I asked, the visibility limited.

"Northside of Casa Grande. Theater is back there. Door over here goes down to the wine cellar."

"Locked?"

"The spirits are behind a steel door with a combination lock."

"I am warned."

Tom used a crowbar to pry up the top, then placed a thick iron bar under the hatch to prop it open. He handed me a flashlight.

"That's McCann, all right," I said, finding a body half-curled inside.

It only took a moment to see the skull had been cracked. Blood soaked the scalp, with streaks running down his forehead. The eyes stared vacantly. I could not see any other injuries. I did see a scrap of wet paper clutched in his dead hand. There was blood on the heavy lid and along the edge of the sarcophagus. Had McCann been shoved into the coffin after being hit on the head, or had the marble top crashed down on him as he tried to get out?

"When did you find him?" I asked.

"'bout an hour after the movie, sur. When you all was singin' in the gallery. I was sweepin' up the butts when I saw him stuck there, his head all crushed. Pried up the top to drag him out, but he fell back instead. Decided to tell Mr. Hearst. I did right, didn't I?"

"Yes. McCann was killed instantly. There's nothing you could have done," I said, though I couldn't be sure if it was entirely true. I would need a closer look at the corpse for that.

"Maybe we should move him into the house? Gots a cold storage room underneath the pantry. Preserve him good 'til we know what to do," Tom suggested.

"Where did you hear about cold storage?"

"I likes readin' them detective stories. They's always studyin' the bodies for clues."

It was a good idea, for I could hardly be seen inspecting the remains once the gardeners returned in the morning.

"Get a cart. And find something to rope off this area. We don't want anything disturbed."

"No, nothin' disturbed. I understand completely, sur," Tom agreed.

He ran off, ready to help. I wondered if Hearst kept a fingerprint kit on the premises. If not, I could gather a brush and powder from the pantry, then lift latent prints with Scotch tape.

While Tom was preparing to move the body, I ran back to my room, finding my Brownie in the leather bag. I only had three flash bulbs, which would need to be used sparingly. I photographed McCann as he lay in the box, another as he was halfway out, studying how the lid might have crushed his skull, and one of the ground surrounding the crime scene.

Tom returned with a two-wheeled service cart from the kitchen. Before moving the corpse, I tested the weight of the lid. The iron bar suddenly slipped out, forcing me to brace my feet and use both hands to stop the lid from crashing down.

"Tom, some help," I said.

He rushed forward, and between the two of us, we pushed the lid back up. Tom held it in place while I put the iron bar back underneath a corner.

"It's heavy, but not terrifically heavy," I said, a little out of breath. "I could lift it myself if I was in better shape."

"Yes, sur," Tom said.

I noticed that he had held the lid open all by his lonesome, even though he was at least ten years older than me.

"Was this iron rod here when you found the body?" I asked.

"Over there, Mr. Hammett," Tom said, pointing to a gouge in the dirt about four feet away.

"If the lid was nearly closed, how did you find him?"

"The top was crooked. I was 'fraid someone may have been foolin' around and cracked it. When I come closer, I see this silk scarf hanging down, half in, half out. Caused me to study on it."

"That was very enterprising of you," I said, trying to make it sound like a compliment. Though I wondered how Hearst's most prized servant seemed to spot so many obscure clues. Was he covering for someone? And did Hearst know who it was?

We rolled McCann through a back door and down a ramp into a chilled storage room. Shelves were being used to store flour, spices, and bread molds for the pantry. A string of lightbulbs hanging from the ceiling cast multiple shadows. We used a waterproof tarp to cover the body.

"What does you think, Mr. Hammett?" Tom asked, weary from the late-night activity.

"I'll know more in the morning, but it looks like McCann was pushed backward into the marble coffin. As he started to climb out, the lid came down on him."

"You can tell that?"

"Look at the stains on his knees. The mud on the back of his jacket. He was down, crawled back up, then got whacked. Whoever he was with ran off."

"Murder?"

"Maybe an accident. Probably not."

"Does you know who it was?"

"Too many footprints. Even found one of my own cigarette butts."

I didn't mention the note found clutched in McCann's grimy claw. The paper was soaked from mud and would need to be unfolded carefully. And in private.

It was nearly sunrise when I needed to wrap up my inspection. Gardeners were arriving to resume work on the courtyard, but there were only a few of them. Not the small army I had seen the day before. Apparently, Hearst really had closed the road until the mystery was solved. One worker, the project leader, was a tall Mexican named Carlos.

"We need to leave these marble boxes alone for a few days," I told him before leaving.

"Miss Marion wants them planted with roses for the birthday party," Carlos protested, telling me why this one had been left propped open.

"Leave these two alone for now. And the one around the side," I insisted.

I mentioned all three to throw suspicion off the one in question.

"Only Mr. Hearst tells us what to do," Carlos replied with a frown. "Shall I call him down here?"

Carlos looked the planters over, saw the rope Tom had placed across our crime scene, and reluctantly nodded. But he wasn't happy about it.

I caught a few hours' sleep, dwelling on the case until my eyes finally closed. I woke to find Bill Powell sitting next to the bed.

"Hair of the dog?" he said, offering me his flask. The brass container had been refilled, though where he was getting the bourbon remained unknown.

I took a quick sip, but not too much. It was going to be a long day.

"Turn in late?" Bill asked. "I saw Alice in your room."

"Wish she'd been able to stay, but I got a call from the boss," I said, pouring water from a pitcher on the dresser to wash my face.

"About another Thin Man movie?"

"No. Can you keep a secret?"

"I'm the best there is."

"Someone killed Sharkey McCann last night."

"Killed? As in, he's dead?"

"Yeah. In the mystery writing business, killed means he's dead."

"Wow. Who did it?"

"That's what Hearst wants me to find out. On the sly. He's afraid of another scandal like Thomas Ince."

"Gosh, I'd sure like to help. Can I be Watson?" Bill requested.

"Do you have a deerstalker cap?"

"Holmes wears the deerstalker cap. Watson wears a bowler."

"Don't use a British accent."

"Sure thing, Sherlock. What's our first move?"

"We're going to have a talk with Weissmuller. He disappeared from the screening last night and looked like he'd been in a fight when he came back."

"No one is going to arrest Tarzan for killing a snake," Bill said.

I dressed casually, as was expected of guests at the Ranch, and we walked toward Casa Grande looking for breakfast. Bill wanted to see the crime scene, so we veered left near the northwest corner. The fog that had enveloped the hill overnight was dissipating but retained a ghostly resonance.

"That's it, huh?" Bill whispered.

"Looks like he was crawling out of the sarcophagus when someone slammed the lid on him," I explained.

Bill crept closer, ducking under the yellow rope Tom had strung between two trees, and knelt down. The coffin had been intricately carved by long-dead Minoan artisans, and even after two thousand years, the nymphs and olive vines were still vivid.

"Don't see any blood," he remarked, running his fingers along the clean surface.

"Wasn't much. I kept a sample before the butler wiped it down."

"Destroying evidence?"

"Not destroyed. I have a photo. The morning fog would have gotten it anyway."

"Did you look inside?"

"Of course. Took a photo of that, too."

"What was Sharkey doing out here? Kind of secluded once the sun goes down," Bill wondered, for it was a dozen feet from the main path and partially screened by tall bushes.

"That's a good question. When we know that, it will probably solve the case," I predicted. Foolishly, as it turned out.

Bill backed off and started poking around, looking at the maze of footprints that I had largely given up on. Then he stopped, stared down into a lush flowerbed, and straightened up holding a cane.

"Hey, isn't this Thalberg's?" Bill said, waving it around.

"Damn it, Bill. That could be evidence. Don't smudge the fingerprints."

Using my handkerchief, I took the ivory-handled cane away from him. It was a nice hardwood walking stick inlaid with silver. Expensive.

I knelt to probe the area where the cane had been lying but didn't see any other artifacts. The only footprints were mine and Bill's, and there was no sign of a struggle. The cane had been thrown into the bushes. Why could only be guessed at.

We got to breakfast late. The morning room looked like another grand museum on a smaller scale, with hundreds of art pieces and every kind of ancient furniture. We sat on thick benches at a heavy oak table, finding fresh bread, butter, French's Mustard and Del Monte Catsup. I heard the kitchen though doors to my right and saw a billiard parlor down the hall to the left. The other guests were already out on the grounds, enjoying their weekend. Not accustomed to eating before noon, I picked at the pancakes and scrambled eggs. The coffee, which I drank black, was excellent.

Marion suddenly appeared wearing a green polka dot dress with lots of red ruffles. Her hair was worn up, and she smelled of French perfume.

"How is the chow, gentlemen?" she asked.

"No complaints, dear," Bill said, holding up his fork with a sausage attached.

"Quite good," I agreed, declining to display my food.

"Everyone had a late night. Especially you, Dash," Marion said.

I noticed a slight nervous stutter to her voice that hadn't been there the night before. It was well-known that Marion worried over this occasional impediment, particularly as it might affect her acting career. Most of the time, it was barely noticeable.

"Mr. Hearst had business to discuss," I said.

She looked at me as if there was something special she wanted to ask, glanced over at Bill, then thought better of it.

"Have you any plans for the day?" Marion asked.

"Thought I'd just poke around. The grounds are so interesting," I answered.

"Me, too," Bill said. "I'm tired of having fun."

"That will never happen. Certainly not here," Marion said. "Is there anything I can get for you? Tom seems anxious to be of service."

"I'm thinking about writing a new detective story," I said. "About a Hollywood fixer who comes to a bad end."

Marion showed the briefest flash of distress but recovered quickly. She was truly underestimated as an actress. And it confirmed my suspicion that Hearst had said something to her. Unless she knew something without Hearst telling her. With the kitchen staff nearby, I decided not to press her.

"Has Mr. Thalberg been around this morning?" I casually asked.

"Irving had a bad night. I think he's sleeping in," Marion said. "Norma's up, though. Already out on the tennis court with Maureen and John. How about you, Bill? You like to play?"

"In a bit, perhaps. I have a little errand to do first," Bill replied.

"Good, I'll see you up there," Marion said, making a graceful departure.

"A little errand first?" I softly inquired.

"If McCann was up to no good, shouldn't we search his room?" Bill suggested.

"Capital idea, old boy. Capital," I said, surprised I hadn't thought of it myself.

We finished up. With only a few bucks in my pocket, I was relieved not to have to leave a tip. Financially, I should have been doing fine. My stories to *Collier's Weekly* had paid $2,000 each, *The Thin Man* had paid a little more than $20,000, and I was getting $500 a week for writing the secret agent cartoon. But the money seemed to disappear as fast as I made it. I wondered if solving this case would allow me to hit Mr. Hearst for a raise.

Holding the cane in my handkerchief, I walked back toward the kitchen, which was shiny and gigantic, the white tile floor well-scrubbed. There was only one cook and one server; a Frenchman in a tall chef's hat named Julien, and a middle-aged Hispanic woman he called Sara. I supposed the usual staff was significantly larger but told to stay home this particular weekend. I nodded, continuing through the pantry and down to the storage rooms. Tom intercepted me in the hall.

"All is quiet, Mr. Hammett," Tom said, indicating the large closet where we had stashed the body.

"We've got more evidence," I said, holding up the cane. "We'll need to dust it for prints before returning it to Mr. Thalberg."

"I keep it safe, sur. Real safe," Tom said, putting on a pair of white gloves and holding the cane at the bottom. He retreated behind a wooden door into the room where we had stored the evidence.

"He's really in there?" Bill asked.

"Better be. Unless he wasn't dead and walked out."

"Can I see?"

We followed Tom toward the back where the storage room was lit by a single low watt lightbulb. A locked cabinet to the right held the fingerprints I'd lifted, only some of which had been transferred from tape to a suitable gray paper.

"Who have you caught so far?" Bill inquired.

"I don't have any sets of prints to compare yet. We'll work on that this afternoon," I answered.

Glass jars in a lower ice cabinet held the blood samples, bits of hair from the victim, the blood-stained silk scarf, and some mud I had found under his fingernails. I doubted any of it would prove useful.

"This should be intriguing," I said, reaching for a covered tray. "We found a note in his hand, but it was so wet, I couldn't chance unfolding it. It should be dry enough to read now."

I slowly took the metal lid off the tray, wondering what mystery might be found.

"What the hell?" I said a bit too loudly. "Tom! Tom, come here."

Tom came running, his expression surprised, for I'd not raised my voice in his presence before.

"Yes, sur?" he asked.

"What happened to the note?" I demanded.

The tray was empty except for a stained paper towel in the bottom.

"I don't know. I don't know. No one been here, far as I know," Tom said.

I quickly checked the rest of the evidence we'd gathered, finding nothing amiss. Only the note had vanished.

"Lock this room up. A lock that only you have the key for. No one else. Do you understand?" I said.

"Yes, sur. I understand," he responded.

"Nothing more can go missing. You don't want to be held as an accomplice after the fact, do you?" I warned.

"No, sur. No more than you," Tom said. We were both on thin ice, and he was bright enough to know it.

"Let's be careful," I concluded.

"If someone stole the note, think they've ransacked McCann's room, too?" Bill asked.

"Jesus Christ, I'd better get over there," I said. "Tom, where is it?"

"Casa del Sol, sur. To the left and toward the back," Tom replied.

"Make sure this room gets locked up," I said to Bill. Not that I didn't trust Tom, but I couldn't afford another mistake. "Come quick as you can."

I hurried back through the vast pantry and out the kitchen door, startling the cooks. The fog had lifted off the mountaintop but was still lingering in the surrounding valleys. I turned toward the bungalows at the edge of the hill, entered the middle guesthouse, and ran down the halls, almost tripping on a thick Persian rug.

The first room I checked was empty. I slammed the heavy oak

door and raced to the next one, bursting in. I saw a leather suitcase on the bed, and some men's clothes strewn over a chair. There was a strong smell. Aftershave? And then there was a brief motion out of the corner of my eye. A blur. I started to turn my head, but the next thing I knew, I was lying on the floor.

———————

"You okay, Dash?" Bill asked, kneeling next to me.

"What?" I asked, rubbing the back of my head.

"Looks like you got conked. Just like in the movies."

"What did he hit me with? A blackjack?"

"Florsheim. Size ten."

He held up a men's shoe with a thick leather heel. Highly polished. I saw it had been wiped clean of prints.

"Did you see who did it?" Bill asked.

"Did you?"

"Didn't see anyone."

"Is anything missing?"

"Haven't had a chance to look," Bill replied. "Are you sure you're okay?"

"Is there any blood?"

"Only a lump."

"Got worse back in my Pinkerton days," I said, slowly sitting up. It was a bit of an exaggeration, but I had a reputation to protect.

Bill went through the clothes on the chair, checking the pockets. I noticed the scent of aftershave again. There was a subtle cheapness about it. A table behind the door held toiletries in a porcelain dish, and a bottle of Murry & Lanman's had tipped over. I tightened the cap back on and set the bottle down next to a tube of Barbasol.

Sitting down on the bed, I poured the contents of the suitcase out on the checkered quilt. There was a Kodak camera, several letters, a receipt book with a record of his trip to New York, and an unsigned contract for Katharine Cornell to appear in the Barretts movie. It appeared McCann's mission to recruit Cornell had been a failure.

"There has to be more," Bill said. "McCann was no fool. He wouldn't leave the good stuff out in the open."

"Unless he was a fan of Edgar Allen Poe," I said, looking at the old roll top desk near the window.

"Poe? The Raven?"

"In this case, The Purloined Letter."

"I don't know that one," Bill admitted.

"Poe's version of a detective story. Auguste Dupin…"

"Who?"

"The dick from Murder in the Rue Morgue. Hoping for a big reward, the cops search a room, looking for a missing letter. Dupin finds it hidden in plain sight."

I glanced around the room and jumped for the desk. There was a business envelope pressed between two leather bound books, but a peek inside revealed the envelope was empty.

"Someone else reads Poe, too," I said.

"That can't be all," Bill insisted, looking under the mattress.

I sat back down on the bed, wishing for an ice pack, looking inside the envelope again. It wasn't torn or bent. Not like it would be in a hurried search.

"There's nothing. Nothing at all," Bill complained, plopping down in a big leather chair.

He took out a cigarette and offered one to me, but I declined. Something wasn't right.

"I'll be a son of a bitch," I said, going back to the desk.

I grabbed one of the leather-bound books, gave it a shake, and then picked up the other one. Several small envelopes fell out on the floor that Bill quickly snatched up.

"Feels like undeveloped film," Bill said, running his fingers along the contours.

"Don't risk exposing it. Hearst has a dark room. We can inspect the negatives there when I develop the film from my Brownie."

"This is getting good. Think it will solve the case?"

"It might lead us in the right direction, unless they're just dirty pictures McCann took on his trip," I replied.

Tucking the envelopes in my breast pocket, I returned to my room and made sure my camera was unmolested. Which it was. I had run out of flashbulbs but still had eight exposures left on the roll and intended to use them. Bill found a bucket of ice and wrapped cubes in a towel. It felt good.

"So, it looks like the killer is on to you," Bill said, taking out his flask. "He might be planning to bump you off."

"How do you know he's not planning on bumping off both of us?"

"No one hit me on the head."

"Next time I'll let you go through the door first."

Bill handed me the silver flask and I took a swig. The bourbon helped. He took a more modest sip and put the flask away. We didn't want to be caught breaking the rules, especially the draconian decree about not drinking in our rooms. Even though I doubted Hearst would chase me off the mountain with so much else going on, there was no point in inviting trouble.

"What's next, Mr. Spade?" Bill asked.

"Thalberg hasn't appeared yet, and Johnny was looking disheveled last night. Let's mosey up to the tennis courts and see how they're doing."

"I'll put my tennis shorts on. That should keep them from

suspecting."

"Mr. Powell, there is no reason for them to suspect anything unless you decide to look suspicious."

Bill went to his room for a tennis outfit. The Ranch supplied both the clothes and the rackets. Not being a tennis player due to my questionable lungs, I washed my face in the bowl on the dresser and caught my breath. When I discovered the mysterious necklace still stuffed in my jacket pocket, I determined to find a good hiding place for it. But where?

There was a knock on the door.

"Come in," I said, looking for a weapon if I needed one.

It was Alice, conservatively dressed in a charcoal gray wool suit with a knee-length skirt and flat shoes. Her long auburn hair was tied up in a bun. Wire-rim eyeglasses gave her a studious look.

"You must have gotten in very late," Alice said. "I stayed up as long as I could. I'm not a guest here, you know. I have a job."

"It's okay, sugar. I'm very sorry. Mr. Hearst kept me longer than I expected."

I waved her in and she took a seat next to me on the bed. She smelled good. Possibly an expensive perfume like the one Marion liked. I supposed it had been a gift.

"What happened to you?" she asked.

"What do you mean?"

"Your hair is all tangled, and ..."

She reached toward the back of my head, feeling the lump. I yelped.

"It's nothing. I fell down."

"Someone should look at that. There's no doctor here, but Mrs. Fuentes knows first aid. She should. Sara has four rambunctious boys."

"Maybe later. What can you tell me about Irving Thalberg? Why does he employ Sharkey McCann? How well do you know him?"

"Golly. Sharkey McCann?" Alice said, unpleasantly surprised. "I've only seen him around the offices. He asked me out a few times, but he's too much of a player for my tastes. A bit slick, too, if you know what I mean."

"And his relationship to Thalberg?"

"McCann's just an errand boy."

"A well-paid errand boy?"

"Dash, you know how Hollywood is. Dog eat dog. Producers like Mr. Thalberg need men who will carry out confidential assignments."

"Does Mr. Hearst have such an errand boy?" I asked.

"Mr. Hearst doesn't need one. He owns thirty newspapers and six magazines. Anyone who crosses him will know the consequences soon enough."

"I wasn't implying anything. I'm sure Mr. Hearst is a good man. Have you heard of any disagreements between Thalberg and McCann? Or between McCann and Weissmuller?"

"Why do you ask?" she inquired, looking me in the eye.

"Some questions have come up."

"Then I suggest you ask Mr. McCann yourself. It's not my place to gossip."

"Fair enough. I don't want to get you in trouble. How about lunch together?"

"A picnic?"

"A picnic sounds fun. No horses."

"I'll ask Sara to fix us a basket. But leave Mr. Powell behind. His eyeballs... tend to wander."

"It's just his way. Besides, I hear he and Jean Harlow are an item.

Or don't you read the glamour magazines?"

"Clipping them is one of my jobs for Marion. Those magazines are horrid things. Filled with lies."

"I know they haven't been kind to Miss Davies. Especially about some of her recent films. And rumors of her relationship with Hearst have been leaking out."

"Only the most disreputable rags print that trash, and they might not be in business much longer."

"Did McCann... that is, does Sharkey make money on the side selling rumors?" I asked.

"If he does, I haven't heard about it. And Mr. Thalberg wouldn't tolerate it," she firmly answered.

"Want to play some tennis?"

"I've got work to do in the office," Alice said, still a little put off with my interrogation. "Lunch is at noon. Not noon o'five. I've heard how you are with deadlines."

Just as Alice was leaving, Bill returned wearing a white polo shirt, white shorts, and white canvas shoes.

"Nice to meet you again, Miss Fowler," Bill said, tipping his visor.

"Good morning, Mr. Powell," Alice said, ducking out quickly.

"That gal has a caboose on her," Bill said with a whistle.

"I don't have time for chasing cabooses. There is a murder to solve."

"Are you sure it's murder now?"

"Someone stole the note. Someone blindsided me in McCann's room. That usually means a killer is covering his tracks."

"Let's find the rogue."

"Ready to go," I said. "And Bill, you may want to lay off Alice. I think your charm is lost on her."

"But not yours, old man?" Bill replied with a sly wink. "No

problem. I won't trample another man's turf."

We walked through the big courtyard where Carlos and a smaller Mexican were trimming the exotic plants. As we passed, Carlos beckoned me over.

"Catch up in a minute," I said to Bill, sending him on. The smaller Mexican took a powder, too.

"We are watching you, Señor Hammett," Carlos said. "The road is closed. There are no phones. Everyone on the mountain is trapped while white men search for... what do they call them in your books? Patsies?"

"I don't know what you mean, sir," I politely replied, withdrawing my arm from his grasp. He had a strong grip, the product of hard physical labor.

"Know that you will not place blame on any of my people."

"Sir, I am not looking for trouble. Just asking a few questions on behalf of Mr. Hearst. If no one has done anything wrong, I will make no accusations. But if you know something, this is the time to come forward."

"We are watching," Carlos said again before going back to trimming the bushes.

I went around the north side of the mansion, passed the roped off sarcophagus, and skirted the movie theater. A pathway led to the famous tennis courts, which were laid out over a roof of some sort. The two courts were walled in with not much room for spectators, though I did see a few tables and wicker chairs. I recalled photos of Charlie Chaplin, Joan Crawford, Clark Gable, and Dolores del Río whacking the ball with Marion and Hearst, who appeared to love the exercise.

Bill had arrived ahead of me, making a fourth with Norma as they played Johnny and Marion. The guests all had white tennis outfits supplied by the Ranch, including the shoes. I noticed high wattage light fixtures, not realizing Hearst might want to play at night. Or maybe in the fog. The April morning was cool, as it tends to be in Southern California near the ocean, but the players were working up a sweat. Maureen was watching from one of the tables with a towel draped over her shoulders.

"Tired already?" I asked, sitting next to her.

"Just catching my breath. Everyone takes the game so seriously," she replied in her charming brogue.

"I'm glad to see Johnny's okay after that fight last night."

"Oh, it wasn't a fight. Not really. Just a disagreement."

"Did Sharkey throw the first punch?"

"I don't know. I didn't hear that," Maureen answered, looking confused.

"Don't know what?" Johnny asked, running past as he chased an errant ball.

"About you and Sharkey getting into a fight," Maureen explained.

Johnny stopped, glared at me, and then handed his racket to Maureen.

"Take over for me, darlin'. Mr. Hammett and I must have a word."

Maureen scampered off, looking delicious in the short white skirt.

"Come with me," Johnny ordered, pointing to a staircase.

The stairs led down below the tennis courts where, to my surprise, there was an indoor swimming pool. And not just any pool. This one was huge, probably eighty feet across, styled in some Roman fashion. Like a giant ancient bathhouse. From floor to ceiling there were thousands of shimmering mosaic tiles, colored in orange and blue with specks of gold. The muggy cavern was illuminated by sunlight shining down through glass bricks in the tennis courts above, which acted as a skylight. Like the Neptune Pool, this pond was heated. The pool was surrounded by several marble sculptures, apparently Greek and Roman gods. The only thing missing was satyrs and nude nymphs.

I followed Weissmuller off to the side, where I noticed dressing rooms and private showers. We stopped in the junction.

"Okay, Hammett, what's your beef?" Weissmuller demanded, his arms crossed.

Tall and broad-chested with dark brown eyes, the jungle king could be intimidating. But he wasn't a thug, and I was no babe.

"Sharkey McCann is dead. I want to know if you killed him?"

"Dead? I didn't even hit the son of a bitch, much as I wanted to."

"What did he have on you? Why the secret meeting?"

"That's none of your damn business."

"When you returned to the movie screening last night, it looked like you'd been in a fight."

"We may have scuffled. Pushing and shoving," Weissmuller admitted.

"Where did this occur?"

"On the path, around the corner from the front doors."

"Near a marble coffin?"

"There was one nearby. He snuffed out a cigar on it before... before our talk got serious. But he was fine when I left. Sharkey even ordered me to get along. Said he had another appointment."

"With who?"

"He didn't say, and I didn't ask."

I thought it a very convenient explanation, absent any useful details. And I didn't know him well enough to guess what might provoke him to violence. His screen persona was formidable, and he looked natural in the role.

"How did you know when to meet Sharkey?" I asked.

"He sent me this note," Weissmuller said, unfolding a piece of stationery common to the guest rooms. It was simple, written in haste, just saying to meet outside once the movie started. I tucked the note in my pocket.

"I can't say you did it, and I can't rule you out. But I won't say anything to embarrass you. If nothing comes of it, your incident with McCann can remain a secret."

"Not that secret," Johnny said.

"What do you mean?"

"After the movie, I told Marion what happened."

I let Johnny go back to the tennis court, taking a final look at the decadent bathhouse before wandering up to Casa Grande. Beer was available in the kitchen, and though not my preference, it was better than drinking water.

It was one big kitchen, larger than most people's houses. The ovens made fresh bread. Rotisseries could cook a dozen chickens at the same time. Cabinets held a wide variety of spices, powders, oils and extracts. I doubted most hotels served as many guests so efficiency.

There was not a large staff this weekend, only Julien and Sara, who were already preparing lunches. It did not seem to be a highly organized affair. A radio was playing music.

"Aren't we all gathering for the midday meal?" I asked.

"Each goes their own way at La Cuesta Encantada. Only the dinners are mandatory," Julien explained in a heavy Parisian accent. He was a large man, about my height, with broad shoulders and long arms. He was quick with his hands, using the stove to make a variety of dishes.

"But no eatin' in your room, Mr. Hammett," Sara said.

"Wouldn't think of it, Mrs. Fuentes," I replied.

"I am preparing a basket for you and Miss Alice. Fried chicken," Sara added. It turned out she was Carlos's older sister, about fifty years old, short and a little plump. Many of the Ranch employees were related.

Anna Lee entered, a graceful twenty-year-old Negro woman in a black outfit decorated with white ruffles. She was the only maid working the weekend.

"Mr. Thalberg would like some tea," Anna Lee ordered, reaching for a silver tray.

Sara produced a warm kettle and poured a deep green tea into an antique cup.

"Make that two cups," I said, taking the tray from Anna Lee. "You're busy. I'll take Mr. Thalberg his tea."

"Thank you, Mr. Hammett," Sara said, pouring a second cup. "You will find Mr. Thalberg in Casa del Mar."

"Which one is that?" I asked.

"You are staying in Casa del Sol. Casa del Mar is on your left," Anna Lee explained.

I nodded my appreciation and carried the tray out the main doors and across the plaza. The Spanish-styled guest house had one floor accessing the gardens but expanded into three floors as it encroached down the mountainside.

Casa del Mar had a shallow entry leading into a sitting room as elaborately decorated as Casa Grande. Now that the morning fog had finally burned off, there was a spectacular view of the ocean. I balanced the tray in one hand and knocked on Thalberg's door with the other.

"Come in," Thalberg said.

I expected to find him in bed, or just getting up, but he was sitting at a large desk in a blue silk dressing gown with stacks of file folders.

"Pressed into service, Dash?" Thalberg said.

I sat in a two-hundred-year-old chair, seeing scripts, budgets, shooting schedules, and enough studio projects to keep five men busy.

"Looks like Sharkey didn't land your actress," I said, gingerly handing him a cup of tea.

"Katharine still might sign. She just doesn't like the idea of Hollywood. Prides herself on being a stage performer," Thalberg answered, holding the teacup with both hands and taking a sip. He wasn't in good health. Wire-rim reading glasses rested on the bridge of his nose.

"If she won't sign, does that mean Marion will get the role of Elizabeth Barrett?"

"Marion's not right for the part. Everyone knows it but W.R."

"He seems pretty worked up about it. If not Marion, who?"

"Possibly Norma."

"Your wife? Hearst really isn't going to like that."

"Can't be helped. I have to do what's best for the film. I always have."

"How does Sharkey McCann fit into that? By failing to sign Cornell, did he lose a bonus? Did you fire him?"

"Sharkey knows I pay for results. If he makes less this time, he'll make more next time."

"Did you lose your cane?"

Thalberg took off his glasses and turned his chair toward me.

"I must have left it in the theater."

"You didn't come to the theater last night. Or Mr. McCann."

"He had a report for me. We had a brief conversation."

"How brief?"

"Dash, what is this all about? Why all the questions?"

"Mr. Hearst has me checking into an incident that happened on the grounds last night. Did you see or hear anything unusual?"

"No," he answered a bit too quickly. "I smoked a cigar in the garden where Norma wouldn't catch me and turned in early."

"Was McCann smoking a cigar, too?"

"Come to think of it, he was. A Cuban," Thalberg said, finishing his tea. I had barely touched mine.

"Norma looked a little upset later in the evening. Was it the note that disturbed her?"

I pointed to a folded piece of paper on the nightstand. It was the same stationery used for Weissmuller's missive, and folded the same way.

"She didn't say anything to me," Thalberg said.

Without permission, I picked up the note and took a quick look. All it said was to meet in the garden about halfway through the movie. No names were mentioned. Thalberg studied me the whole time but never objected to the intrusion on his wife's privacy. I tucked the note in my breast pocket.

"Thank you, sir," I said, preparing to leave.

"You can call me Irving. I like your work, Dash. I like it a lot. You wrote Thin Man for Hearst. How about writing something for me?"

"I have a few ideas."

"Send them over," Thalberg encouraged.

I gathered up the silver tray carefully, being careful not to jiggle the teacups, and headed back for the kitchen. The teacup would provide an excellent set of fingerprints. Though Thalberg had not been completely honest with me, the more I thought about it, the less I was convinced he could be guilty. And I really did need to start writing again.

Chapter Four

THE STEW THICKENS

Late in the morning, we heard the sound of a powerful airplane buzzing over the compound, circling twice before landing in the field north of the parking lot. The area had a small hangar with a fairly primitive runway.

"Do you recognize it?" Bill asked, having changed into a brown leisure suit.

We'd gotten a good glimpse of a small red monoplane with an oversized engine. A speedster.

"Lockheed Vega," I said. "You don't suppose we're being visited by Wiley Post, do you?"

"Amelia Earhart, maybe," Bill said.

"Really? Amelia Earhart?"

Bill laughed. "It's not Amelia Earhart. Hearst has newspapers flown in for his review."

"I assumed he would cancel the Saturday delivery."

"Looks like you were wrong."

Bill and I loitered in the courtyard, curious about the new visitor, smoking and pretending we weren't drinking. Within half an hour, the tram came up the hill. Hearst emerged from his cathedral and went down to greet it, lingering on the tar covered roadway. The pilot was a tall lanky fellow about thirty-five years old, pretending to be Charles Lindbergh, leather football cap and all. He handed Tom a large sack of newspapers, listened to something Hearst had to say, then shook the mogul's hand. Rather than get back on the tram, the pilot grabbed a duffle bag off the seat and walked in our direction.

"Hey, fellas," he said in a distinctly Midwestern drawl. "Looks like I'll be here a day or two. What's all the mystery?"

"No mystery," Bill said. "Mr. Hearst thinks the road's unsafe. Doesn't want a lawsuit for killing a movie star."

"Didn't see nothin' wrong with the road, and I ain't no movie star. Name's Rocky Knowles, best pilot west of the Rockies. Maybe the best pilot anywhere," he introduced, offering hardy handshakes. "I always make the weekend run, rain or shine. Fog or no fog."

"You wouldn't be a teetotaler, would you?" Bill asked.

"I'd rather be dead," Rocky said.

"Want to take a walk?" Bill offered.

We strolled down a steep walkway, passed a gold statue of a nude woman kissing a frog, and paused on a balcony overlooking ravines and rangeland. We could see herds of cattle, antelope, buffalo and zebras. The hillsides were thick with pines and oaks. Bill took out his flask and three small paper cups, filling each to the brim.

"To the gods of the air," Bill said.

"To Mr. Hearst, who pays too much for a pile of worthless newsprint," Rocky added. "I got a buddy up here somewhere. Name's Sharkey McCann. Anybody seen him?"

I stopped halfway from draining my cup. Bill nearly choked, spitting some out.

"How do you know McCann?" I asked.

"He's always got business somewhere, and always needs to get there fast," Rocky explained. "We keep a plane ready at Grand Central Terminal for him. I got a message saying he might need a ride home from this pig farm."

"Haven't seen Sharkey roaming around this morning," Bill said. "But this is a big place. He could be anywhere."

I declined to comment.

"No objections to a fine imported Scotch, I hope," Rocky said, taking a pint bottle of Martin's from the pocket of his leather flight jacket.

"Looks like you're not afraid of Mr. Hearst's ground rules," I remarked.

"I'm an employee, not a guest. And Mr. Hearst is welcome to fire me any time he wants. I can make just as much money flying for Jack Warner."

I took the bottle and gulped. With the end of Prohibition, it was finally legal to import quality spirits again. Though the speakeasies I patronized tended to have better stock, there was still a lot of bathtub gin running around.

"I've got a case in my plane. It's consigned to Hearst, but I may be able to sneak out a bottle or two," Rocky suggested.

"Count me in," Bill said.

As much as I would love a genuine Scottish whiskey, I didn't have the cash. And I knew Rocky wasn't offering such a prize for free.

Just as it was time to return, Rocky took my elbow and led me off to the side. Bill went on without us.

"If you've got it, I can deliver it. Fifty-fifty split," Rocky whispered.

"Have what?" I asked.

"The package. The one Skinny the Rat had at the Ambassador. Bugsy wants it back, but there are others who will pay more."

"Skinny was nervous, but he didn't give me anything valuable."

"Maybe he clued you in on where he hid it?"

"Something about a pancake house on Fairfax."

"Rachael Macao? No, that's a wild goose chase. The trick's real name is Saucy LaRue, part-time call girl and full-time jewel thief. Good with her hands, if you know what I mean."

"How do you know all this?" I inquired.

"Word got around after the Rat took a midnight splash into the Venice Canal wearing cement overshoes, but those New York knuckleheads didn't know the canals are only four feet deep. Skinny chipped his way out and gave me the low down for a quick trip across the border."

"What is this package?"

"If you don't know, I ain't saying," Rocky answered. "But remember my offer. If the wrong people find you with it, things won't go well."

We walked back to the Neptune Pool where Norma and Maureen were taking a dip. They looked like nymphs in their tight bathing suits. Bill had decided it was a good time for a swim. I had work to do, tipping my hat to the ladies and moving on to Casa Grande.

Getting a feel for the mansion, I slipped in the side door I'd used that morning, crept through the kitchen seeking to remain unobserved, and looked for the ramp leading down into the basement. I was still in the pantry when I heard voices and thought to wait a moment.

"I know you're uncomfortable, but we don't want Miss Marion to get in trouble, do we?" an educated male voice said. It was familiar, but I couldn't place it.

"But do we need to keep him *here*?" a Hispanic female responded. It was Sara.

"The body needs to remain cool. The blood samples, too. The fingerprints need to stay safe. Mr. Hammett will know what to do when the time is right," the man said. And now I knew who it was.

"Goddamnit, Tom, what the hell is this?" I barked, barging into his office.

Sara saw my anger and ran off. Tom stood his ground.

"Sur? I's don't know what ya means," he answered.

"Don't give me that crap. I heard you talking to Mrs. Fuentes. You speak better English than I do."

"Ya must of misheard, sur."

"I misheard nothing, and unless you want me to think you're tied up in McCann's murder, you had better start explaining."

Tom sighed, loosened the buttons on his black dress coat, and sat down on a flour barrel.

"This is America, Mr. Hammett. Not France. Blacks are expected to keep their place. I like this job, and though Mr. Hearst prides himself on being open-minded, no white man is that open-minded."

"So you're just putting on for old massa?"

"What do you know about putting on for old massa?"

"I was a detective. Don't you think I know a con when I see one?"

"I'm not conning anyone. I work hard. And I'm loyal to Mr. Hearst."

"Then explain yourself."

"I grew up in Alabama. Just south of Tuscaloosa. Graduated from the Tuskegee Institute after studying under Professor Carver. Speaking like an educated man in Alabama will get you lynched, so I came west. But most times, it's not that much better here. I applied for a job at the Ranch because it allows me time in the greenhouses."

"Greenhouses?"

"I'm a botanist."

"Do you know chemistry?"

"Of course."

I backed up, leaning against the wall, wondering if I was getting the straight story. And decided I was. Nothing in Tom's demeanor spoke of deception.

"Did the note really disappear?" I asked.

"Yes, sir. It did," he replied.

"But you know who took it, don't you?"

"Only a suspicion, and I'd rather not say unless it becomes necessary."

"I have my suspicions, too. Do you have a last name?"

"Wheatley. Thomas Madison Wheatley."

"Well, Mr. Wheatley, I would appreciate your help processing these fingerprints. And when we're alone, dispense with the Stepin Fetchit."

"Yes, Mr. Hammett."

"You can call me Dash, whenever you think it won't blow your cover."

"I'd like that, Dash. And I've got a better way to store these fingerprints, if you don't mind my suggestions."

"Let's get to work," I agreed.

I only had an hour, not wanting to be late for lunch. Alice had already warned of dire consequences. Fortunately, Tom's chemistry background made the process more efficient, as I suspected it would. Each print was moved to a yellow 3x5 file card and marked with the location where it was found. We locked everything up tight and Tom kept the key.

"We need prints from everyone who was on the grounds last night," I said, washing my hands in the sink.

"The staff is on record in Miss Morgan's office. I can match those," Tom offered.

"Who?"

"Miss Julia Morgan. She's the architect who's building the Ranch."

"A woman?"

"Yes, sir."

"Well, that's fine. I guess. Then we'll just need prints from the guests."

"I have a plan for that, too. You just trip up the killer, I'll get the evidence."

"Those detective stories you read have really come in handy."

"Some of them stories were yours," Tom replied.

I headed back to the plaza, going through the main house with a quick project in mind. First, I had to find Sara and ask for some hairpins, a bottle of lemon juice, and a cup of flour. Fortunately, the big museum was empty, allowing me a few moments of privacy. I studied the ancient furniture, the antique vases, the painted wood carvings, the imposing oil portraits, the Persian carpets, and finally focused on the five-hundred-year-old tapestries hanging on every wall. Most featured kings, queens, dukes, and duchesses. Lots of royalty. When I ran out the front door ten minutes later, the necklace was no longer in my pocket.

I reached our meeting place at one minute before noon, congratulating myself for being on time. It was Alice who arrived five minutes late.

"You smell great for an office girl," I said, admiring the flowing white dress and yellow sunbonnet.

"And you smell like donuts," she replied. "I thought by this time you'd reek like a saloon."

Anna Lee emerged from Casa Grande with the picnic basket promised by Sara. I smelled the fried chicken and peeked inside to see biscuits, corn on the cob, and a bottle of white wine. There was even a checkered blanket to sit on.

"Thank you, Anna," I said, tipping my fedora.

"Watch out for ants, Mr. Ham-mett," Anna Lee said. Then she curtsied and rushed back into the cathedral, for the small staff had much to do.

"Where would you like to dine, Mr. Ham-mett?" Alice asked.

"Someplace where we can watch the zebras," I replied, for zebras are not something city dwellers get to see every day.

We started walking down the main road toward the ocean, then veered off into a rolling grassland. I noticed hoofprints from horseback riders.

"W.R. has hundreds of animals roaming the Ranch," Alice said as we strolled side by side. "Lots of deer, buffalo, and the famous zebra. The feed boxes along the roads are placed there so guests can see them better. There are even a few giraffes, though we usually find them in the wooded section on the other side of the ridge."

"What about the lions and tigers? Any chance of watching them bring down their prey?"

Alice laughed.

"No tigers at the moment. But W.R. has a lion in the menagerie, along with a family of black bears, a pair of leopards, and a bunch of really annoying monkeys. He's even planning on buying an elephant."

"Sorry I'll miss out on Jumbo," I said.

"Me, too. It would have been fun to see Mr. Weissmuller ride him."

"The fracas last night between Johnny and Sharkey, do you know what it was about?"

"I shouldn't say. It's really none of my business," Alice said.

We found a shaded knoll overlooking a grassy pasture and unfolded the blanket. Six zebras lolled around about fifty yards away, chewing the spring flowers. Beyond them was a herd of gazelle.

"This is good chicken," I said, munching a leg.

"Everything Sara makes is good," Alice agreed, the juice from a thigh dribbling down her chin. "It's good Sara packed napkins, too."

I opened the wine, an acceptable French vintage, and poured two glasses.

"To life in paradise," I offered.

"And to our patrons," Alice added.

We sipped. I ate a biscuit.

"I know Miss Davies told you about Sharkey," I said.

"I don't know what you mean. What about Sharkey?"

"He was found dead last night. Under suspicious circumstances. Which is why I've been asking so many questions. And why you've avoided answering. Did Miss Davies tell you to stymie my investigation?"

"Of course not. She wouldn't do that."

"So how about answering some questions?"

"Is Sharkey really dead? How did it happen?"

"Got hit on the head. Might have been with a chunk of marble, or maybe a garden tool. Or even a cane. I'll know more when I have time to inspect the remains."

"His remains? They aren't in your room, are they?"

"No, not in my room. But Mr. Hearst did ask me to find out what happened before he has another Thomas Ince on his hands."

"Why do you think Johnny did it?" she asked.

"I'm not saying he did anything. I'm just gathering information."

"I know Johnny got a note at dinner, maybe from Mr. McCann. He left during the movie and came back about half an hour later."

"What did the note say?"

"I don't know. Really, I don't."

She probably didn't, and I already did.

"What can you tell me about Thalberg and Johnny? Any trouble about contracts? Is Johnny trying to get out of making another jungle movie?"

"I don't think so."

"Could McCann have been applying a little pressure on Thalberg's behalf?"

"No, nothing like that. I'm sure of it. Johnny likes being Tarzan. It's made him famous."

"There was some kind of trouble between them."

"I work for Marion, not MGM. I wouldn't know about that."

"Can you think of anyone else who might have a problem with McCann?"

"Just about everybody. He was a very rude and disagreeable man. You saw how he provoked W.R. at dinner."

"Over the Wimpole movie. I remember. Does Mr. Hearst get angry like that often?"

"He doesn't like being insulted, if that's what you mean."

"So he has a temper?"

"You're not saying—?"

"I'm just asking questions. What about Mr. Thalberg? Did that disagreement at dinner get him upset?"

"Mr. Thalberg doesn't want a breach with W.R. That could mean problems between MGM and Cosmopolitan."

"Maybe Thalberg was unhappy with McCann stirring the pot?"

"Mr. Thalberg is a sick man. How could he hurt anybody?" Alice said.

"That's not much of a defense," I replied.

"Mr. Thalberg doesn't need a defense. Not from me. He's a great man. A genius."

"I suppose he is. It was just a thought."

"You had better watch how much thinking you do out loud. I'm just a secretary, but you're messing with some of the most powerful men in Hollywood. Mr. Hearst is one of the most powerful men in the world. Being a famous writer won't stop them from destroying your career."

"Warning taken, Miss Fowler."

We finished lunch, and the wine. I may have had a little more than she did. Alice was careful to pack up everything, bones and all, for Mr. Hearst took a dim view of leaving trash on his estate. I carried the basket as we walked back toward the main house.

"How long have you worked for Marion?" I inquired.

"A little more than two years. After graduating from Vassar, I got a job at Paramount in Manhattan doing distribution, but it wasn't... it wasn't... Marion rescued me from some very boorish supervisors. Brought me out west. Made me her personal assistant."

"Vassar is an expensive school. Are you a New York girl?"

I knew she wasn't. Not with her Midwestern mannerisms.

"Michigan. My father was an executive at Packard but lost everything in the Crash. He died a year later. Mom a year after that."

"That's rough," I said. She was not only an orphan, but an only child, judging by her temperament.

"What about you? Everyone knows Dashiell Hammett's detective stories, but the man is an enigma."

"Nothing special. Born in Maryland. Got a job with the Pinkertons when I was twenty. Took a couple years off during the war to drive an ambulance but caught the Spanish Flu. Spent most of my army career in a Tacoma hospital. Married my nurse. Moved to San Francisco. Started writing."

"And now you're on the Enchanted Hill, investigating a murder."

"Seems like we're both on the Enchanted Hill," I said, taking her hand.

Alice had to go back to work, for Hearst still had an empire to run, and Marion Davies was an important part of that empire. I was a bit dusty from sitting in the field and thought to change clothes, returning to Casa del Sol.

There was a noise in my room, and it wasn't the maid. I paused outside the door, listening. Someone was moving things, possibly ransacking. I had no intention of rushing in and getting conked on the head again, so I pushed the door open slowly.

It was Rocky Knowles, wearing his leather aviator jacket, going through the contents of my satchel.

"Can I help you with something?" I asked.

Knowles whipped around, startled.

"Where is it, Hammett?"

"I told you, I don't have the dingus."

"The what?"

"Never mind, because whatever you're looking for isn't here. Did you try McCann's room?"

"Went there first, but somebody already tossed it. As you well know. Did Hearst buy him off? Or you?"

"What makes me a suspect?"

"I've been nosing around. Heard you've been asking about Sharkey's business."

"And just what was his business?"

"Information."

"Is it possible Mr. Hearst asked your friend to leave the Enchanted Mountain? McCann upset his guests at dinner last night."

"Those bitches," Knowles snarled under his breath.

"Who?"

"None of your damn business. Hey, wait a minute. If Sharkey got the heave ho, why is his bag still here?"

"Maybe you should ask him."

"You know more than you're saying, Hammett. I'm going to find out what it is."

"Fair enough. In the meantime, I'll thank you to leave my socks and underwear alone."

I wasn't sure if Knowles would. He looked angry enough to keep searching my room whether I approved or not. There was a tap on the door.

"Hey, Dash, what's keeping you?" Bill said, barging in. He looked Knowles over, and Knowles stared back.

"We'll pick this up later," Knowles said, pushing past Bill and out the door.

"What was that all about?" Bill asked.

"Caught Rocky searching my bags."

"Looking for the negatives?"

"Possibly."

"Did he find them?"

"No, they aren't here."

"Are they...?"

"They're in a safe place."

"I guess this means that Sharkey and Rocky were partners," Bill guessed. "Does he know about the murder?"

"Not yet, but he suspects something's wrong. He probably thinks I'm up to my elbows in his business."

"Aren't you?"

"I suppose. I just haven't figured out what his business is."

———

At first I thought the marble lid had killed McCann, but now I wasn't so sure. I asked Bill if Nick Charles might want to solve that mystery.

"We aren't going to dissect the body. Just take a closer look at the wounds," I explained. "The lid falling on him might be an accident, but if he was killed by the cane, we might be looking at first degree murder."

"I'm game," Bill said, following me into the plaza.

It was a few hours past noon. The sun burst through the clouds, revealing a warm day and blue sky. I noticed Marion and Norma on a bench deep in conversation and decided not to interrupt them.

"Think The Thin Man will revive your career?" I asked.

"Revive? Hell, there's nothing wrong with my career, old man. I'm making four or five pictures year. I'm witty, sophisticated, and just started dating a goddess. On the sly, I hope you know."

"No one will hear it from me," I assured him, though his relationship with Jean Harlow was already fodder for the gossip

71

mags.

We slipped through the side door where the staff was cleaning up from lunch, bringing dirty dishes from the morning room. Tom appeared with empty water glasses, intending to put them under lock and key before the fingerprints were smudged.

"We need to take a look," I said to Tom with Bill standing behind me.

"Yes, sur. A course ya does," Tom said in his groveling accent. I tried not to look annoyed. Bill didn't give it a second thought.

Tom led us through the pantry and down into the basement storage rooms.

"I's gots lots ta do, Mr. Hammett. Mr. Hearst ain't ate yet," Tom apologized.

"We'll be fine. Thank you, Mr. Wheatley," I said, touching the brim of my hat.

Tom glanced at Bill, looking embarrassed, and hustled off. I opened the thick wooden door and turned on the lone light bulb.

"Chilly in here," Bill said, tugging his jacket tighter.

I pulled the canvas tarp back that was covering the body. McCann looked like he'd been in a bar fight, the round face puffy and purple. His white Panama suit only had the barest trace of blood along the collar. I picked up a hand, feeling the fingers and checking under the nails. There were traces of mud, but no skin or hair. If he had grabbed his assailant, it left no clues.

"What are those stains?" Bill asked, pointing at the fingertips.

"Soot from the kitchen stove. Tom and I used it to take his fingerprints," I explained. "We took prints at the crime scene, too. Once we have prints from all of the guests and workers, we'll sort out who the best suspects are."

"Placing any bets?"

"Not so far."

I didn't wish to disrobe the body, but did loosen the clothes enough to probe for additional injuries.

"What do you think?" Bill asked, helping to hold the shirt open.

"Nothing substantial. The head injury appears to be the cause of death."

I bent over, using a flashlight to study an abrasion just back from the left temple. There were traces of white in the hair, possibly marble dust. I used a swab to collect a sample, Bill holding the glass tube. I would try to match it later. The right side of the skull showed damage, too, but nothing so obvious. The skin wasn't broken.

"Clobbered by a stone slab?" Bill said.

"Seems likely, though we can't dismiss a shovel. Or a cane. We should—"

"Oh my God, is that Sharkey?" a female voice asked.

Bill and I turned to find Maureen standing in the door, a fresh croissant in her hand. She was staring with eyebrows up and mouth hanging open. I quickly drew the tarp over the body.

"What are you doing down here?" Bill asked.

"Looking for Sara. What are you doing down here?"

"It's not what you think," Bill said.

Of course it was. Rather than offer an explanation, I waited to see how Bill would handle the situation. Grim as it was, I found it hard not to smile.

"Sharkey is dead. Is that why you asked John all those questions? Did John kill him?" Maureen asked.

"No, John didn't... he didn't... we... don't think. Probably," Bill said, stammering worse than Marion when she was nervous.

"But somebody killed him. Was it murder? Is this murder?" Maureen nearly shouted.

Bill took hold of her arms to shush her. Having worked on *The Thin Man* together, I saw they had established a bond.

"For God's sake, Mo. Don't yell it to the whole house," Bill warned. "We don't want to alarm everyone, do we?"

"No, I guess not," Maureen said, calming down. "But why is he here? What are you doing?"

Bill didn't know what to say. He turned to me.

"This was probably an accident," I said with confidence. "But Mr. Hearst is worried it may reflect badly on his guests. He asked me to do a preliminary investigation before we call the police. I am a trained detective, you know."

"Then John isn't in trouble?" Maureen pressed.

"He said there was a harmless scuffle, though if we knew what the disagreement was about, it might clear him," I said. "Is there any chance he might tell you?"

"You want me to be an informer?" she asked.

"There is nothing wrong with helping a friend," I insisted.

Bill took Maureen into the hall, whispering intently. I couldn't tell how much he was telling her. Or not telling her. Or even if he was telling her the truth. I wouldn't. And it didn't matter, as long as she wasn't going to make a scene.

Maureen returned alone, sitting on a stool while giving the problem some thought. Hailing from Ireland, being an informer was no small thing to ask. Only 5'3" and thin-boned, she looked more delicate than Jane, but the blue eyes blazed with a fiery strength. At that moment, I thought her the sexiest woman I'd ever seen.

"I'll find out what I can," she finally agreed. "But whatever it is, I won't tell the police. Or anyone else, except you, Mr. Hammett. And if I don't like what I hear, I won't even tell you."

"Fair enough. I'm glad to know you can keep a secret," I said, helping her off the stool. "It's important not to say anything for now."

"I understand. But you better have a talk with Bill. The way he was wringing his hands, I thought he might be the killer."

Tom returned a moment after Maureen left, looking tired. I wasn't sure how much sleep he was getting.

"Almost got those fingerprints done," he said, showing me the file of cards. "Everyone at dinner will be handling the crystal. Anna Lee and I can mark each one. Keep them separated."

"We shouldn't be bringing Anna Lee in on this. Miss O'Sullivan was just here. She saw the body."

"The missy knows, too?" Tom said.

"Too?" I asked.

"Sir, just about all of us who work on the hill know about Mr. McCann. I don't think no one told Julien yet, but Sara knows. And Anna Lee. Carlos. Little Jose. Alberto. Hard to keep it mum in such a small group. But you can count on their discretion. No one would do anything to hurt Mr. Hearst or Miss Marion."

"Does this mean Carlos won't bash out my brains with a shovel?"

"Oh no, sir. If Carlos thinks you're trying to pin the killin' on his Mexicans, he bash your brains out good."

"But what if one of them is guilty?"

"Don't think Carlos cares about that. Not a wit," Tom warned.

"Sounds like you're not making any friends, Dash," Bill chimed in, suddenly appearing from the hallway.

"The only friends I need here are ones who can sign a paycheck. You're doing good work on these prints, Tom. And I like your plan for dinner. Thank Anna Lee for me."

I led Bill through the pantry and out of Casa Grande. We stopped for cigarettes under a giant oak.

"Okay, so Johnny knows. Maureen knows. W.R. knows. The help knows. Marion knows. Anyone left we should tell?" Bill asked.

"Don't be a smart aleck. Knowles is still in the dark. Sort of. And I still don't know how Thalberg fits into all of this."

"What about Norma?"

"What about her?"

"If Irving is mixed up in this, she might be, too."

"I hadn't thought about that. And she did leave the movie theater for twenty or thirty minutes."

"And she had access to Thalberg's cane," Bill suggested.

"How well do you know her?"

"I've never slept with her."

"That's not an answer."

"We've talked on the lot. Attended parties. Been to some premieres. The usual Hollywood stuff."

"Get her alone. See if there's a trail to follow. I'll see if we can eliminate Johnny as a suspect or move him to the top of the list."

"Could Tom have done it?" Bill asked.

"Tom?"

"If Sharkey was embarrassing Mr. Hearst, that's motive. You've seen how loyal he is. He had means, opportunity, and he was the one who found the body. And he's sticking to you like glue, keeping close watch on all the evidence. And did you notice how his English improved? Something is going on with that rascal."

"I guess we should add him to the list. After all, he is the butler," I conceded.

Bill went to look for Norma, thought to be in the stables. From what I understood, Hearst owned a number of stables with many fine horses living in comparative luxury, but I hadn't been riding in years. I had no intention of riding a bucking bronco now.

I headed toward the Neptune Pool, hoping to find Maureen prying Weissmuller for information. The path was lined with tiled planters and drooping trees. For a moment, I thought someone was following me. Making a quick turn, I saw Little Jose trimming a bush with long clippers. Alberto had a cart filled with trimmings. The rake Carlos liked to use was propped against a marble coffin, but there was no sign of the gardener.

I proceeded to the pool, finding Thalberg sunning himself in a beach chair wearing a straw hat. Knowles was kneeling next to him. Whatever the discussion was about, Rocky didn't seem happy about it. I don't know if his face was red from anger or too much drinking, but his posture was agitated. Thalberg appeared calm. Frozen-faced, but calm. No one else was in the area.

"Hammett! Goddamn it, you and I need to talk," Knowles said, jumping up. "But first I want to know where Sharkey is. The road is closed, so I know he didn't go down the hill."

"I heard McCann and Shearer were going horseback riding. All very hush hush," I said. "You might catch them at the stables if you hurry."

Knowles huffed and rushed off, both fists clenched. I went to see Thalberg.

"McCann on a horse? I guess Rocky doesn't know his partner in crime very well," Thalberg said with a relieved smile.

"Partner in crime?"

"You'll figure it out."

"You could help."

"I'm in this deep enough already. No need to dig any deeper."

"So it's true. McCann had something on you. Maybe Rocky knows what it is, or maybe he doesn't, but without McCann's proof he has nothing. Is he still trying to shake you down?"

"Sharkey was a fixer. Good at his profession. Rocky is a thug. Men in my position don't cave to thugs."

"If Knowles finds Norma at the stables, will she be okay?"

"Have you met the stable master? Red Brand?"

"The wrestler?"

"A retired wrestler who loves horses, and an old friend of W.R.'s since their days in New York. You'll find W.R. doesn't forget his friends. Or his enemies."

"I'll need to catch up with Mr. Brand. Ask him a few questions," I said, wondering why Tom hadn't mentioned him.

"Be careful. Red doesn't have much patience for questions," Thalberg warned.

As I walked toward the plaza looking for Tom, I noticed a small party sneaking off into the woods. It was Marion, Johnny and Maureen. Marion was holding a camera. Johnny was loaded with equipment. All were dressed in jungle khakis and wearing floppy hats.

I recalled Maureen saying something about publicity photos and decided to tag along, keeping a discreet distance so I wouldn't be seen.

"TARZAN AND HIS MATE"

Chapter Five

NOT SPEAKING FRANKLY

A rough gravel road led toward a zoo on a low hillside northwest of the castle, one of several such enclosures surrounding the compound. Some of the animals needed to be fenced off for their own protection. Some of the animals needed to be caged because they were dangerous.

Before the group headed into the woods, there was another distraction. At a crossroad, Norma suddenly rode up on a spirited stallion, golden brown with a white stripe down his nose. She handled the beast like a true cowgirl, reining in within a few yards of Marion. Norma looked great in a tight leather riding outfit, especially when she rose up in the saddle.

Marion waved Maureen and Johnny on, staying to speak with

Norma. I was too far away to hear details, but Norma was agitated. Marion seemed disturbed, but remained calm. Norma passed her a note, a folded piece of white paper. It didn't look like the missing note that Sharkey had been clutching, though I couldn't be sure. Marion only gave it the briefest glance before tucking it into her vest pocket.

There was more noise. Not a horse, but a flatbed truck. Norma looked back, and then urged the stallion up the hill into an arched bridle trail that the truck couldn't follow. I heard someone call it a pergola, whatever that that was supposed to mean. Rocky drove up and jumped out of the old Ford, angry that Norma had given him the slip. Then he turned on Marion.

I still couldn't hear everything that was going on, but Rocky was shouting something about being cheated. His fists were clenched. I considered intervening, for Marion looked like a waif compared to the hulking pilot, but I didn't want them to know they were being observed. I did pick up a hefty tree branch.

Marion started marching back in my direction, her knee-length boots kicking up dust, and then she veered toward the base of the hill below the Neptune Pool. Rocky was following, gesturing aggressively. I heard him say, "I'll get paid. One way or another." Marion whirled around, arms crossed, and stood her ground. Rocky loomed over her.

I couldn't stay hidden any longer, emerging from behind my tree and walking briskly down the hill toward the confrontation. I need not have bothered.

As if on cue, Carlos appeared from a wooden tool shed wearing thick work gloves. Rocky took a step back as the big Mexican interposed himself between him and Marion. Rocky pointed at Marion and started arguing again, the words garbled. Marion wasn't impressed, and Carlos didn't care.

"Thank you, amigo," Marion said, heading for the trail where Maureen and Johnny had gone.

Rocky turned to follow, but Carlos blocked him. Having dropped my tree branch, I slowed my pace, getting within a few yards. Marion disappeared into the forest. I don't think she saw me.

"Out of my way," Rocky said, trying to go around Carlos.

Carlos didn't say anything. He just continued to prevent the bully from following Marion. And then Rocky threw a punch, catching Carlos on the jaw. Carlos ducked a second punch, and then pushed Rocky back using both arms. When Rocky stepped forward again, Carlos raised a clenched fist.

"Whoa, fellas, I think that's enough," I said, getting between them.

"Mind your own business, Hammett," Rocky said.

"You don't want to do this, Mr. Knowles," I warned. "This isn't your home ground. You don't have friends here."

"I have one friend here. Somewhere. And when I find him, the rest of you are going to be sorry," Rocky replied.

The fight was apparently over. Rocky walked back up toward the big house, leaving the truck in the middle of the road.

"Are you okay?" I asked.

"I did not need your help, Señor Dasher," Carlos said.

"Knowles could cause trouble for you. This is still a white man's country."

"Whose word would the sheriff take, the gringo's or Miss Davies's?"

"She didn't see the fight."

"That is not what she would tell the law."

"Has she lied for you before?"

"You ask too many questions."

And with that, he walked away, making sure Rocky didn't reverse course toward Marion.

I sat in the truck, tucked my hat down from the warm sun, and smoked a cigarette. I'd have taken a snort if I had brought a flask, and I wondered what happened to Bill. Once Carlos was gone, I drove the flatbed truck another quarter-mile and abandoned it on a turnout, trying to discern which way my quarry had gone.

It would have been nice to have a map. As far as I knew, no one had made a map of the grounds, though there were probably drawings in Julia Morgan's office. Forced to guess, I took the lower road to the north, figuring I could go around the hill and come back up the main road if I got lost.

This was not an ordinary forest. There were plenty of tall pines, oaks and cottonwoods, but patches would appear of palms and date trees, flower beds, hay bales and buckets of oats. Fences screened off pastures and spring meadows. At one point, I saw a giraffe head poking above high hedges, and another time a herd of antelope pranced by. None of the creatures looked dangerous, though I did pick up a rock just in case.

My trail rose along a sharp bend with a broad view of the surrounding countryside. Below was rolling grasslands. Deep woods filled the hill behind me. The mountain blocked any sign of the ocean, and the cathedral had disappeared. I'd forgotten to bring water. Hopefully, I wouldn't need to drink out of a horse trough.

If Marion was taking jungle photos and looking for wild animals, it wouldn't be on this remote dirt road. I looked for a path into the forest, occasionally ducking low branches. I wasn't a total babe in the woods, having spent some time in rustic settings, but was more adapted to city life. My street shoes weren't doing so well, getting scuffed. My jacket was roughed up, too, and even developed a tear on the elbow. At this rate, I'd look like a hobo before making it back to the mansion.

I found an old shack at the crest of the ridge. Footprints showed it had been visited regularly, and there were plenty of cigarette butts. There was even the recently smoked stub of a Havana cigar. To the east, there was a clear view of the castle, and to the south was the coast highway. If I had binoculars, it would have been possible to look through the windows of Casa del Sol. I wondered if the shack was some sort of guard station or observation post. Below me was a dirt road leading to one of the animal enclosures, and movement among the trees.

I crossed underneath the Greek arches forming the pergola, a covered trail made of cement columns lined with flowers and fruit trees. The sounds of hoofs warned me a rider was approaching.

"You made a successful escape, Mrs. Thalberg," I said, moving out of her way. Norma pulled up and dismounted before me, letting her stallion catch his breath. She was wonderfully attired in a white long-sleeved blouse, tight britches, and tall black leather boots. She wore a wide brim cowgirl hat and carried a riding crop, though I doubted she used it. Except maybe on Knowles.

"Isn't this a strange place to find you, Dash? We must be a thousand yards from the nearest tavern?"

"I forgot my flask."

"I don't carry one."

"My bad luck. Cigarette?"

"Thanks," she said, looping the horse's reins over a trellis to keep him still. We sat on a convenient marble bench, probably a thousand years old made on some Greek island. I lit smokes for both of us.

"I spoke with Irving this morning. He looks busy."

"Irv is always busy. He's not just a genius, he works harder than anybody."

"He must have been disappointed that Sharky didn't land Katharine Cornel."

"She might still come on board."

"If not, will you be Elizabeth Bennett? Or Marion?"

"That's not my decision. They give me a script, and I do the script. And I do them better than most. I'm sure Marion tries her best, too."

"Are you friends? You seem like it?"

"Of course we're friends. And sometimes, friendly rivals."

"A rivalry you've been winning lately. W.R. thinks your husband is showing too much favoritism."

"Men must play their games. What games to you play, Dash?"

She slid over on the bench, bumping my hip, and looking up with big, luscious eyes. It took a moment to realize she was putting me on.

"Less dangerous games than you," I replied. "Can I ask you a question?"

"Yes, you may."

"Did you kill Sharkey McCann?"

"No."

"Do you know who did?"

"I do not, and I don't want to know. Though the SOB should get a medal."

"Does Marion know who killed Sharkey?"

"That would not be any of my business."

"You are charming."

"You are not without charm yourself. Though if you want to solve Sharkey's death, you may need to be more clever than charming."

"Tell me what you know."

"Write a girl detective character for me. A smarter one than the character you're writing for Maureen."

"I'm not writing any characters for anybody, at the moment."

"And that's your story?"

"That's my problem."

"I'll see you at supper, Dash. Don't get lost," Norma said, untying her horse and putting a foot in the stirrup.

"If I write a girl detective for you, will you tell me what you know?"

"I already have. Bye, Dash."

She disappeared down the trail back toward the castle, her bottom bouncing up and down in the leather saddle. She looked great. I crossed over the ridge and down toward the road. That's where I found Marion and her photo crew.

The narrow dirt path leading down to the road wasn't quite overgrown but provided sufficient cover to keep my presence secret. After reaching the bottom, I moved among the trees, trying to get within hearing distance. There had been enough suspicious activity between Marion and Johnny that I wondered what their connection might be. And was Maureen as innocent as she pretended?

We came to a series of cement buildings, probably used to store food for the animals. There was a monkey cage nearby. I slipped behind a low wall as Marion waved her party to a stop.

"This is a good place," she said.

"I'm not going to pose with wild baboons," Johnny protested, standing close enough that the noisy apes were reaching through the iron bars. They were skinny creatures with long, hairy arms and grasping fingers.

"They aren't baboons. These are spider monkeys from South America," Marion said.

"I'm not posing with chimpanzees either," Johnny added. "They bite."

"Jiggs isn't so bad," Maureen said.

"Jiggs isn't so good either. You just haven't seen his mean side," Johnny said.

"He always has cigarettes for you," Maureen persisted.

"The cigarettes are for himself. He only shares so I'll light them for him," Johnny explained.

"Are you talking about Cheeta?" Marion asked.

"His real name is Jiggs," Maureen answered.

"He smokes cigarettes?" Marion said.

"And cigars," Maureen answered.

"Well, we're getting a new Cheeta for the next movie. Jiggs is a scene stealer," Johnny complained.

"Are you ready to get in costume?" Marion asked.

"What costume?" Maureen said with a laugh.

She suddenly pulled a pile of brown rags from her pocket and began stripping down to almost nothing. Johnny averted his gaze toward the end, but I couldn't. Maureen O'Sullivan was one heck of a beautiful woman, especially when nearly naked. She did keep on a thin bra and tight flesh-colored underwear. The top she put on looked like wolf fur, fairly open in the front but tight enough to prevent her breasts from popping out. The bottoms were just two leather flaps, one in front and one in back, tied together with black string, leaving her thighs bare. I suppressed an urge to whistle.

Johnny wasted no time either, removing his great white hunter outfit for his more famous garb. His costume, to the extent that two long pieces of hanging cloth held together by a rope belt could be called a costume, revealed a magnificent physique. Three years in Hollywood hadn't ruined the Olympic swimmer yet, though I had no doubt that the late-night parties, heavy drinking, and the attentions of aggressive women would eventually bring him down-to-earth.

I shouldn't have been surprised, but I was. Marion opened a large shoulder bag and took out a make-up kit, complete with a round mirror. She set it on a concrete wall and helped Maureen with her hair, blush, eyebrows and lipstick. She even added streaks of brown rouge to Maureen's shoulders, making it look like dirt.

Meanwhile, Johnny roughed up his hair, using Brylcreem to keep it messy. He also touched up his eyebrows, added coloring to his cheeks, and used a gray lip balm to produce a more fearsome appearance. They were at it for nearly twenty minutes, causing me to sit down while wishing for a smoke.

"Has Mr. Hammett been pressing you with a lot of questions?" Marion got around to asking.

"He sure has. He thinks I killed Sharkey McCann," Johnny answered.

"Did you?" Marion asked.

"No. I just warned him to mind his own business," Johnny said.

"But you did hit him?" Maureen inquired, using an innocent tone.

"I wouldn't say that I hit him. It was more of a suggestion," Johnny replied.

"He was alive the last time you saw him?" Marion asked.

"Was he alive the last time *you* saw him?" Johnny countered.

"Excuse me?" Marion said.

"While I was smoking in front of the house, I heard the two of you going at it around the corner. Quite a row," Johnny said. "You mentioned that Mr. Hearst knows how to deal with his kind. Not the first time I've heard that, too."

"I just wanted him to back off," Marion said.

"So did I," Johnny explained. "At least Hammett doesn't think you killed Sharkey. Not yet, anyway."

Marion paused at the implication. And then she smiled.

"We should find him a better suspect," Marion said. "What about you, Maureen? Do you have an alibi?"

"Me? I didn't even know the *mac soith*," she said.

"You're young, innocent, and Dash likes you," Marion added. "If he thinks you're the killer, he might look the other way."

"I didn't kill him. I've never killed anyone!" Maureen declared.

Marion and Johnny started laughing. Marion gave her a hug.

"I was just teasing, dear," Marion explained. "Shall we get to work?"

Maureen and Johnny really looked great in their jungle costumes. Not the same as they had appeared in the movie without the careful lighting and film editing, but nevertheless quite striking.

Marion was also quite the photographer. With years of experience shooting guests at the Castle, she had a practiced sense of position and framing. They started in front of the monkey cage, interacting with the eager primates as the beasts reached through the bars for food. They earned a few peanuts.

After the monkey cage, they moved down the dirt road toward a huge tent made of green netting. It was filled with birds, mostly parrots. I followed discreetly until they went through a swinging door, locked it behind them, and entered a second door, moving freely inside. Some of the birds sat on perches, waiting to be fed. Others flew among tree tops. And they were real trees, the broad branches reaching out in every direction. I was able to watch from the outside but couldn't get close enough to hear their conversations.

The next scene was an artificial lake in a wide ravine that even had a waterfall. White-tailed deer lingered by, sipping water until

Marion chased them away. A pair of zebras soon took their place, standing ankle deep in the shallows.

"Are you expecting me to ride one?" Johnny asked.

"Would you?" Marion hopefully answered.

"No. I confine my riding to rhinoceroses," he said.

"How about you, honey?" Marion asked, taking Maureen by surprise. "Will you ride a zebra? Maybe a Lady Godiva shot?"

"I will jump out of a tree and let John catch me. That's as far as I go," she said.

"Let's try that pose," Marion suggested.

Maureen didn't actually jump out of a tree. She crawled up on a boulder, adjusted her skirt for modestly, and slowly tipped over until falling into Johnny's arms. The drop was three feet, at best. They both grinned, and it looked sexy as hell. Marion was snapping one shot after another. Maureen and Johnny waded into the lake, standing close enough to the zebra that they all looked like friends. The zebras didn't care for it and wandered away.

"Nude bathing scene?" Maureen asked.

I don't know if she was joking. I really hoped she wasn't. Marion waved them on to the next location without comment.

Following wasn't easy without being seen, but I managed to keep an eye on them. In a particularly thick part of the forest, Marion had them sit on a tree branch, angling the shot so they looked high off the ground. They weren't. Johnny was able to hop down with ease and lower Maureen.

"Where are these photos being published?" Maureen asked.

"Every Hearst newspaper in the country, if I'm lucky," Marion said. "And I'm going to ask Irving to have MGM distribute stills to the theaters. That's why they need to be good."

"How is Mr. Thalberg doing?" Maureen asked.

"Not well, I'm afraid. He fell down last night. Norma says his back hurts."

Thalberg had not said anything to me about falling down the night before, and his back seemed fine when we'd met. He hadn't even mentioned his missing cane. I wondered if Norma was telling the whole story. Did she even know the whole story?

I wasn't sure what else could be learned by spying on my host and her guests, and it was getting toward late afternoon. Once Marion lost the light, they'd be heading back to the mansion.

Backtracking slowly, I gained enough distance to straighten up and looked for a promising route. I wasn't far from a large concrete arena and saw a wide cement path leading past it back to the main road.

I paused to look down into the enclosure. It had a large, grassy yard with animal cages embedded in the wall on the far side. A shallow creek ran down the middle, with a few large rocks for decoration. The walls were tall and steep, possibly ten or twelve feet, and with good cause. There was an African lion lying in the shade on the far side, his tail swishing away flies. The arena was generously strewn with straw, though I doubt that's what the lion ate.

There was something down below on the ground. A folded piece of paper, probably blown in by the wind. Another mysterious note? I knelt for a closer look, wondering how to retrieve it. And got a closer look than I expected.

I sensed no movement behind me, just the last moment sound of boots crunching dry leaves, and then I was flying forward into the pit, given a firm push. I instinctively stretched out my arms, seeking not to land headfirst. A pile of rushes helped, but I landed heavily on my left side, pain shooting through my neck and shoulder. With a kick, I rolled over to my right, sitting with my back against the concrete wall.

I twisted to hold my head up, struggling for breath. The shoulder may have been separated. The pain had caused my hand to curl into a tight, useless fist. I looked up, hoping to catch a glimpse of my assailant, but saw only treetops.

With any luck, there would be a staircase somewhere, for I'd never be able to climb a ladder with my bad arm. To my right were three iron cages embedded in a cave. The circular wall rose steeply on all sides. Only belatedly did I remember there was another occupant in my unwanted prison. The lion.

It was a tough spot. Yelling for help might stir the lion to action. Not yelling for help would leave me stranded. I doubted anyone knew where I was, having crept through the forest in secret. I had no idea when the lion was normally fed, but I'd seen no workers in the area. I sincerely hoped I didn't smell like a zebra.

Very painfully, I took off my tweed jacket, bunching it in my lap. Then I removed my tie, using my good hand and teeth to make a sling. Sliding my bad arm in was difficult, but necessary if I was going to move around. That done, I wrapped the jacket around my right arm to protect it from large animal bites.

The lion was growing curious. He gradually moseyed to the edge of the shallow creek, staring in my direction. With any luck, I thought he might be toothless and declawed. An eager licking of his chops soon proved he had longer fangs than I did. A scratching at the ground showed sharp claws. I wondered if he might be the lion MGM always used to introduce their movies, perhaps trained not to attack mystery writers. By the glare in his amber-colored eyes, I doubted it.

I slowly stood up, my back to the wall, and edged toward the cages. If one of the gates were unlocked, I might slip inside and pull it closed behind me. I didn't see any bears or tigers waiting for me.

The lion was no dummy. He splashed across the stream and casually moved into my path. I backed up, looking for a boulder to hide behind, but there was nothing substantial. I considered picking up a rock to throw at him, though it seemed a futile strategy. Even the slender tree branch I found hardly felt like a weapon with only one good arm to swing it.

I must admit, it was a good-looking lion. Long in the body, tannish brown, with big paws and a full mane. There was intelligence in the eyes, and a casual patience to his demeanor.

The lion maintained a slow pursuit. If it was a race, I wasn't going to win. When I made another try for the cages, he sauntered in front of me like it was a big joke. It became clear he had the better odds and knew it.

"Help!" I yelled, now back where I first fell in. "Help! I'm in the lion pen. With a lion!"

The lion sat down for a moment to scratch his ear. He was not flustered. He yawned, then growled softly and began to rear up, the tail switching back and forth. I waved my tree branch while moving to my left again, trying to stay out of reach.

"Help! Lion pit! Real lion!" I shouted.

My adrenaline was up, and I was beginning to sweat. Not good, for I'd heard that predators smell fear. The lion wrinkled his nose, quickening his pace.

I made a dash for the first cage, having no choice, but the lion got there first, almost knocking me down. I scrambled away, jumping over a rock, falling in the creek, and crawling back to my starting position. I was madly waving the tree branch. The lion sat down, watching me from ten feet away.

"Okay, Leo. What do you want?" I breathlessly asked.

Patting my vest pocket, I found my cigarettes and pulled out my brand-new Zippo lighter. I snapped the flint wheel with my thumb, sprouting a small flame. It took a moment to realize that the lion wasn't going to be afraid of it, so I lit a cigarette instead. It felt like a firing squad.

As the smoke drifted in the lion's direction, his nostrils flared. I couldn't tell if he was repelled or angry.

"How about a smoke?" I offered.

The lion wasn't inclined, but he was growing bored with the game. He approached with more determination, causing me to stand rigid against the wall, holding my breath. Just as he was about to pounce, there was a distraction.

I don't know where she came from. It was just a blur jumping in front of me. The lion was startled, too, choosing to take a step back. It was Jane. No, I mean Maureen, half-naked in her jungle costume, black hair fanning out across her shoulders.

"Back! Back!" she demanded, waving a heavier branch than I had.

The lion did move back, at least temporarily. Maureen continued threatening with the leafy club, showing no fear. A second later, there was another thud. This time it was Johnny, also in his jungle rags except for a canvas trail hat. He held a branch, too, longer and more dangerous looking.

"Numa! Unk! Unk!" Johnny said in guttural growls, taking deliberate steps forward.

The lion gave ground, took a look back, and started for the middle cage in an anxious hurry. When the gate closed, I looked up to see Marion watching from the top of the wall. There was a bearded man standing next to her, dressed like a gamekeeper.

"Are you okay, Dash?" Maureen asked, turning in my direction.

I slumped down on my butt, more relieved than I thought possible.

"That was a close one," I replied.

"Mr. Brand says Mike is only dangerous when provoked, though hitting him with a stick probably wasn't smart," Maureen said.

"There was no hitting. Is that Mr. Brand?"

"Yes. He had just joined us when we heard you calling for help. He said if John and I made a lot of noise, the lion would go back in his pen."

"I'm glad you did. You are a hero, Miss O'Sullivan," I said, struggling to stand up. "You, too, Mr. Weissmuller. Thank you."

"What's wrong with your arm?" Johnny asked.

"I think the shoulder separated when I fell in."

Johnny approached me like a grim giant, the dark brows bent and lips snarled. He took my arm out of the sling and probed the shoulder with his powerful fingers.

"This is going to hurt," he warned.

And it did. With a swift twist, he put the shoulder back in place. I lost my breath but discovered there was significantly less pain when I began to breathe again.

"How did you do that?" I asked, giving it a rub.

"Ten years of sports injuries, Dash. Or do you think we athletes are so dumb that we never pay attention?"

A smaller gate opened at the far end of the enclosure where Marion entered, followed by the broad-shouldered gamekeeper. She ran in my direction, a first aid kit in her hands and eyebrows bent with worry.

"Dash, are you okay? How did this happen?" she asked.

I nearly explained that I'd been pushed in but then thought better of it. Only my assailant knew what had happened, and that might give me an edge later.

"Got too near to the edge," I said. "How did you get in?"

Maureen pointed to a rope dangling down the side of the enclosure. Had it been there all along? Even if it was, I couldn't have climbed it.

"You should be more careful, Mr. Hammett," Mr. Brand said. He was taller than I, with thick powerful arms. Good for corralling stray beasts. The bushy red beard was turning gray at the edges.

"Dash," I said, reaching to shake his hand.

"Red Brand. The big cats are my babies," Red said, returning the handshake gingerly. "We're short-staffed this weekend, so I've been riding the circuit. Otherwise, Mike would have been in his shelter already. He's fine now that he's eating."

"Your intervention was well-timed," I said. "Lucky for me you were in the area."

There was a look in his gaze that, for the barest instance, made me wonder if Brand's sudden appearance really was a coincidence.

"Do you need first aid, Dash?" Marion asked.

"Not really..." I started to say.

She opened the first aid kit. Among the ointments and bandages was a pint of Early Times.

"I guess I do, Miss Davies," I said, unscrewing the top for a gulp.

It was a smooth bourbon, better than Old Forester.

"Anyone else?" I asked, offering the bottle.

To my surprise, Marion went first, using the cap from her canteen for a cup. She passed it to Maureen, who took a modest sip. Johnny just sipped, too. Mr. Brand abstained, being on duty.

"We don't need to say anything about this, do we?" Marion asked. "It's for medicinal purposes only."

"Medicinal only," I agreed.

"Not a word," Maureen said as Marion locked the bottle away.

"How did the photoshoot go?" I inquired.

"Well, I think," Marion said. "I'll know more when I develop the negatives."

"May I use your darkroom?"

"Taking pictures with your Brownie?"

"Yes. A few," I replied.

She nodded agreement, leading me back toward the gated stairwell. While crossing the artificial creek, I saw the folded note lying in the damp grass and scooped it up, hoping no one would notice. As we passed the lion cage, I paused to look. Mike was having dinner, and it wasn't me.

———

Our group walked back toward the mansion except for Red, who still had a zoo to feed. Maureen and Johnny strolled ahead carrying the equipment, leaving me one-on-one with Marion.

"Care to tell me what you are doing out here? And how you really wound up in that pit?" she asked.

"I was investigating."

"You mean spying. On me?"

"On everyone."

"You can't suspect everyone. Or maybe you can. We might all be in on it together."

"Agatha Christie already wrote that one."

"Pops expects more than a story from you. And whatever the story is, he expects your discretion."

"What has he told you?"

"You are the persistent scoundrel," she said with a charming laugh. "All Pops has said is that you're trying to find out what happened to Mr. McCann before we have another scandal. It's been ten years since Thomas Ince got sick on our boat. He had ulcers and a bad heart, but all sorts of terrible rumors have plagued us ever since. Elinor was with him when he died. At home. In his own bed. His son was with him. Even his own doctor, but none of that matters. This thing with Sharkey might be even worse."

"Ince was a respected filmmaker. He practically invented Westerns. Sharkey McCann was a felonious messenger boy. It won't be much of a story unless the killer turns out to be someone famous."

"How long is the list?"

"It will get smaller," I promised.

I saw Maureen had stopped at the crossroad below the castle, waiting for us to catch up. Marion and I quickened our pace.

"You're having bad luck today," Maureen said, generously brushing trail dust off my rumpled coat.

"You are no longer a jungle girl," I said, seeing she had returned to her civilian garb. Much to my disappointment. Maybe Marion would let me see the photos.

"Can't run around the Ranch half-naked," Maureen said.

"Just in America's movie palaces?"

"That's different and you know it. Celluloid isn't the real thing."

"But being a movie star is, isn't it?" I said. "I guess you need to make a lot of sacrifices for fame. Long hours. Lack of privacy. Unpleasant personalities."

"It looks better in the glamor magazines," Maureen agreed. "What sacrifices for fame have you made, Mr. Hammett? Long evenings at the nightclubs. Heavy bar tabs. Run-ins with the cops. Waking up with women you don't recognize?"

"Mystery writers are not so sought after," I said, though she had come very close to the truth.

"But your skills are. Have you ever been forced to take on an unwanted client? Someone with money and power, who can ruin your career if you don't get the results they want?" Maureen asked.

"Mr. Hearst hasn't been that tough on me," I quickly replied. "But I think someone has been threatening other careers. John's. Marion's. Mr. Thalberg. Norma. Maybe even you, Miss O'Sullivan. Has anyone been standing up in your defense?"

"I have you, Dash. I don't need anyone else," Maureen said, taking my good arm as we went up the steps toward the Neptune Pool. "But I would like to ask a question. If I *was* the killer, would you rat me out?"

"No," I replied.

"Thank you. You are quite the gentleman."

"You and Bill get along fine. You made The Thin Man together. You've made two movies with Weissmuller. And now you've been cast in the Wimpole movie, if not with Katharine Cornell, then Marion or Norma. Any insight for me?"

"I don't know much about casting. When they first talked to me about Tarzan, I thought they were going to hire Clark Gable."

"Wouldn't that have been a hoot? Who would you rather see playing Elizabeth Bennett? Norma or Marion?"

"That's not a fair question."

"I have my reasons."

"Marion is wonderful in those comedies she makes. And she's no lightweight. She's starred with Bing Crosby. Leslie Howard. Clark Gable. She's making a Civil War movie with Gary Cooper. But Lizzy Barrett? I don't know. Maybe Norma does that better."

"It could mean an Academy Award nomination. Norma has three. Marion has none."

"Dash, what are you saying?"

"Maybe someone wanted Marion for the role bad enough to push Katharine Cornell out of the picture? The contract Sharky brought her is still unsigned."

"Marion doesn't have any trouble finding work. Norma doesn't have any trouble finding work. I don't. Johnny doesn't. Bill doesn't. How are you doing?"

"I'm working on a new mystery. The star might be a spunky girl detective who learns who killed a slimy Hollywood fixer. Know anyone who might be good for the part?"

"I'll give it some thought," she replied.

Norma had finished her horseback ride and reached the pool ahead of us, resting at the edge of the decking in a reclining lounge chair. Alice was loitering near the water, too, wearing a delectable black swimsuit.

"We girls need to change," Marion said, waving Maureen on. "Dash, come up to the house. We'll have Sara look at your shoulder."

"Thank you, Miss Davies," I said, choosing to linger behind for a moment.

"I hear you fought a lion," Alice said. Her breath was scented with sweet wine. "What were you trying to do? Beat Johnny out of the next Tarzan movie?"

"It wasn't exactly a fight, though that furry scamp did cause me to run out of cigarettes."

"Well, I don't have any cigarettes on me," Alice said, stepping back with her arms held out. I could see she didn't.

"Bill Powell will have some," I said.

"So why did you jump in the pit? Just wanted to tease the poor beast?" Alice asked.

"No, that's not what I wanted."

99

"What do you want?"

I glanced around, saw no one but Norma, and pulled Alice close, hoping for a kiss. She felt good in my arms.

"Mr. Hammett, you are very bold," Alice said, disengaging herself.

"May I have hope?"

"It never hurts to hope," she replied with a pixyish smile.

I wanted to find clothes that were not torn and sticky with sweat but decided to find an aspirin first. And maybe a bottle of Jack Daniels. Bill met me in the courtyard before the cathedral doors.

"Heard a lion stole your cigarettes," he said, handing me a pack of Camels.

"The lion had help," I replied, rushing to light one up.

"What does that mean?"

"Someone pushed me in the pit. While I was trying to get a gander at this."

I took the damp note from my pocket, still unfolded.

"Is that the one stolen from the pantry?" Bill asked.

"I don't think so. Not crumpled enough. This was blowing around the animal pen."

"What does it say?"

"Nothing. It's blank," I said, showing him both sides.

"Blank? Invisible ink?"

"Don't know. But I do know there are a lot of secrets going on around here."

"Plotting the murder or covering it up?"

"Or both?"

"Come on, they aren't that clever," Bill said.

"Not like us detectives, huh?"

"I've played Philo Vance and Nick Charles. And I figured out how to get a date with Jean Harlow. That puts me in a rare sphere."

"Let's hope you still have a job after this is over."

"The question is if Dashiell Hammett will have a job after this is over."

Bill walked back with me to the mansion, taking a side door leading to the kitchen. Julien and Sara were preparing dinner, the Frenchman at the stove while Sara bundled silverware into paper napkins. Marion sat me on a stool near the oven.

"Mr. Hammett hurt his arm," Marion announced.

Sara stopped her bundling to probe my shoulder with her thick fingers. Having a brood of rowdy sons had taught her more first aid than most doctors.

"Ice," she commanded.

Julien took a moment from chopping up birds to bring a bag from the ice box. The cold hurt at first, but I got used to it. Sara made me take off my shirt and wrapped a long piece of linen around my shoulder, securing it with a hairpin.

"Any whiskey?" I asked.

The staff looked the other way, not wanting to get fired. Marion led me back into the bathroom and produced a pint of Jim Beam, I'm not sure from where.

"We don't talk about this. Not in the main house," Marion warned.

"With the greatest discretion," I said, taking a stiff shot before returning the bottle. "Can I see your dark room now?"

The dark room wasn't in the main house. I followed Marion out the side door and across a rear courtyard stacked high with lumber waiting for the next phase of construction. At this rate, I thought, the castle was never going to be finished.

"They are rebuilding my darkroom. Again," Marion said with exasperation. "Pops has a temporary room set up in Julia's office."

We went into a small architect's office on the ground floor of the south wing. Behind the office was a curtained room, complete with developing trays and a red light.

"Everything you need is here, Dash. Just make sure to close the door and draw the drapes," Marion advised.

"Where is Miss Morgan this weekend?" I asked.

"Julia is in Paris. Some sort of class reunion."

"She's quite the pioneer, isn't she?"

"It's a hard world for women in any profession."

"So Pearl Buck has told me."

"I hear you are mentoring a woman playwright. Lillian Hellman?"

"Yes. She's very talented. I suggested a plot from a mystery book I read. Bad Companions."

"What is the play about? Maybe W.R. can buy the rights."

"It's about a schoolgirl who accuses two of her teachers of being lesbians. The charge is false, but it leads to one teacher committing suicide and the other being abandoned by her fiancé."

"Perhaps that's not something W.R. would want after all," Marion quietly advised. "Are you going to be using the dark room now?"

"It will have to be later. I don't have the negatives with me."

"Be on time for dinner. W.R. has questions," Marion warned.

Though I needed fresh clothes and a shower, I decided to check on my corpse first.

"He's still there," Tom said, meeting me at the storage room door.

"And our evidence?" I asked.

"Nothing's been touched. Made sure of that."

"Tom, why didn't you tell me about Red Brand? What other secrets are you keeping?"

"You wanted to know about suspects, Dash. Mr. Brand wasn't on the hill Friday night. He lives in the village on the other side of the highway."

"I thought Mr. Hearst closed the road."

"Do you think that's the only road up to the Ranch? It's for guests, like you."

"I see. I'm sorry if I jumped to conclusions," I said, offering my hand.

"You've got to be suspicious," Tom graciously replied, returning the gesture.

"By the way," I asked, "You didn't kill Sharkey, did you?"

Tom's eyes opened wide. His arms dropped to his sides. I studied the reaction, having experience in reading posture. Then Tom smiled.

"You're awful good, Dash. No wonder your books are so popular."

"You're no slouch, Mr. Wheatley. Have you finished cataloging the fingerprints?"

"Just about. Got some fragments that need extra care."

"Carlos erased the footprints around the crime scene."

"We've got the photos. Just need to develop the film."

"I only had the one. Probably not very good," I lamented.

"Then it's good I borrowed Miss Marion's camera and took ten more," Tom said.

"If you ever want a job as a Pinkerton, I'll give you a recommendation."

"I'm a might ripe in years for that. And I like this job. But wouldn't mind consulting on a script every now and then."

"Everyone wants another Thin Man movie. Maybe I can pick your brain?"

"I've got a few ideas."

Chapter Six

GRILLED SUSPECTS

I finally made it back to my room, gratefully showered, and wrapped myself in a thick cotton bathrobe provided by the Ranch. A pack of fresh ice was in the silver bowl on my dresser, which was very thoughtful of someone. There were giant pillows on the bed, allowing me to sit up with the ice on my shoulder while I made a list of suspects in my notepad.

From a writer's point of view, solving a crime is easier when you already know the ending. In this instance, I was not so fortunate. A few minutes later, Bill arrived with a stack of magazines from Hearst's library. Some were gossip rags, others were industry journals.

"Took a while to find everything you wanted," Bill apologized.

"I'm surprised you found any of it," I said.

"Think I'm dumb?"

"No, I think you're an actor."

"I'm smart enough to know murders don't happen for no reason. Are we working with a motive?"

"My best guess is blackmail. Lots of notes passing. Packets of negatives. Clandestine activity. If we keep digging, I'll bet some compromising photos show up. The question is what secret is so damaging that it's worth committing murder for?"

"What usually works in your books?"

"Blackmail is not a common crime. Not like in the magazines. The average joe can't afford to be blackmailed; they don't have the money. And those who do have the money don't talk about it."

"Makes sense. So who are your suspects?"

"What about Maureen?"

"Maureen?" Bill asked in surprise.

"Working on the least likely. Easier to weed out the also-rans that way. What's the dirt on her? Closet drinker? Nude photos?"

"Rumor says she's dating John Farrow."

"The Australian playboy?"

"They say Farrow's settled down since almost getting deported last year. Writing screenplays for RKO now."

"It would be hard to blackmail anyone dating John Farrow. No juice there," I said.

"Shall we cross her off the list?"

"We're not crossing anyone off the list yet, but Maureen does have a good alibi."

"Which is?"

"She was sitting next to me throughout the entire movie."

"Fine. Next victim," Bill agreed.

"Thomas Madison Wheatley."

"Who?"

"The butler."

"Pretty cliché, don't you think?"

"He's clever, well-read in murder mysteries, and fiercely loyal to Hearst. If he thought Sharkey had something on his boss, he might be capable of anything."

"Nothing here on the employees except their payroll records," Bill said, flipping through a ledger book. "Wheatley, Thomas. Hired as a gardener, April 9, 1922. Promoted to butler, February 1, 1926. Appointed Chief Steward, January 2, 1930."

"It wasn't Tom," I said.

"How do you know?"

"He's not really a butler. He's a manager. Managers don't kill people; they let others do it for them. And if he got someone to do the deed, we'd have never found the body."

"No dice on the butler. Who's next?"

"William Horatio Powell."

"Okay, now you're just being ridiculous. I was in the movie theater the whole time."

"My timeline could be off. Maybe Sharkey was killed before the movie and the cold kept the body fresh? Or maybe you snuck off and got him after the show while I was lighting my cigarette."

"I didn't kill Sharkey, and you know it."

"Yes, it was just a fun thought. How about Norma?"

Bill picked up a copy of *The Hollywood Reporter*. Hearst's library was well-stocked.

"She married Thalberg in '27. One of the biggest weddings Hollywood has ever seen. I was there. She stood by him when he got sick. Other than the usual jealousy, I've never heard a cross word against her."

"You're friends?"

"Yes, good friends."

"Okay, we'll cross her off the list," I said.

"I thought we weren't crossing anyone off the list?"

"Norma is too little to knock down that marble top. She's an elf. But then, if she had help?"

"Norma's back on the list?"

"Back on the list," I decided. "What about Miss Davies?"

"Marion..."

There was a knock on the door, not loud enough to be Rocky. Still hurting a bit, I let Bill jump up to answer it.

"Hello, Alice," Bill said, swinging the door wide.

"Hello, Mr. Powell. How are you feeling, Dash? I brought more ice," Alice said in her charming Midwestern accent.

Miss Fowler was dressed in a long white cotton robe from the pool, her swimming suit on underneath. I assumed. She carried a large silver bowl covered with an embroidered cotton towel. She had a bright look in her vivid blue eyes. The long auburn hair was damp but not wet. She set the bowl on my end table and drew the towel off. There was ice all right, and a pint bottle of Bacardi imported all the way from Cuba.

"You *are* a welcome sight," I said, straightening up from my pillows.

Alice poured each of us a glass, adding ice cubes, and passed them out with great delicacy. I wasted no time taking a sip.

"I haven't had rum this good since visiting Key West," I recalled. "Hemingway wanted me to go marlin fishing. I wanted to stay on dry land. But not too dry."

"Hemingway hated what Paramount did to A Farewell to Arms," Alice said, sitting on the bed next to me. "I really liked Gary Cooper, though. He was so romantic."

"I liked Helen Hayes," Bill said, smacking his lips.

"Miss Hayes is at MGM now. She made several movies for Mr. Mayer last year," Alice said.

"I saw her playing Mary of Scotland on stage at the Alvin Theatre around Christmas," I mentioned. "I wonder if she knew Sharkey McCann? Maybe we can pin the murder on her."

"That wouldn't be very nice," Alice said, scrunching her thin eyebrows.

"Don't worry, sweet stuff. Your heroine has a solid alibi. She's still performing in New York," I said.

"You have a cruel streak, Mr. Hammett," Alice complained.

"All detectives do."

"Speaking of which, should we get back to business? You were asking about—" Bill started to say.

"Irving Thalberg," I interrupted, giving him the evil eye.

It took Bill a moment to realize I didn't want to discuss Marion in front of Alice, but he soon took the hint.

"Didn't von Stroheim once threaten to punch Thalberg in the face?" I asked.

"Yes, and Thalberg dared him to do it," Bill confirmed.

"That's a bit rough and tumble. I hear he likes parties. And the ladies," I said.

"Mr. Thalberg would never step out on Norma. Not ever," Alice insisted. "He just likes to socialize. He calls it keeping his finger on the pulse of America."

"You're not going to find America's pulse at a party in Beverly Hills," I remarked.

"Irving is very smart. He reads philosophy," Alice defended.

"Enough to concoct a plausible murder scheme?" I asked.

"Come on, Dash. You've seen the shape he's in. If Norma is an elf, Irving is an elf's shadow," Bill said.

"Irving has trouble walking. It was even worse after he lost his cane," Alice said. "Marion had to loan him one of Mr. Hearst's antique walking sticks."

"I'll concede he's a poor suspect, but not impossible. And he seems to know more than he's letting on. Bill, you and I will need to draw him out, either at dinner or afterwards."

"He usually plays pool with W.R. after the meal," Alice said.

"I play a mean game of pool, too," I confessed. "Did you have any luck getting Johnny to talk?"

"A little," Alice admitted. "He and his wife aren't getting along. He's afraid the bad publicity will hurt the new movie."

"Unlikely," I said. "Unless word gets out that he's beating her."

"John wouldn't do that! He's nice. Really nice," Alice protested.

"I haven't heard any of that either," Bill said. "This report says he was born in Hungary in 1904, but his parents brought him to America six months later. He learned to swim at the YMCA. He won three gold medals at the Paris Olympics in '24, and then two more in Amsterdam in '28. Even got a bronze medal in water polo."

"Now that is a rough sport. Lots of punching," I said.

"A lot of elbows, to be sure. I haven't heard there's much punching in water polo," Bill disagreed. "Everything we've got on Weissmuller says he's a straight arrow."

"Those are the ones you have to watch out for," I said.

"John did not kill Mr. McCann. He couldn't have," Alice insisted.

"Somebody did. If not Weissmuller, then who?" I pressed.

Alice lowered her head, embarrassed to be put on the spot.

"We can't completely dismiss the staff. Especially Carlos," I said. "But I feel they are unlikely suspects. Unless they were acting on someone's behalf, the servants here just aren't the types to attack a guest."

"They are staff, not servants," Alice corrected me.

"Of course," I replied. "I didn't mean any disrespect."

"By someone's behalf, do you mean Mr. Hearst?" Alice asked.

"Hearst is a powerful man, accustomed to getting his own way. And he might not need anyone's help. With all the swimming and horseback riding he does, Hearst must be in pretty good shape. Did he have a grudge against McCann?"

"He's not happy that several glamor rags have started publishing stories of his relationship with Marion," Bill said.

"Everybody knows about that," Alice said.

"For years, publishers had a gentlemen's agreement about leaving the private lives of public figures alone. That seems to be breaking down," Bill explained.

"If Hearst wanted to get rid of Sharkey, he has plenty of ways to do it without killing him," I decided. "But he also wants to avoid a scandal. Let's find out where he went during the movie. Maybe he knows more about this than he's saying."

"I can speak with Julien and Sara," Alice offered. "Mr. Hearst often goes to the kitchen during the movies to check on preparations. And sometimes to answer phone calls. He's always busy doing something."

"Very good. Sounds like everyone knows their assignment," I concluded.

"Dash, there is someone missing from the suspect list," Bill said.

"Who?" Alice asked in surprise.

"Mr. Dashiell Hammett," Bill said. "How do we know *you* didn't kill Sharkey?"

"Now why would I kill Sharkey McCann?"

"Oh, I don't know," Bill continued. "Maybe he was going to reveal the plot of your next book. Or maybe he was cutting in on a broad you like. Hell, maybe you just didn't like the son of a bitch. And who better to get away with a murder than you?"

"All good points. Put me on the list," I said, finishing my rum.

"I'll check with Tom. Find out what the schedule is for tonight," Bill said. "Are you still planning on developing those negatives this afternoon?"

"Yes, we'll need to know what Sharkey was trying to hide."

"Negatives? Pictures?" Alice asked.

"Found them in McCann's room. After someone clobbered me trying to find them first," I said.

"Florsheim, size 10," Bill smirked.

"I've heard that joke enough."

"Do you think it was Mr. Knowles who hit you?" Alice said.

"Probably, though it's hard to imagine a shoe being Rocky's weapon of choice," I replied.

Bill left his pile of magazines and newspapers on the desk, going to find the butler. Alice stayed.

"Marion is wondering if we should call a doctor for your shoulder," she said.

"I've been hurt worse. Mostly in bar fights. Tell Marion that Sara did fine. And your rum was a blessing."

"I will leave out the part about the rum, even though she already knows. Marion keeps an eye on everything."

"Let's not let her know too much," I urged, pulling Alice close for a kiss. She didn't lean in, but she didn't pull back either.

"Marion and I don't gossip about our private affairs."

"Marion has affairs?"

"I didn't mean it like that. It's a figure of speech. She has always been faithful to Mr. Hearst."

"Has Hearst always been faithful?"

Alice appeared shocked by my question.

"Mr. Hearst is an old man."

I took that as a yes, as far as she knew.

"I've got to get dressed and down to Julia Morgan's dark room," I reluctantly announced. "You might want to put on some clothes. It gets cold late in the day."

"Can I help with the pictures?" she asked.

"I've arranged for some help, thank you. See if Marion might be a little more forthcoming. Anything she says will be held in confidence."

"Really?"

"I'm a writer, not a cop," I said.

———————

After sending Alice on her way, I found a shirt without holes in it, put on my dress coat, and left a note for Anna Lee to have my tweed jacket mended. It would look good with patches on the elbows. After a final sip of Bacardi, I stashed the bottle in a planter near the window.

A few steps down the hall brought me to the linen closet. I glanced in both directions, made sure no one was watching, and opened a drawer at the bottom filled with pillowcases. The negatives were hidden in a brown notebook containing my new novel. Or what would be my new novel, if I ever started writing it.

The sun was still up as I emerged from Casa Del Sol, but the air was cooling fast. With this part of the coast prone to heavy fog, I wondered how much visibility there'd be come dark.

The stone path going toward the movie theater took me past the crime scene. I paused to glance at the marble sarcophagus, but I didn't wish to show excessive interest. The rope Tom had put up was gone. On the far side of the plaza, the gardeners were raking leaves while pretending not to watch me.

Down on the tar-coated road leading toward the tennis courts, visible through the trees, I spied Marion and Norma on a bench deep in conversation. Norma appeared the more animated of the two, waving her slender arms. Marion seemed composed. I didn't see any notes passed.

I had intended to go around the main house, but to avoid Marion seeing me I decided to cut through the morning room instead. It was a mistake. Just as I was able to see Julia Morgan's office across the rear courtyard, W.R. Hearst intercepted me at the back door.

"Mr. Hammett, you're staying busy," Hearst said in a grumpy tone.

"I have a lot to keep me busy, sir."

"Have you solved Sharkey McCann's death?"

"Not yet, but narrowing down the possibilities."

"The sheriff needs to be called Monday morning. That gives you until tomorrow night," he warned.

"What is it you would like to have tomorrow night, if I may ask?"

"Answers. Answers I can use with the authorities."

"Answers or the truth?"

"I want the truth."

I doubted the father of yellow journalism wanted the truth if it proved inconvenient. Or damaging to someone he cared about. And I wondered what that meant for me.

"Dash, have you been drinking?" Hearst suddenly asked.

"It's medicinal," I replied. "After falling into the lion pit, I separated my shoulder. Weissmuller put it back in for me."

113

"Who got you the booze? Bill Powell?"

"I can't rat anybody out, sir."

He stepped back, looking me over. My jacket was rumpled, and my trousers stained at the knees. I'd washed but neglected to comb my bushy hair. Gray stubble showed I hadn't shaved in two days. Either I was beginning to look like Sam Spade or an Okie.

"Which cat almost got you?" he asked.

"Mr. Brand called him Mike."

"You got lucky. The males aren't aggressive predators like the females. Sheba would've have gutted you like an angry theatre critic. Not that Mike wouldn't have gotten around to it eventually."

"That would explain the nice conversation we had."

"See that your luck holds, Mr. Hammett. Stay off the hard stuff. The last thing I need is a drunk stumbling through my business."

"Yes, sir. I'll watch myself," I promised.

He studied me for another moment, unable to hide his doubts, and then disappeared into the kitchen.

Julia Morgan's office was on the ground floor of the south wing, a small space filled by filing cabinets and a drafting table. The space behind her office had been converted into a temporary darkroom, as evidenced by the crude shelving. Tom was already arranging the developing trays.

"Just another minute and we'll be ready to go, Mr. Dash," he said. "Make sure the curtains are closed tight. Don't want the negatives ruined."

"A wise precaution, Mr. Wheatley. The negatives we found in McCann's room are 35mm. Will that be a problem?"

"Nothing will be a problem. Miss Marion likes to see her photos fast, not wait until some flunky gets around to it. Sometimes she makes copies for the guests."

We started with the film from my Brownie, taking our time. I couldn't afford to screw up. The shots were good, under the circumstances. Better for an overview of the crime scene than targeting specific evidence. Some of the black and white prints were blown up to reveal more detail, but they didn't show anything I hadn't already seen.

"The sheriff might need these eventually. Let's mark them with the date and time."

"Easy to do," Tom confirmed, holding a grease marker. His handwriting was better than my chicken scratching.

"Okay, now let's see what McCann was up to," I said, taking the negatives out of the brown envelope carefully.

"Color film. This is going to be tricky. Better make contact prints," Tom announced, looking at the negatives before putting the first one into the developer.

It was not a quick process. We needed to keep the chemicals finely balanced as each image went through the stop bath, fixer, wash, and was finally transferred to paper. The shots were good. McCann must have been using an expensive camera.

"Lots a girls, Dash. And not all of them completely dressed," Tom said, working the trays like a pro.

"Do you recognize anyone?"

"Not so far."

"Looks like beach scenes," I said, looking at a photo on the drying rack.

"Santa Monica. These were taken near Miss Marion's beach house. See here? And here? It's the one Mr. Hearst built for her."

"That's a beach house? It looks like a palace," I said, seeing a huge three-story Georgian mansion at the foot of a giant cliff.

"They say it has a hundred rooms, but I've never counted them.

If you think the Hollywood stars flock to the Ranch, you should see one of their parties down there."

"Sharkey must have been taking pictures and saw something he shouldn't," I guessed.

"Maybe this," Tom said.

As the image came into focus, we saw Marion and Norma sitting on a park bench, scantily clad, and holding hands. Norma was leaning forward, perhaps saying something intimate. Marion appeared composed, eager to hear what Norma was whispering.

"It's just girl stuff," Tom quickly said, knowing what I was thinking. "The ladies do more touching than we do. It doesn't mean anything."

"Maybe not, but I can see why they might find it embarrassing in the wrong hands. Are there any more?"

There were three photos in all. A second showed them sitting closer on the bench, but no longer in conversation. The third had them resting back against an ivy-covered brick wall, Norma's head on Marion's shoulder.

"This is Hollywood, Mr. Hammett," Tom said, getting formal with me. "No one cares much about what women do. No gunsels here."

"I don't see anything worth killing over," I agreed. "But we're seeing the pictures for the first time. We don't know what Sharkey said he had, or how Marion or Norma might react. For that matter, we don't know how Hearst or Thalberg would react if they were clued in."

"What should we do?" Tom asked.

"Make two copies of each, then we'll destroy the negatives."

"Destroy evidence?"

"We don't know that these photos are evidence. And even if they are, I don't think Marion or Mr. Hearst wants a horde of ham-fisted cops pawing over them. Is that what you want?"

"No, sir. That's not what I want."

"You keep one set. Hide them good. I'll take the other to Marion and see what she has to say. Hopefully not a confession."

"You can't suspect—"

Casting suspicion on Marion caught Tom off-guard, much to my satisfaction. Perhaps he was not so unflappable after all.

"Don't be so serious, Mr. Wheatley. We're investigating a mysterious murder in an exotic location with a cast of intriguing suspects. It doesn't get better than this."

"Sir, how much you been drinkin'?"

"Not enough."

While Tom was finishing up, I stepped outside for a cigarette. I could see the tennis courts and the purple mountains looming behind them.

Something wasn't right. The photos were interesting, but as Tom said, hardly worth the time of someone like Sharkey McCann. I thought back on Sharkey's request for a meeting after the movie. What had he been after? And why would someone kill for it?

———

I wasn't looking forward to confronting Marion. I liked her, and doubted she had anything to do with Sharkey's murder, but she might know who did. From what I understood, she was in the gothic study on the third floor where I had met with Hearst the night before. I slowly made my way up the winding concrete stairs, careful not to trip. The dim lightbulbs weren't much help.

To my surprise, neither Marion nor Hearst was at home, but Irving Thalberg was, stuck in a big, overstuffed easy chair going through a stack of magazines.

"Good afternoon, Mr. Thalberg," I said, sitting on a stool next to him.

"Irving to my friends. Still looking for Sharkey's killer?"

"I guess word is finally getting around."

"Hard secret to keep in such a small group. Marion told Norma. Norma told me."

"And who told Marion?"

Thalberg smiled, a twinkle in his dark, studious eyes.

"It might have been W.R. Or maybe you aren't as clever with your subtle questioning as you believe?"

"Who was Sharkey McCann to you, if I may inquire?"

"A delivery boy. And I didn't know about the blackmail until last night. Not that I'm surprised. There are only two kinds of people in this town; those who keep secrets, and those who sell them."

"Which are you?"

"I keep secrets, Mr. Hammett. What I sell are stories."

"So tell me a story."

"In exchange for what?"

"If Norma's the killer, I'll give her a pass."

Thalberg laughed. "You might be better at this than I am, Dash, but I have nothing for you. Norma didn't kill Sharkey, and neither did I. Even if I did leave my cane behind after reprimanding him."

"In the garden next to the marble coffin?"

"Same place."

"Was Norma with you?"

"No, she and Marion had already left."

"What did Sharkey have on them?"

"Photographs."

"Of what?"

"I think you already know. At least, you think you do. In

Hollywood, nothing is ever as it seems."

I noticed him shiver, the big vaulted office being drafty. I found a plaid blanket to wrap over his shoulders. He offered a grateful nod.

"What's got you so busy?" I asked, glancing at the magazines.

"A story Rocky is spreading around. Sounds like a tall tale to me, but I wanted to check it out."

"Any luck?"

"No. Sharkey and Rocky were always getting mixed up in treasure hunts, none of which ever played out. Even this last venture of Sharkey's was destined for a bad end, though Rocky seems to think he has some leverage."

"Does he?"

"Not with me."

"Comes across like a tough character."

"Perhaps. But if he tries to put the arm on W.R., he'll find out what a tough character really looks like."

I had a lot more questions, but Thalberg drifted off to sleep and I didn't have the heart to wake him. I was just getting up when Marion entered.

"Dash, what a surprise," she whispered, drawing me to the far side of the room. "Did Irving confess? After beating that poor man with his cane?"

I should have realized she was joking, but the sore shoulder still bothered me, and I was trying to fathom Thalberg's enigmatic hints.

"Let's get you another aspirin," she said, opening the top drawer of a massive oak desk. I swallowed it with water this time.

"I found some film negatives in Sharkey's room," I said.

"Where?"

"Hidden under the leaf of a book. You didn't think to look there."

"No, I missed that one."

119

"Did you whack me over the head with a shoe?"

"Florsheim, size 10?"

"Bill is going to have a problem with me if he keeps telling that story."

She laughed.

"No Florsheim, Dash. I would have used a blackjack."

That was probably the truth. The lady had grit.

"I suppose you used my darkroom to develop the film?" Marion asked.

"Yes. You are in three of them. You and Miss Shearer."

"And now you think Norma and I are having an affair, Sharkey found out, and either I or Norma killed him rather than pay blackmail?"

"I'm investigating a death. I don't think anything until I have facts."

"Well then, here is a fact. Norma and I are not having an affair. We were never having an affair. Norma likes men, and I'm pretty fond of them, too."

"Then—"

"Dash, get me the negatives and I will be more forthcoming."

"I've destroyed the negatives. There are two sets of prints. I was planning on giving one set to you, and the other to Miss Shearer."

"Very generous."

"I'm not selling them, if that's what troubling you. I just wanted you and Norma to know what Sharkey had."

"We'll speak again, after dinner. When you have the pictures."

"Where should we meet? The garden next to the sarcophagus?"

"You *are* a rogue. No wonder your books are so popular."

She opened the desk drawer to put the aspirin back and I noticed a marked-up newspaper article. There was a photo of a necklace.

"What's that?" I said, pointing.

"The latest mystery."

"Diamond heist?"

"Not any diamond. The Silver Blaze," she said.

"Can I see?"

"Are you a diamond expert?"

"You'd be surprised."

"Then surprise me."

"I have a friend in San Francisco. Al Samuels. When I was writing The Dain Curse, he clued me in on the good stuff. I even dedicated the book to him."

"Did you seduce his daughter?"

"That's none of your business."

Marion smiled and took several articles cut out of New York newspapers, laying them on the desk. The black and white picture didn't do it justice, but it was the same necklace Skinny the Rat had given me in Los Angeles.

"The Silver Blaze?" I asked.

"It's a story going around on the lot. Many in the industry are Jewish, you know," Marion explained.

"I don't follow."

"This new government in Germany is making life difficult for Jews. Hamar Schacht, an industrialist with government connections, helped the Rosenthal family leave the country. In exchange, Rosenthal sold him the Silver Blaze."

"Fancy necklace. Four white diamonds and one large blue stone woven in a platinum setting?"

"That's the one. They say it was once the property of an Austrian Duke."

"Sounds like something Mr. Hearst would like to acquire?"

"Not if it's stolen," Marion replied.

I took a quick read of the article that Marion had underlined with a red pencil. Rosenthal had acquired the Silver Blaze in 1919 and then sold to Schacht last summer. The following November, when the luxury ship SS *Deutschland* collided with the American cargo vessel SS *Munargo* in New York Harbor, the necklace disappeared in the confusion.

"All very interesting," I remarked, dropping the newsprint back in the drawer. "Suspects?"

"The ship's crew. Longshoremen. The mob. The cops. Take your pick."

"Any idea what it's worth?"

"No one wants to say, but it must be worth at least $25,000."

"Sounds like a lot of trouble for a trinket," I said. "I'll have those photos after dinner. Let's avoid the garden."

Going back toward the pantry, I stumbled upon Rocky sitting in the kitchen working on a pitcher of brown beer. He saw me before I saw him.

"Hammett! Goddamn it, McCann is missing, and so is his notebook. What have you done with it?" he growled.

"Me? Why would I have anything to do with it?"

"Because you're the only one up here with any brains, except Miss Davies. I know you're up to something."

"Are you looking for McCann's notebook, or the photographs?"

"So you do know the score. Trying to cut yourself in?"

"I haven't seen the notebook, and Marion has the photographs, so I guess you're out of luck. McCann's probably caught a ride back to L.A. by now."

"What about the other?"

"The other what?"

"I'm really beginning to lose patience with you."

I walked up to the white wooden table where Knowles was sitting. Julien and Sara were watching from the hot stove as they prepared dinner. French game hens, by the delightful smell. Sara looked concerned. Julien looked like the sort who worried about nothing.

"Let me show you how impressed I am," I said, helping myself to a glass of beer. And then I poured it over his head.

"What the...?" Knowles howled, jumping from the chair.

I set myself, fists ready, looking for the best place to land a punch. Knowles was big and looked tough, but I'd taken on worse. Maybe not lately, but I had.

Knowles took a step, coming around the edge of the table. I moved a tiny half-step back for position, but then the brute slowed to a halt, looking at me with an angry but conflicted glare. Beer was dripping down through his thick brows, forcing him to wipe his eyes with his sleeve.

"Monsieur?" Julien said, suddenly standing at Rocky's side with a towel.

"Gracias," Rocky said, running the towel over his bushy hair.

"May we get you a fresh shirt, sir?" Julien asked.

"No thanks, Frenchie, I'll get my own shirts," Rocky answered. "But don't think this is over, writer-boy. I won't get what I want by beating you down now, but a reckoning is coming. You had better get me my prize before something bad happens."

Rocky stormed out of the kitchen, leaving his half-empty beer glass behind. Julien burst into a grin. Sara smiled softly and turned back to the stove.

"A most unpleasant gentleman," Julien observed.

I offered Julien a thankful nod and headed downstairs into the storage corridor, finding the door to the cold room unlocked. Tom was inside.

"Have the photographs?" I brusquely asked.

"Yes, two sets," Tom said, handing me two vanilla envelopes. I glanced inside, seeing clearly developed 8x10s.

"The negatives?" I inquired.

"Burned."

"We need to watch out for Knowles. He was in on the blackmail and awful unhappy not to be getting what he expected."

"I heard. We ain't that far from the kitchen, you know. What's this prize he's all heat up over?"

"I can't say for sure, and it might be best you don't know."

"It might be best that I do know. It's my job."

I had to give it some thought. Though not anxious to discuss stolen property, Tom had proven to be my most reliable ally.

"Knowles may be searching for a stolen diamond necklace, hoping for a big payoff. There's a jewel thief involved, wrecked boats, Austrian princes, Jews and Nazis."

"Is yous makin' all this shit up?"

"Not by half."

"So where is it?"

"I've told Knowles I don't have it."

"So where is it?"

"In a safe place."

"We still gots a little matter of a murder to solve, Mr. Hammett. We'll get all the guests tonight at dinner."

"That should narrow it down for us."

"You got a suspect, don't you?"

"We'll need to see where this goes. I've been wrong before."

I still had some time before dinner, just enough to rest up and clear my head. I noticed the groundskeepers wrapping up their work day as I entered the courtyard. Carlos was giving me the eye. The Mexicans had Sunday off, and being Catholics, would likely spend the whole day in church or a fiesta, which suited me just fine.

"Your guys are off the hook," I casually mentioned in passing.

"We never should have been on a hook," Carlos grouched.

"That wasn't my call. I'm just doing Mr. Hearst a favor."

"We trust Mr. Hearst. He will do right by us."

"I expect so," I said, quickly moving on.

Behind me, I heard them muttering in Spanish. I knew a few words. Enough to know their comments were not kind.

My room was quiet when I returned, no one standing behind the door ready to bash me on the head. I rushed for the shower, took a shot of Bacardi, and stretched out on the firm bed. I was nearly asleep when a familiar perfume, still laid on a bit too thick, caused me to stir.

"You've had a long day," Alice said.

"Maybe it will make a good script."

"You'll need to change the names."

She dropped off her long coat, wearing a frilly white cotton dress underneath. "Make room," she said, crawling into the bed and pulling up the heavy quilt.

"Bring your nightgown?" I asked.

"Left it in my room."

"You must be curious."

"Of course I am."

"I'll know more this evening, when Tom and I have gathered the fingerprints. Maybe we can meet here later for a nightcap?"

"That would be nice," she said, putting her head on my good shoulder.

And then I fell asleep.

_____

I woke up feeling someone next to me, but it wasn't Alice. A woman. Cheap perfume. Her long hair was brushing my face as she knelt over me, and then I felt a blade pressed against my throat.

"No stallin', Hammett. Where is the dingus?" a cool, throaty voice said.

"Dingus?"

"The dingus. The goods. The ice. The real thing. I know you've got it."

I pushed the knife aside, turned on the bedside lamp, and took a look at my would-be assailant. She was pushing forty with ruddy cheeks and deep brown eyes made blurry by lack of sleep. Her long black hair hung down from her bony shoulders.

"Who the hell are you? Hearst really does need to get some security up here," I complained, reaching for my half-filled shot glass. It was empty. Either Alice or the intruder had beat me to it.

"Who I am is unimportant. Give me what I want or you'll be regretting it."

"I don't claim to know what you're talking about. If it's the negatives, they've been destroyed."

"Negatives of what?"

"Two major Hollywood movie stars having a lesbian love affair."

"Good for them. Now give me what I what."

"I know you're not after the plot to my next book. If you're looking for a certain diamond necklace, it's not here. And even if I had it, there's no reason I'd give it to you."

"I have a knife," she pointed out.

I smacked her in the face with the back of my hand, grabbed the knife, and got ready to hit her again. She didn't resist. I had the impression she was accustomed to getting roughed up.

It was an Italian switch-blade with a tiger-striped Bakelite handle, popular on the Jersey boardwalks. I folded the knife up, slid it into my pocket, and reached for the bottle of Bacardi on the floor.

"Care for a snort?" I asked, offering the shot glass.

"Won't turn it down," she said, taking a sip. "Smooth."

"Hemingway sent it to me."

I went to the nightstand, dipped a towel in the cold water left over from the melted ice, and pressed it against her cheek. She adjusted the towel closer to her eye.

"You hit like a girl," she said.

"Yeah, I've been told that."

"What do you want for the... the...?"

"Stuff that dreams are made of?"

"Enough to keep a girl in high heels," she said, trying to smile.

"You must be Saucy LaRue."

"Dorothy to my friends."

"Good with your hands and fond of stolen merchandise."

"Gosh, you really are a detective."

"So what is a nice gal from Brooklyn doing in California attacking strangers in the night for a stolen necklace? You can't front something that well-known."

"After the reward."

"And who is the benefactor? Same buyer that Rocky Knowles hinted about?"

"Where did you see Rocky?"

"He's got a room overlooking the airfield. Swaggering around talking about dire consequences."

"They are dire, especially for you," Saucy said.

127

"I may be able to cut you in, but only if you spill what you know. I'm not afraid of Rocky. Or a girl with bad hair."

"There is someone you should be afraid of."

"And who would that be?"

She looked at me like I must be dense.

"Okay, Homer, here's the scoop. Sharkey setup Mrs. Schacht for the heist."

"Sharkey?"

"We met through a mutual friend."

"By the name of Bugsy Siegel?"

"Ain't naming no names."

"Go on."

"Well, it all worked like a charm. The longshoremen arranged a collision in the harbor, I made the grab in the confusion, and took it on the lam. But some Huns got on my tail, so I ditched the ice with Sharkey."

"How did the Rat end up with it?"

"Don't know that part, but after Skinny dumped the Blaze on you, he ratted you out to Siegel. Now they say Bugsy's looking for blood, and it's your blood he wants. Clear enough, smart guy?"

"Why would one necklace be that important? It's shiny enough, but not big league."

"Don't know either, and I don't care. I just want my cut."

I poured her another drink. It all made sense, though I was sure there was more to the story. There always is.

"Does Mr. Siegal know I'm up here vacationing at Versailles?" I asked.

"Probably not yet."

"How did you know?"

"My pal Maisie Walker passed it along."

"Stay here, I'll be back in a minute."

"Not joining me?" she asked, patting the bedcover.

"Sorry, snickers. Can't afford you."

LaRue was going to be a problem, but one that needed to wait. Oddly, I felt somewhat refreshed despite the rude awakening, sore shoulder, and modest hangover. I was trying to map out how the evening would go, and what to do with what I was learning. If I hoped to get more work from Hearst, I'd need to tread carefully on some delicate toes.

My best suit had been cleaned, pressed, and hung in the closet. Fresh socks and underwear lay on the dresser. I detected the scent of lilac water in the wash bowl. All very thoughtful.

"I can't get you an invitation to dinner," I said, adjusting my blue silk tie, "but I might get you a room where Knowles won't see you. We can discuss the missing property later."

"You know where it is?" Saucy said, crawling to the edge of the bed.

"Let's just say I have a clue, and I'm not greedy. Do we have an understanding?"

"You're my best bet. At the moment," she agreed.

Her word was worth nothing, of course, but postponing a situation was better than inviting one prematurely.

"THE BARRETTS OF WIMPOLE S!"

Chapter Seven

UNINVITED GUESTS

I rushed into the courtyard, finding Maureen, Johnny, Norma and Thalberg formally attired, at least by Ranch standards. No one was wearing a tux. Bill caught up a moment later, out of breath.

"You didn't say anything about a roommate," he whispered.

"Not my roommate. Maybe yours, if you can afford her."

"She doesn't look like a working girl."

"She's a jewel thief, and she likes knives."

"What's she doing here? In your room?"

"That's a long story."

We entered the grand museum as a group, greeted by Tom at the door. He was dressed more formally than any of us, wearing a black dress coat with a ruffled gray collar and white gloves.

"Welcome, welcome," Tom said, taking our hats and scarves. "Refreshments is coming. Just takes a seat."

The Assembly Room was drafty despite a crackling fire in the massive marble fireplace. Bill followed Norma over to sit at the piano, the mood somber. Just twenty-four hours before, Sharkey McCann had arrived through those same doors, and now everyone in the room knew he was dead. Even if they didn't know the precise circumstances. It felt like a dark cloud, but no one was mourning. It was more the tension of not knowing what was going to happen next. When Bill tapped out a familiar dirge on the keyboards and sang "dum, dum, ta dum," it didn't go over well.

Norma finally became impatient with the morose atmosphere, playing a popular tune from *42nd Street*. She had a deep, throaty voice, singing "I Only Have Eyes for You" to Bill so seductively that it was embarrassing. Thalberg didn't seem to mind, plopped in an overstuffed armchair once owned by a French duke. Still in her kitchen whites, Sara brought Irving a drink and made a fuss over him. I noticed Bill strolling around the perimeter of the room with Johnny and Maureen gazing at the three-hundred-year-old Flemish tapestries.

"See one you like?" I asked, giving Bill a nudge with my elbow.

It would have been a silly question for me. My cottage in Florida could never accommodate such massive weavings, some ten or twelve feet tall. Bill Powell's lush Spanish villa in Whitley Heights offered considerably more room.

"Not exactly my style," Bill answered. "Besides, Carole would have used them for carpeting. And had a good laugh over it, too."

I knew Bill and his comedian wife had divorced the year before but managed to remain friends. It spoke well of his character.

131

Hearst arrived from his secret door on schedule, lingering near the piano in good spirits. He was particularly attentive to Norma, with whom Marion had been spending a lot time. He sat next to Thalberg for a moment, sharing a copy of *The Hollywood Reporter*. He joked with Johnny, gave Maureen a hug, and offered me a genial nod from across the room.

After the pleasantries had been satisfied, Hearst herded everyone into the Refectory, pushing me and Bill along while boasting of the greatest meal we would ever have. Unlike the night before, Norma was seated next to Marion, who sat next to Hearst, with Maureen on his other side.

The men were all sitting on the other side of the table, Thalberg across from Hearst, Johnny to his right, and Bill and then I to his left at the lower end of the pecking order. There was an extra place setting next to Johnny that I hoped meant Alice would attend, but was disappointed. Arriving late and full of bluster was Rocky Knowles.

"Thank you for inviting me, Mr. Hearst," Knowles said, tucking his table napkin into his collar. He was still wearing the buckskin flight jacket but had dispensed with the leather football helmet.

"I hear you've made yourself unwelcome in my kitchen, Mr. Knowles. I trust you shall respect my table?" Hearst said with jovial caution.

Knowles nodded, wisely choosing not to counter the slander. If slander it was.

"How are you, Dash? How is the shoulder?" Marion asked as Tom placed baskets of bread, butter and honey on the table.

"Not bad at all, thank you. A bit sore, perhaps."

"How did you fall in that pit?" Thalberg asked. "Didn't you see the lion?"

"Yes, I saw the lion. As for the pit, you might ask Rocky," I said.

"Mr. Knowles?" Marion inquired, scrunching her eyebrows.

Everyone turned to see what Rocky had to say. He appeared pleased with himself, a bread roll in one hand and a butter knife in the other.

"What would that have to do with me?" Knowles said.

"Please. I know it was you who pushed me," I replied.

"Pushed?" Marion said. "On purpose?"

"How do you know it was Rocky?" Hearst asked.

"Johnny and Red Brand were with Marion and Maureen. Bill was meeting Norma at the stables. The gardeners were still in the plaza. And Irving can't walk that far. Only Rocky had motive, means and opportunity."

"It was just a joke," Knowles said. "You should have seen Hammett flapping his arms. You'd have thought he was a parrot."

Knowles laughed, waving his elbows up and down.

"That's terrible," Maureen said, glad to be sitting far away from him.

"Dash and I play games all the time. Tag. Gotcha. Hide and Seek," Knowles said. "He knows I meant no harm. Don't you, Dash?"

"It was all in good fun, Rocky," I agreed. "I may even have a surprise for you before too long."

The main course was broiled game hens, mashed potatoes in gravy, and sautéed asparagus in garlic sauce. Very tasty. A fine Bordeaux was served, Rocky emptying his glass and getting a refill before Bill and I even had a taste. I glanced at Hearst, wondering why he was allowing such boorish behavior. The tycoon was annoyed, but not enough to say anything. Did Rocky have something on him? I looked across at Marion, but her cheerful smile betrayed nothing.

The far door opened with a squeaking shudder. Tom appeared, his expression a mixture of nervousness and a hint of delight.

"Mr. Hearst, you have a new guest. He asks permission ta see you," Tom announced from the door.

Mr. Hearst stood up with a curious look as a squat, overdressed Bavarian entered, his black tie and tails far exceeding the occasion. He wore a white cravat, a gold medallion over his breast pocket, and even had a monocle dangling from his right eye. It was the outfit of a foreign diplomat. He was followed by a tall, strait-laced assistant in a gray army uniform. It wasn't an American uniform. More European. The soldier's decorations were subtle, befitting a diplomatic mission, but I did notice a swastika sewn above the left breast pocket.

"Good sir, my name is Ernst von Münch, attaché to the German Consulate in San Francisco," the balding visitor said, approaching to shake hands. His attempt at an ingratiating smile was offset by a weaselly glower in his light blue eyes. "This is my aide, Lieutenant Wilhelm Kemper."

Kemper came to attention and clicked his heels. I put him at twenty-five years old, fresh-faced and eager to please. Possibly raised on a farm, judging by his posture and broad shoulders.

"What can we do for you, Herr Münch?" Hearst asked, returning the handshake.

"We have business to discuss, Mr. Hearst, but my mission should not trouble your distinguished company," Münch replied.

"Would you join us?" Hearst invited.

"By all means," Münch agreed.

But a subtle glance by Hearst warned that not all were so welcome. Lieutenant Kemper took the hint and quietly withdrew, likely to have dinner in the kitchen with the help. That wasn't going to go over well with Julien.

Marion switched places with Norma to sit next to Münch, being the good hostess, which placed the German diplomat directly across from me and Bill. She also made a round of introductions as Hearst remained subdued.

"So, what brings a lousy stinking Kraut to Shangri-La?" Knowles asked from the end of the table.

Needless to say, everyone was shocked, regardless of how some may have agreed with him. Münch was not flustered. He probably assumed Knowles was a veteran of the AEF, harboring a grudge from The Great War. And for all I knew, that was correct.

"I am new to your beautiful country," Münch graciously explained, fiddling with the monocle as Sara brought him a plate. "I flew above the Atlantic in the Graf Zeppelin last month, and then took your marvelous rail network to the West Coast."

"And took pictures of our military bases, I bet," Knowles said.

"Perhaps, a few," Münch said with a grin.

"That is sufficient, Mr. Knowles," Hearst warned.

"Yes, sir," Knowles meekly acknowledged, reaching for more wine.

"You are a long way from San Francisco, Herr Münch," I remarked.

He looked at me with an unspoken thought, his gaze searching.

"I enjoyed The Maltese Falcon, Mr. Hammett," Münch said. "Perhaps the Black Bird can still be recovered?"

"I hear your *Führer* specializes in miracles," I responded.

Being sympathetic to the German communists, the election of a new fascist government in Germany the year before had come as an unpleasant surprise. It was bad enough that Mussolini was still in power after fourteen years, even if the Italian trains did run on time.

"Herr Hitler has brought pride back to the Fatherland," Münch said. "After years of humiliation, we are finally asserting our rights."

"What rights would those be?" Hearst inquired.

"The rights of Germans in German lands, and a pure German heritage. And the right to travel abroad without being robbed," Münch said, glancing in my direction.

"Hitler has moved rapidly to secure his power," Hearst said. "Perhaps you can provide an interview for my newspapers? Let the American people know what to expect from the new leadership."

"I am at your service, sir," Münch agreed.

Talk returned to more familiar topics. What to wear at the upcoming *Tarzan and His Mate* premiere. How to look composed on the red carpet while a thousand light bulbs are popping in your face. What new projects did Irving have cooking? When Bill mentioned *The Barretts of Wimpole Street*, Marion quickly changed the subject.

Throughout dinner, I noticed Münch keeping an eye on me, as if evaluating how I should be approached. As a henchman of the new Reich, I supposed he would attempt to bully information from me, though it would be in vain. As a Pinkerton, I had barged into seedy bars, walked dark streets, and wrestled with violent suspects. I thought it was Knowles that Münch should worry about. The thuggish pilot glared down the table in a soft rage, fondling his butter knife like a dagger.

"I read in the paper that Hitler—" Bill started to say.

"Which paper?" Hearst interrupted.

"The *Times*," Bill confessed, a rival of Hearst's *Los Angeles Examiner*.

"We won't be discussing politics at the table tonight," Hearst said.

"I was just curious," Bill pressed. "As you know, Mr. Münch, Hollywood is a company town. Most of the studio heads are Jews.

Didn't—"

"Mr. Powell, I said that will be enough," Hearst insisted, half-rising from his seat. "If Herr Münch has anything to say about the Jews, he can say it to the Examiner. Maybe that will give you an excuse to buy my newspaper."

I wondered what Thalberg was thinking. Though born in Brooklyn, he was the son of German Jewish immigrants. Nothing showed in his expression, neither anger nor any particular interest in what Münch had to say. As far as I knew, Thalberg was the only Jew among the weekend guests. His wife was known to be Protestant.

The meal proceeded without references to Hitler's ambitions in a world still racked by the Crash of '29, which was too bad. I was hoping to learn if Germany was meddling in Spanish politics as Hemingway predicted they would.

Dessert was a light lemon soufflé. There would be no movie this Saturday night, probably because of McCann, but nothing was said. Knowles still seemed in the dark about his friend's fate, and it was none of Münch's business.

Most of us adjourned to the Assembly Room, Knowles being excused. Hearst and Münch did not follow, apparently having a private conversation elsewhere. Marion arrived just as Norma, Maureen, Bill and I were starting a bridge game in the alcove near the long bay windows.

"Dash, Pops wants to see you in the Billiard Room," she requested, though from Hearst nothing could really be treated as a request. I excused myself, asking Thalberg to sit in for me and not lose any money. I was joking but wasn't sure if he knew that.

We passed back through the Refectory to the Morning Room and made a sharp left down the hall into the Billiard Room. The kitchen was just behind me in the other direction. I noticed Knowles in the junction trying to make nice with Anna Lee. I didn't think he was so open-minded. By appearances, Anna Lee was showing mild interest.

Like the Castle's other rooms, the billiard parlor was cluttered with artifacts, wood carvings and dangling chandeliers. The high Spanish ceiling was painted with elaborate scenes of dukes and knights. Old Flemish tapestries hung on the stone walls. There were two game tables, one six-pocketed for pool, the other pocketless for billiards.

Hearst and Münch stood near a tall marble fireplace, Münch with a glass of white wine, Hearst holding a cup of coffee. Marion discreetly disappeared.

"Dash, I think you need to hear this," Hearst said, sounding displeased. "Herr Münch, would you please explain this problem again?"

"Of course, sir. I am acting on behalf of General Göring," Münch replied. "He was in negotiations with Hamar Schacht to buy a piece of jewelry when it was stolen by gangsters in New York Harbor. He has requested the consulate's assistance in recovering the item. This is why I have come to you, Mr. Hearst."

"Why would you think I know anything of this?" Hearst asked.

"Mr. Hearst, you are a famous collector of precious relics. Perhaps the most famous. Certainly the Silver Blaze, once owned by Archduke Ferdinand, would add luster to your collection?"

"Sir, I am not a thief," Hearst curtly responded, taking a step back. "Nor do I traffic in stolen goods."

"Not even with the famous Dashiell Hammett as your agent?" Münch said.

"Not even," Hearst replied. "Dash, do you know anything about this?"

"I read about the theft in the newspaper, Mr. Hearst. The Examiner. But I don't have any personal information about a supposed robbery."

"Supposed? Are you denying the Silver Blaze was taken from a citizen of the Reich?" Münch pressed. And he had an effective angry glare, one eye staring indignantly through the monocle. Maybe his anger was genuine, but I doubted it.

"I understand that the necklace was extorted from Franz Rosenthal. That hardly makes it Herr Schacht's legal property. Or General Göring's, for that matter," I said, adding the last bit just to rile him. Hearst gave me a frown.

"We aren't lawyers, Dash. If you know something about this, you need to speak up," Hearst said.

"We aren't cops either. I'm under no obligation to return property that isn't mine to someone with a doubtful claim on it."

"Then you do have it?" Münch said.

"I wouldn't go so far as to say I have it," I answered, jiggling my coat pockets.

"Mr. Hearst, I must demand the rights of German citizens be respected!" Münch said, reaching for a pool cue from the wall. It was a posh stick, ivory-handled with silver inlays. For a moment, I thought he might try using it as a weapon, but then he leaned over the pool table, pretending to line up an imaginary ball.

"Do you play, sir?" I asked.

"Billiards was invented in Germany," he said.

"Are you familiar with 8-Ball?" I inquired.

"Of course," Münch said.

"Then we should have a stake match. I will play you for information. Best two out of three. You win, I'll tell what I know."

"And if you are the victor?"

"Then I get that fancy eye-piece of yours."

"My monocle?" Münch said, clutching it against his chest.

"Sounds like a fair bet," Hearst said with a wry smile.

There was a knock on the door, and Tom appeared with Lieutenant Kemper in tow, now wearing a conservative blue business suit. I noticed a gold swastika pin on his lapel. Hearst nodded to Tom that is it was okay, allowing the chiseled aide to enter.

"Lieutenant Kemper will be my second," Münch announced.

I noticed Knowles still lingering in the hallway, flirting with Anna Lee, occasionally glancing in our direction.

"Very well. Rocky, would you please come here?" I said, wiggling my finger at him.

Carrying a beer stein, Knowles quickly followed Kemper through the door.

"Rocky, we are about to play a high stakes game. Will you be my wingman?" I requested, nodding toward the Germans.

"I'm your guy, Dash," Knowles agreed, giving the Germans a dirty look.

"May I assist?" Kemper said, reaching for a triangle to rack the balls.

"Your accent is more Wisconsin than Berlin," I remarked.

"My parents immigrated to this country when I was a child," Kemper explained. "I was raised in Racine before going to college in Berlin."

"And joined the German army?" I asked.

"These are troubled times for the Fatherland," Kemper said.

"Let me guess. Your parents are members of the Friends of Germany?" I said.

"What do you know of the Friends, Mr. Hammett?" Münch asked.

"I know the organization was ordered by your Rudolf Hess to spread anti-Semitism in America, and its leader was deported last October for being a foreign agent," I replied.

"Herr Spanknöbel may have grown too enthusiastic in his duties," Münch said, "but the Friends are not political. They merely seek to preserve their German heritage."

"Bunch of goddamn Hun traitors. We should hang every last one of those sons of bitches," Knowles sneered.

Kemper took umbrage at Knowles's remark, his dark brows furrowing and fists clenched, but Hearst intervened.

"Mr. Knowles, you will respect my guests or find yourself flying for Jack Warner instead," Hearst warned. "And the cheap son of a bitch doesn't pay half what I do."

"Yes, sir. I'm sorry, sir," Knowles meekly if insincerely replied.

I selected a pool cue from the rack, a thin stick far less ornate than Münch's but likely to be more effective.

"Shall we lag for the break?" I asked.

I let Münch win the lag by a few inches, wanting to see his play before committing myself. He was a bit paunchy leaning over the table but snapped off a good break, sinking a stripe. He followed with two more before missing a close corner shot.

I gave Hearst and Rocky a confident nod and spent several moments circling the table as I pretended to line up my first shot. Which had been obvious at once. Playing the solid balls, there were several easy shots, and then some tough ones before getting to the eight-ball. But I wanted to watch how Münch reacted to my inspection, following his gaze to see if he perceived the game in a similar vein. The room was very quiet.

My best angle caused me to stand in front of Kemper, who seemed to creep up more than necessary as he looked over my shoulder. Hearst watched from the fireplace. Knowles had taken a seat on a tall barstool in the opposite corner. I sank three solids to even the score, then grazed a stripe before hitting my target, surrendering the initiative, for the rules said that failing to strike my own ball first counted as a scratch. Münch placed the cue-ball at the far end of the table, knocked in his final four balls, and then tapped in the eight-ball for the win.

Having won the first game, it was still Münch's turn. He gave me a curious look.

"You may have the honor, Mr. Hammett," Münch graciously conceded.

Kemper quickly racked the balls, but I took my time making the break, watching Münch out of the corner of my eye. He was a cool character, but his aide wasn't. Kemper fidgeted, wrung his hands, and kept reaching into his pockets. I noticed a familiar bulge under his jacket, likely a small caliber pistol in a shoulder holster.

My break shot was strong, but no balls dropped in, giving Münch several good options. He went on a streak, sinking all but the ten-ball before running out of angles. He nestled the cue-ball behind the eight-ball, hoping I would scratch, but I got off a sharp bank shot and started a run. Soon we were both down to single balls, and it was still my turn.

"Two-ball in the side pocket, and then the eight-ball in that corner," I announced, using my cue as a pointer.

I studied the shot carefully despite Kemper suddenly walking around to the other side of the table to distract me. Münch and Hearst pretended not to notice. Knowles frowned, moving to the edge of his chair. The two-ball dropped nicely, and the cue-ball crept slowly down the length of the table, just barely tapping the eight-ball in with a touch of drama. Several in the room let out their breaths, including me.

"You play well, sir. We will see if you play well enough," Münch said, adding more chalk to the tip of his stick.

"Care to raise the stakes?" I asked.

"What is your proposition?" Münch said.

I gave the room a discerning glance, letting everyone know I had something special in mind. And then I walked Münch down to the far corner where we wouldn't be overheard.

"If you win the third game, I will take you, and only you, to the person holding the Silver Blaze," I whispered.

"And if you are victorious?"

"Then I will ask you a specific question, and on your honor, you must answer it. And it stays between us."

Münch stepped back, looking me over. There was the barest hint of a smile on his thin lips.

"I like you, Mr. Hammett. It's a wager."

We lagged for the final match, which I won. The break went nicely, dropping the three-ball, but I was unable to run the table. My five-ball drifted to the edge of a corner pocket, protected by the eight-ball. Münch did well running the stripes until down to his last two balls, both hugging that pesky eight-ball, which would knock in my last ball if given the chance. And worse, he created a narrow line down the side for me to make my final shot.

"Tough one," Münch said, circling the table looking for an angle.

He didn't have a good play on this shot, but if he could get me to scratch, he could angle his last two balls away from the eight-ball and possibly win. But if I didn't scratch, he would risk giving me my opening. Münch walked to the rack of antique cues, searched them out, and selected a new stick. He didn't bother to chalk the tip.

"Fifteen in the corner," he announced, though there was no way that would happen. He'd have to bounce it over the eight-ball first.

Münch set himself along the side of the table, raised the butt end of his cue high, and drove down with the tip. To everyone's surprise, instead of hitting the cue-ball, the stick tore a four-inch gash in the green baize fabric. The cue-ball angled off, and both of his remaining balls rolled toward the center, where they'd be easier to play.

"My apologies, sir," Münch said, standing back from the damaged table.

I glanced at Hearst, who appeared unhappy, and then noticed the gash lay right across my only good line of play. I turned back toward Münch, seeing him with the slightest trace of a satisfied grin. Kemper wore a big smile, pleased with his boss's cleverness.

It was my turn, the cue-ball now blocked from the five-ball by a ravine. I considered calling a foul, but that was the last resort of a sore loser, and Dashiell Hammett was no quitter. A drunk, an adulterer, and sometimes a hack, but never a quitter.

I circled the table three times. Once to see the best angle, and two more times for show. I paused to chalk the cue, patted my pocket to see if my cigarettes were still there, and snuck a wink at Rocky, letting him know I was having fun. Rocky frowned, thinking I was taking it all too lightly. Hearst was frowning, too, perhaps getting a bit impatient.

"Five-ball in the corner," I announced.

The cue-ball traveled straight, jumped a bit when it hit the ruffled edge of the tear, and bounced the five-ball into the pocket before rolling back into the center.

"About time," Rocky said, letting out his breath.

"A superb shot," Münch congratulated.

I couldn't tell what Hearst thought. Kemper said nothing.

"Eight-ball in the corner," I said, sinking the final shot without drama.

I set the cue stick in the rack and stepped back next to Rocky, waiting to see what would happen.

"How'd you do that?" Rocky quietly asked.

"If you've seen the pool tables on the Lower East Side, you'd know a little hole or two isn't much of an obstacle," I whispered.

Münch passed his cue to Kemper before walking in my direction. He didn't look particularly upset.

"Your trophy, sir," Münch said, reaching into his breast pocket to retrieve the monocle. When he handed it to me, I fumbled and almost dropped it, causing Münch to pinch the lens between his thumb and index finger, leaving a clear fingerprint. The monocle was heavier than I expected because of the round gold frame. I wrapped the prize in a handkerchief.

And then Münch took a small leather container from his pocket, revealing a second monocle just as nice as the one he lost. He put it up to his eye.

I could not suppress a smile. The German was a rascal. We walked back toward the empty corridor that led to the movie theater.

"Your question?" Münch asked once we were alone.

"You sent someone here to scout out the location of the Silver Blaze. Who is it?"

Münch stepped back in surprise. He shouldn't have been. It was an easy deduction. And I would know if he lied.

"We were offered the services of Mr. Ambrose McCann, who accepted the commission," Münch revealed.

"Offered by who?"

"Ah, you only won one answer, Mr. Hammett. Only one."

Münch made a quick turn on his heels and returned to the

Billiard Room, where he nodded to Mr. Hearst.

"Good evening, gentlemen," Münch said with a grateful bow.

Münch and Kemper began to leave, but Knowles suddenly got up from his stool, bumping into the Wisconsin turncoat. I can't say for sure if Knowles deliberately incited an altercation, or if Kemper was the provocateur, but it quickly didn't matter.

"Goddamn Hun," I heard Rocky grunting as he pinned Kemper against the second billiard table.

Rocky raised his arm to deliver a punch. Kemper pushed Rocky back, belting him with a shot to the jaw. Rocky staggered, caught his balance, and charged forward again, fists flying. None of them were landing with any force, possibly because he was drunk.

Kemper deflected a blow, and then another, keeping his arms up and feet apart. He'd had experience in the ring, even bobbing and weaving to avoid getting hit. I considered intervening, and then thought better of it. Münch was enjoying the fight, standing next to Hearst. Hearst looked a little exasperated. I supposed fisticuffs among his guests was not an ordinary event.

Experience in a boxing ring doesn't always give an edge over a street brawler. Rocky threw some low punches that had Kemper huffing for breath, then turned the Wisconsin German around, intending to drive his head into the wall. But before he made good, Hearst grabbed his shoulder, pulling them apart. As I suspected, he was strong for such an old man.

"That will be enough, Mr. Knowles," Hearst demanded.

Rocky wanted to keep fighting, but when Münch suddenly got in the way, he relented. Though Hearst's voice was often high-pitched, there was something very menacing about the way he growled.

"Sorry, Mr. Hearst. The Kraut started it," Rocky said, blood dripping from his lip.

Kemper neither confirmed nor denied the accusation, brushing down his jacket. I assumed Hearst would toss Rocky off the ranch for his bad manners, but no such declaration was made. I took Rocky by the elbow and drew him off into the hallway. Julien and Sara had been watching, but they dispersed quickly. Rocky and I continued out into the cool night air through a side door.

"Thank you, Mr. Knowles. That proved entertaining," I said, offering a cigarette.

"It don't change nothin' between us," Knowles answered, taking out a fancy pewter lighter. "I know you've got the Blazer now, so you can either partner with me, or I'm going to take it."

"I told that Hun the truth. I haven't got the Silver Blaze."

"You know where it is, which is just as good. What really happened to McCann? Did you put him under because he found out about the necklace, or is he helping you find a buyer?"

"Maybe you aren't such great friends after all?"

"We served in the 95th Squadron together, which makes us more than friends. Don't mean we can't pursue our own interests."

"I have no intention of interfering with your interests, provided they don't interfere with mine," I warned.

I stubbed my cigarette out on the cement planter, gave him a firm look, and headed back toward the Assembly Room. Rocky would do whatever he was going to do. I couldn't stop him, but he wasn't going to buffalo me.

Chapter Eight

MIDNIGHT QUARRELS

I was hoping to see Alice, who had not appeared at dinner, but needed to complete an urgent mission first. Finding Tom in the Refectory where they were still cleaning up from dinner, I pulled him aside.

"Thomas, does Mr. Hearst have a gun?" I asked.

"Mr. Hearst has a whole room full of guns," he replied.

"I mean a real gun, not a flintlock owned by some duke."

"Oh, no, they are real guns. Pistols, shotguns. Even bought a Thompson before the government tries to make them illegal."

"A pistol will do," I said.

We went up a narrow staircase on the northside, finding a room that was more of a large closet. There were half a dozen hunting rifles and shotguns in the gun racks, though I don't know that Hearst ever used them, having a special fondness for animals. On a shelf below the gun racks, I found a Colt .45 caliber M1911 automatic like the one I'd carried in the war. Tom retrieved a box of ammunition from the drawer.

"Who you planning to shoot, Mr. Hammett?" Tom asked as I was feeding seven rounds into the clip.

"Let's hope it doesn't come to that," I answered, tucking the gun in my waistband and buttoning my coat.

After visiting the armory, I made a quick stop in the upstairs gothic study. The vast room was bathed in ghostly shadows. A fire burned in the marble fireplace.

"Hello?" I called out. There was no answer.

A desk lamp allowed me to sift through the pile of newspapers that Marion had shown me earlier.

The article I needed was still there, two ships colliding in New York Harbor. It spoke of the damage, rescue efforts, and rumors that dockworkers had helped themselves to some of the cargo. I remembered there had been another article mentioning a piece of stolen jewelry, but that newspaper was missing.

———————

The museum downstairs was silent as a mausoleum, so I went out the front doors, encountering Anna Lee while crossing through the plaza. She was carrying fresh towels and linens.

"Long day for you, isn't it, Miss Anna?" I said, doffing my hat.

"I don't mind, sir. Like the quiet once everyone turns in," Anna Lee said. "That Miss LaRue is still in your room. Says she likes it."

Saucy was probably searching my room, hoping to make a big

find. At some point she'd guess I was a step ahead of her.

"Can you please find her another room?" I requested.

"Working on it now, Mr. Hammett. Take me 'bout half an hour."

"Thanks. I'd like to visit with Miss Fowler. Do you know where she is?"

"Likely in B," Anna Lee said. "That is, Casa del Monte. It's the cottage on the right."

Anna Lee rushed off as I went in the other direction. The smallest of the three bungalows was largely deserted, just a few lights on. The foyer wasn't quite so over-decorated as the other buildings, but elaborate enough. Antique furniture. Oil paintings. Persian carpets. Vases stolen from ancient tombs. Having always spent money as fast as I made it, maintaining such wealth continued to amaze me.

I heard a noise from a room in the back overlooking the north road, approaching softly. When I knocked on the door, it slowly opened.

"Crying?" I asked, poking my head in.

Alice looked up from the narrow bed, quickly wiping her eyes.

"It's nothing."

"May I come in?"

"Please," she said, sliding over to make room.

The small apartment was modestly adorned, lit by an old table lamp. There were books and magazines on the oak desk. The bed was covered with a nice, thick Amish quilt appropriate for cold weather.

Alice was still dressed for the office, a brown wool business suit and silk stockings.

"Can I help?" I asked.

"It's just been a hard few days. What are the police going to say when we tell them about Sharkey? It's going to be so embarrassing for Mr. Hearst."

"And Marion? Isn't that who you are really worried about?"

She nodded.

"Marion is thirty-seven now. Unmarried. Her relationship with Hearst is already scandalous. Millicent will never give him a divorce. And Norma is getting the best roles from MGM. What if something happens to ruin her career?"

"I wouldn't worry too much about that. Marion strikes me as a lady who can hold her own."

"You wouldn't say that if you knew everything."

"Maybe I know more than you think. Like the photographs."

She caught her breath, reaching to squeeze my hand.

"You developed them?"

"Harmless fluff. Marion has them now."

Alice seemed relieved, somewhat.

"We should track down Maureen and Johnny. Round up Bill and Norma," I suggested. "It's still Saturday night, and even if you and I aren't movie stars, we should still have a good time."

"Yes," she agreed.

Alice briefly went into the bathroom, shutting the door. When I heard water running in the sink, I poked briefly around her desk, looked in the top drawer, and then opened the closet. As I suspected, there was the familiar whiff of men's cologne. Murry & Lanman's?

"You look great," I said when Alice emerged in an attractive silvery red dress and high heels. She'd put on a stylish black fedora probably bought on Rodeo Drive.

"Thank you, Mr. Hammett," she responded, tipping the hat down until it almost covered one eye, as was the fashion. I found her fur jacket hanging on the door, nothing so fancy as mink. Probably rabbit.

"It's cooling off. I should get my coat," I said.

"Maybe it will warm up later," she suggested with a wink.

On our way to Casa del Sol, we paused near the path leading down toward the Neptune Pool. Though the electric torches were tuned low, seeming to indicate the area empty, we heard voices.

"It's Marion and Norma," Alice said, pausing to listen. "I think Mr. Thalberg is there, too."

"Say hello for me. I'll only be a minute," I said, urging her on.

Alice went off to the right. I kept going, following a winding path through tall bushes and overhanging trees. It looked like a great place for an ambush, though I wasn't expecting one.

I heard more voices as I entered Casa del Sol, apparently coming from my room, only these were not so hushed.

"You goddamn bitch!" Knowles shouted, followed by the sound of breaking ceramics. Possibly a thrown vase.

"Come closer, you son of a whore," Saucy howled.

"Stay back," Bill loudly warned.

I couldn't tell if Bill was talking to Knowles or LaRue, or both, and rushed to find out.

"Who ratted me out? Was is Sharkey?" Knowles demanded to know.

"You're a goddamn idiot, Rock. Sharkey is dead. Murdered by one of your movie star friends," LaRue replied.

"Dead?" Knowles said, stopping whatever he was doing.

I reached the open door, finding Bill bravely standing between the combatants, arms held out and a trickle of blood on his forehead.

"That's more than enough," I said, shoving Knowles back into the wall and joining Bill in the middle of the room. Saucy was holding another vase, hopefully not an expensive one. Another lay shattered on the floor. Her expression was angry but not afraid. I doubt there were many men she feared.

"What's this about Sharkey?" Knowles asked, starting toward me.

"We'll discuss Mr. McCann privately, without an audience," I said.

"Hammett is playing you," LaRue unhelpfully butted in. "If he wanted you to know, he'd already have given out. Everybody here knows the score but you. Even the gardeners."

"Thank you for that, Saucy. You really know how to repay a favor," I said.

She raised the vase as if to throw it. I jumped forward, slapped the vase from her hand, and then pushed her backward so hard she bounced across my bed into the wall. I hadn't meant to be so rough, but didn't apologize.

I turned toward Rocky, fists clenched.

"You want some of this?" I asked.

Knowles wasn't too worried about my fighting skills, being a little taller and heavier, but he was cautious enough to want the right time and place.

"The tennis courts, in an hour," Knowles said.

"The northwest corner of the palace, in the gardens, at midnight," I countered.

"Good enough," Knowles said, disappearing into the hall.

"Are you all right, Miss?" Bill asked, helping Saucy sit up.

"Aren't you the gentleman?" Saucy replied, rubbing the back of her head.

"Want to tell me what that was all about?" I asked.

"Throwing elbows over territory," Saucy said. "The dingus was mine first, even if Sharkey did get a whiff of it."

"What the hell is a dingus?" Bill asked.

"A dingus is a mysterious object from one of my books. An object of great value."

"And it's mine," Saucy added. "Rock thinks I'm helping you sell the diamonds. And I can. No one knows the black market better than I do."

"Diamonds?" Bill asked.

"The necklace has made me very popular. So tell me, Miss LaRue, what does the Silver Blaze have to do with McCann's death? Were you here last night? Sneaking around the gardens, checking out your territory?"

"Me? I had nothing to do with clobbering Sharkey."

"Was it Knowles? He could have slipped into the estate, had a falling out with his partner in crime, and then flown back to cover his tracks. Maybe the two of you are in cahoots?" I pressed.

"Don't try to put the squeeze on me," Saucy said. "Rocky and I were in L.A. last night looking for you. Lots of people saw us. And not the best kind of people."

"Maybe you can prove that. Maybe not. I have until tomorrow night to put the finger on someone."

"Then let's get the dingus and blow this joint. Make life easier for everyone," Saucy said.

"The dingus is the Silver Blaze?" Bill asked. "You stole it?"

"I didn't steal it. It was entrusted to my custody. And now we've got these cockroaches crawling out of the woodwork."

"Hey, I resent that!" Saucy objected. "I've got as much class as anyone."

"Then start showing it. If the necklace does fetch a price, and doesn't end up with the cops instead, I'll see you get a cut. If you stop making trouble."

She had to think about that. I might not be telling the truth, and she might not want to wait. And quite frankly, I really had no idea what to do with the damn thing, having a murder to solve.

"Sharkey's room is empty. I'll stay there tonight," Saucy decided as she got off the bed.

"The dingus is the Silver Blaze?" Bill said.

Saucy and I laughed.

"Sweet stuff, why don't you bring me breakfast in the morning?" Saucy said, leaning close to give Powell a breathless kiss.

"Call me Bill."

"I know who you are, but you look like a cop," she said. "Thanks for standing up for me. Sorry about your head."

Saucy gave him another quick kiss and left, taking her small travel bag.

"Think those two had anything to do with Sharkey's murder?" Bill asked.

"Hardly. But Miss LaRue will be more careful if she thinks there's a murder rap in the air, and we need to buy ourselves more time."

"Do you know who did it?"

"At the moment, it really doesn't matter."

———————

Bill and I tucked our coats tight against the cold April night and went to the Neptune Pool, now lit by a last quarter moon. The clouds had faded over the ocean, soon to return as midnight fog. Bill had unspoken questions I wasn't ready to answer.

The weekend guests were standing together on the far side of the decking, huddled around a brisk fire burning in an ancient bronze brazier. Hearst and Marion had not joined them, which made the conversation easier. There was no sign of Alice, Knowles or the Germans.

"What was that pool game all about?" Thalberg was the first to ask.

I paused to light a cigarette, studying my audience.

"I understand everyone is tense," I finally said. "If something has happened to Sharkey McCann, the situation won't look good for Mr. Hearst. The embarrassment. The press. The accusations. And it won't do any of you much good, either. Not with several of you having motives."

"I did not break that snake's neck," Johnny protested.

"And I believe you, Mr. Weissmuller," I agreed.

"I didn't either. Or Irving," Norma said.

"I'll take your word for that," I replied.

"Then what are you saying?" Thalberg asked.

"I'm saying that the rumor about Sharkey McCann having died here is just that. A rumor. For all we know, Mr. McCann took the train back to Los Angeles."

I made a side-glance toward Maureen. Other than Bill, she was the only one that had actually seen the body. I wasn't worried. Maureen O'Sullivan was no informer.

The gathering seemed stunned, at first. I sensed that, for most of them, my suggestion came as a relief.

"You can talk about it," I offered. "Just remember that once the lid comes off, there's no putting the genie back in the bottle."

I strolled back toward Casa Grande, confident they would come to the right decision. The dark trees overhung the path, and a light fog was beginning to drift in. Just as I reached the plaza, there was a new complication.

"No sudden moves, Hammett," Rocky said, sticking a gun in my ribs.

"What's the score, Rocky?" I asked.

"Tired of your games, Shakespeare."

I looked him over, though the light was poor. He was heavily bundled against the cold, his black felt hat pulled down. The cheeks ruddy. He reeked of good scotch.

"As a matter of fact, I'm glad to see you," I said, taking out another cigarette. Then I patted my pockets, feeling unsuccessfully for my lighter.

"Got a light?" I requested.

Knowles stared at me with frustration, then produced his old pewter lighter. I gave the cigarette a good a puff.

"I may have a job for you," I said.

"I already have a job."

"This would be part-time."

"I don't bump people off, if that's what you're thinking. And I'm no one's muscle, so don't think on that, either."

"Nothing so drastic. Are you ready to see where it happened?"

I led him down the darkened path around the corner of the mansion, stopping behind the hedge where the marble coffin rested. Tom had left a flashlight for me on the bench.

"Your friend met with several people here last night," I said, shining the beam to points of interest. "You know more about those conversations than I do. Following one of the meetings, your friend fell backward into that marble coffin, and as he was trying to climb out, the lid fell on him."

"One of the movie stars?"

"I confess, it would help if I knew. Maybe it was you. Maybe it was Saucy. It might have been Münch and his lackey. I hear the gardener has a bad temper."

"So who killed him?"

"Do we really know if anyone killed him? He might have stumbled. Too much drink. Such a dark garden. A moment of

157

carelessness."

"What are you saying?"

"I don't really care what happened to Sharkey, as long as this can be cleaned up without publicity. That might be worth something to me."

"Like a diamond necklace?"

"Like the opportunity to broker a diamond necklace."

"I didn't kill Sharkey."

"That's not the point."

"Is Saucy in on this?" he asked.

"There have been conversations."

"She don't see a dime of my cut. And I expect a big cut."

He waved the pistol around to emphasize his meaning.

I still had the .45 in my waistband, hidden by the winter coat, and was sure Knowles had no idea I might be armed. At any given moment, when his guard was down, I could have whipped the gun out and blown his brains all over the courtyard. But it wouldn't have solved my problem.

"I can't afford to take a cut at all. It's too hot for me," I said. "You can broker the sale, but I decide who buys it. That's not negotiable."

"So you *do* have an angle? Something even bigger?"

"This is Hollywood, Rocky. Everyone has an angle. But after this is over, you and me being such good pals, I'll expect a case of that Martin's at no charge."

"You'll get your case if this pays off. If it doesn't, I won't be so generous."

We turned back, going to the kitchen. The help was gone, the dishes washed. The counters still smelled of soap. I turned toward the pantry, going down a narrow staircase. The door was straight ahead of me.

"He's in there," I said, pointing.

"With the donuts?"

"No, there's a cold room farther back," I explained.

"You detectives, what a bunch of creeps."

Just outside our destination, I noticed the door was ajar. Cold air was flowing into the hall. Knowles pushed past me, stopping a few feet away.

"Okay, Hammett, what's the gag?" he said.

"What do you mean?" I said, squeezing forward.

"There ain't no body in here."

And he was right. McCann was gone.

"He was here an hour ago," I said.

Knowles looked me over, wondering what to think. Was I playing him? Making up a story? Then he lowered his thick eyebrows, squinting.

"So, you're saying we've got a body snatcher running around?"

"Apparently."

I heard a noise from behind me. Out in the hall. A sound coming from one of the cabinets, which I opened.

"Tom?" I said.

Tom was lying on the floor gagged, his hands and feet tied. His fancy butler suit was covered in flour.

"Knowles, lend a hand," I said, dragging Tom out.

We untied the simple knots of a white rope and brushed him down as best we could. I pulled the rag from his mouth.

"I's sorry, Mr. Hammett. I's real sorry," Tom said. "Someone grabbed me from behind. Took the key."

"They took more than the key, Mr. Wheatley. They took the corpse. Any idea where?" I asked.

"Mr. McCann? Gone?" Tom said, trying to look surprised.

"He's in on it. You know he is," Knowles said, inching forward with clenched fists.

"That won't be necessary, Mr. Knowles," I intervened. "Tom, get cleaned up and start looking. When you find McCann, come and tell me. No one else. Do you understand?"

"Yes, sur. I understands," Tom said, shuffling off.

"He knows, doesn't he?" Knowles said.

"It isn't hard to guess. Don't worry, we'll have McCann back here by morning."

"Body or not, we still have a deal."

"I'm not saying different."

I don't know what Knowles thought of that. He may have been wondering if I was being straight about any of it, or just stringing him along. Truthfully, I hadn't decided.

———————

The day was wearing me out. I didn't even want a drink, but I still needed to know what Tom had discovered about the fingerprints. I went to the cupboard where we'd been storing the evidence, discovering a sketch of the murder scene. Somewhere in all those pencil scrawls was the answer I needed.

"I'm hearing strange stories. Stories that won't look good in the newspapers," Hearst said, coming up behind me.

I noticed the great man was wearing a long purple silk robe, thick wool slippers, and holding a cup of coffee. My host seemed more stressed than tired. Why he was roaming the panty corridors underneath his castle was a mystery. We weren't anywhere near the wine cellar.

"We'll know what happened to McCann by tomorrow," I said.

"I expect no less. Do you have a guess for me?"

"It would be easier if your employees hadn't stolen the body."

Hearst frowned, the thin eyebrows bending deep.

"They are just trying to protect me," Hearst said.

"So am I."

"Does any of this have to do with the necklace?"

I had to think about that for a moment.

"I'd say it's unlikely, though I can't rule it out."

"There's the truth, and there's the truth we print," Hearst said.

He went back upstairs to the kitchen and disappeared. I wasn't sure what to make of his remark. Did Hearst really want to know what happened, or was he looking for a plausible story?

It wasn't hard to guess that the gardeners had stolen the body. Paranoid about being blamed, they probably thought it best that the problem go away.

Bill caught up with me outside Casa Grande, emerging from the fog like a wraith.

"Your suspects are scattered all over the hill," he said, out of breath. "I can't keep track of anyone."

"Münch and Kemper are still in the castle. I think. Maureen is upstairs in the room next to Marion's. Johnny's room is down the hall from Thalberg's in Casa del Mar. I've lost track of Knowles."

"What was it you asked Münch?"

"I wanted to know how he knew the diamonds made their way to San Simeon."

"Did he say?"

"Not exactly, but he gave me a clue."

"This place is full of clues. Not so many answers."

"I know someone who may have answers."

I left Bill standing in the gray haze, not wanting to involve him more than necessary. Casa del Mar loomed on its hillside, holding court over the shrouded valley below. When I heard voices in Thalberg's room, I stopped to eavesdrop.

Irving's voice was obvious. Deep, calm and clear. Professorial. The other voice was female, and it wasn't Norma. The conversation was intense, but I couldn't make out what was being said, so I decided to barge in.

"Good evening, Mr. Thalberg. Good evening, Miss LaRue," I said, pushing the door open.

Neither showed surprise. Thalberg was dressed in his red smoking jacket sitting at the oak desk. LaRue sat cross-legged on the bed, wrapped in a long fur coat, with black silk stockings poking out from underneath.

"Hello, Dash. What brings you out on a cold night?" Thalberg asked.

"Following up on an interesting conversation. Catching up with old friends?" I said.

"Miss LaRue and I have not been previously acquainted," he replied.

"But we're friends now. Aren't we, Irving?" LaRue quickly added.

"Of course, my dear. Good friends," Thalberg said with a pleasant smile.

Saucy rolled off the bed, straightening her coat and pink scarf. She reached out her hand, letting Thalberg give it a kiss, and gave me a catty look as she waltzed out of the room.

"Should I bother asking?" I said.

"Just another treasure hunter. What can I do for you?"

"Herr Münch says McCann told him where to find the Silver Blaze. What did McCann tell you?"

"What does the Blaze have to do with Sharkey's murder?"

"Maybe nothing. Maybe everything."

"I think maybe nothing. Sharkey could be very enterprising, but he was no criminal mastermind."

"Are you saying Münch is lying?"

"Do you have a better explanation?"

"Not yet."

I left the room knowing I'd get nothing from Thalberg. He was accustomed to haughty studio heads, cutthroat newspaper columnists, and temperamental actors. A drunken mystery writer was the least of his worries.

———

I considered going back to my room for a quick catnap. The drinking and long hours were beginning to take a toll, but I wanted to visit Alice first. She met me on the path among the plaza gardens.

"You're getting around tonight," she said, wrapped in her rabbit fur coat.

"It's when I do my best thinking."

"What are you thinking?"

"That this might not work out the way Mr. Hearst wants it to, and that he might be very unhappy with me."

"You are still Dashiell Hammett, regardless of what W.R. thinks."

"A Dashiell Hammett that's broke again."

"You've been making big money since coming to Hollywood. Tens of thousands. Where does it all go?"

"Guess I'm a soft touch," I answered, though expensive hotel rooms, big saloon bills, fancy clothes and compliant female company had a lot do with it.

"You'll find the answers you need, I'm sure of it," Alice said, moving closer. Her blue eyes shone in the tiki lamps, her lips pursed and nose wrinkled. I wanted to kiss her but thought better of it.

"The note that was in Sharkey's hand is still missing. Do you know where Marion hid it?"

"Marion? Why would Marion have it?"

"Miss Davies is a very astute woman. Watchful and well-informed. And protective of Mr. Hearst. She might think hiding the note will prevent a scandal."

"Would it?"

"I don't know. Maybe. Or it might make the situation worse."

"I will ask her, if you want," Alice offered.

"Let's not say anything yet."

I took her hand, leading Alice back to my room in Casa del Sol, where I would find ice for my shoulder. And a sip of good rum.

Chapter Nine

DOWN THE HILL

My respite didn't last long. Just before midnight, there was a knock on my door. It was Tom wearing a heavy wool coat and mufflers.

"I found the information you wanted, sir," Tom said, glancing at Alice. "Sorry to disturb you, ma'am. Real sorry."

Alice and I had been sitting on the wide bed under the quilt, sipping Bacardi while reading my new stories in *Collier's*. She thought them humorous.

"Thank you, Mr. Wheatley," I said, gathering my hat and overcoat. "Sorry, darlin'. Duty calls."

I gave her a peck on the cheek and followed Tom into the hall.

"Near the dock," Tom whispered.

"Can we get down the road in the dark?" I asked.

"We know the way, but it's not a San Francisco trolley ride."

"Never underestimate a good trolley ride."

I followed him through the garden, down a long promenade of marble steps, and passed the gardener's shed where an old black Ford truck was parked. Tom revved up the engine as quietly as he could and released the brake, rolling into the darkness until we were surrounded by drooping trees and thickening clouds of fog. The zoo where I'd nearly been eaten by a lion was somewhere off to my left.

"What have you found out?" I inquired.

"As you suspected, Carlos thought his people were going to be blamed. He wanted to make the evidence disappear."

"Making a case without the *corpus delicti* is difficult, but not impossible. And if the sheriff wanted to blame the Mexicans, he wouldn't need any proof. All he needs is an accusation."

"You don't need to explain that to colored folk, Dash," Tom said.

I settled back in the thinly padded leather seat, one hand on the door, the other on the dashboard. It was a rough ride, hitting every imaginable bump. Several times, I had to grab my fedora before it flew off. And the night was black, allowing little to be seen. How Tom even knew where the road was remains a mystery.

We emerged from the canyon above the main highway, wisps of fog drifting across our path. Beyond was another dirt road, unmarked, and a creaky wooden gate. Tom jumped out to get us through, rolled the heap forward, and closed the gate as if he'd done it a thousand times.

"This village is where the groundskeepers and dockworkers live. A few of the ranch hands, too," Tom explained as we stopped before a weather-beaten general store.

I spied several small houses and cottages, none of them much to brag about. It was as I thought, the poor living in hovels in the shadow of the great man's palace. We got out and walked to the door, Tom knocking lightly. I had read much of company stores, how rich corporations would sell vital products at high prices and on credit, keeping their peasant workers in perpetual debt. Capitalism at its worst.

An old black woman answered, draped in a blue cotton shawl. She nodded and let the door creep open so I could follow Tom inside. She was a tiny thing, bent over and deeply wrinkled, but offered a welcoming smile. The room was kept warm by an old Franklin stove in the corner.

"You brought a guest," she said.

"Dashiell Hammett," Tom replied. "Dash, this is Maybelle."

"Nice to meet you, Maybelle," I said, bowing.

The old woman stepped back, looking me over.

"Your last book wasn't your best," she remarked.

"That's what I keep saying," I responded, gallantly kissing her hand.

She seemed surprised but let it pass.

"Need cigarettes?" she asked.

"I do," I said, making a better inspection of her shop.

Several lamps allowed me to see shelves of toiletries, linen, clothing, and canned goods. Cigars, candy and jars of jellybeans filled the counter.

"A whole carton of Camels for a dollar?" I asked. "They cost $1.25 at the A&P."

"You can buy them by the pack," Maybelle offered.

"For a small store on the coast in the middle of nowhere, your prices are very reasonable."

"Mr. Hearst makes sure we takin' care of," Maybelle explained. "It's a long drive into town, an' even longer walkin'."

"That is generous of him," I said.

"The Ranch ain't like where you from, Mr. Hammett. We family," Maybelle said.

I supposed it was true, to a point. Isolated communities often feel a special bond. I'd felt it while staying with Lillian in Homestead, and while visiting Hemingway in Key West. How far such loyalty would go under the scrutiny of the police could be a different story.

"Tom said I might find something important here," I said, tucking a couple of cigarette packs in my pocket and putting two-bits on the counter.

"They waitin' for you out back," Maybelle said, nodding toward the rear door.

Tom went first, going down a rough plank staircase toward an old dock. I soon felt a salty ocean breeze. The ground was sandy, covered in scrubby plants. A seagull loomed on a post to my right. Lanterns hung outside a creaky wooden warehouse.

"Maybe I should do the talkin'?" Tom suggested.

"And what is it you'd say?"

"Well, you know. We need the body back."

"And if they deny having the body?"

"Pretty sure they does."

"Let's play this one off the cuff," I said.

We reached a heavy pine door but didn't need to knock, seeing it slide aside as we approached. The interior appeared to have only one source of light, a fire burning in an oil drum. Tools hung from the walls: saws, shovels, grappling hooks and meat cleavers. There was a vaguely dank smell. I heard waves crashing on the beach nearby.

Half a dozen weather-beaten men were waiting inside, five Mexicans and an elderly white man. Some sat on stools, others stood back in the shadows. I recognized one of Sara's sons.

"You are a long way from home, Señor Hammett," Carlos said, standing in the middle of the room.

"We are here to get Mr. McCann back. Taking him will cause plenty of trouble," Tom said.

"There is plenty of trouble to go around," the grizzled white man said. He had a long gray beard, wore a sea captain's cap, and held a clay pipe. He looked like a character out of a Jack London novel.

"Mr. Hammett ain't here to cause you trouble," Tom promised.

"He is no friend either," Carlos said.

I walked forward into the warehouse where I could see my audience. The pistol hidden in my waistband gave me some security, though I was convinced it wouldn't be needed.

"Just because I've become famous, you may think I'm rich," I said. "Because I'm seen in exalted company, you may think I'm a snob. And because I was once a detective, you may think I'm a cop. None of this is true. I am a friend of working men. I don't care about their color. And I'm asking for your help."

"You must blame someone. Why not blame us?" Carlos asked.

"Are you guilty?" I asked.

"No, we are not guilty," Carlos answered.

I let the moment linger for dramatic effect, seeing the men leaning forward to hear what I might say. Their eyes glistened in the firelight.

"I believe you," I finally said, hearing them let out their breaths. "But I still need to discover what happened, and in such a way that Mr. Hearst will not be embarrassed."

"It won't be good for any of us to have a scandal," Tom added.

Glances were exchanged. Words not spoken but understood. Carlos waved me toward a large ice chest probably used for storing fish.

"He is in there," Carlos said, declining to open the lid. I took his word for it.

"We need to get him back to the pantry," Tom said.

I paused to think on that, then pulled Tom aside.

"We used the pantry to inspect the remains. I think we've gotten all we can on that score," I whispered.

"You want them to dump McCann in the ocean?" Tom asked.

"I wish it was that easy, but it would create too many questions."

"What are you thinking?"

I walked over to the ice chest and slowly raised the metal top. McCann was still in a partially curled position, rigor mortis having set in. I checked to make sure no one had broken bones to fit him in the box, glad to find him intact. It would be another day or two before the muscles began to relax. Longer if he was kept cold.

"Carlos," I summoned, drawing him over. He did not look down at the body, making me wonder who had actually done the moving.

"*Está muy muerto*," Carlos said.

"That he is. I need you to keep the body cool, but don't let it freeze. Don't let anyone adjust the clothing. It's evidence, and it must stay evidence."

"You are not going to take it?" Carlos asked.

"Not tonight, but it will need to go back up the hill. Tom will let you know when the time is right."

I was playing fast and loose with the law, risking a lot. But rural cops were not famous for their sophisticated techniques, nor for stringent attention to details. All I needed was a good story that would put the incident to bed.

Carlos seemed troubled by my request.

"We would rather the body disappeared," the old white man said.

I gave him another look, wondering what his game was. Why would he care? Was he provoking trouble?

"Sir, if a white man was arrested for this crime, the court would want a body to proceed," I explained. "Courts are not so particular when the defendants are not white, especially here in California. I see six men who know McCann was brought to this warehouse. If just one person talks, the sheriff will arrest all of you. And the testimony will be damning. Is that really what you want?"

"My amigos, if the police ask Mr. Hearst what happened to McCann, what is the Chief supposed to say?" Tom asked. "That his employees stole the body of his guest?"

Tom and I stepped back while the rest of them huddled. There were a few animated gestures, but no loud disagreement. Tom had hit the nail on the head.

"We will keep the body safe, then bring it up when you say," Carlos announced.

"Thank you, that will be very helpful," I said, reaching to shake his hand. Carlos appeared surprised but returned the gesture.

I strolled back out into the night, Tom just a few paces behind. The door closed. Rather than head straight for the truck, I turned down toward the beach, lighting a cigarette.

"That went well," I said.

"They keep their word," Tom said.

"I hope so."

The shoreline lay to our right, the white foam of the breaking waves luminescent. The Pacific Ocean was far more robust than the placid Atlantic waters around Florida. Except during hurricane season.

"I'm going to walk for a few minutes. Think this problem out," I said. "I'll see you back at Maybelle's."

The erratic fog wasn't thick enough to obscure my path as I strolled toward the highway, though the palace on the hill was lost in the darkness. I had a pretty good idea what happened to Sharkey, lacking a few particulars. It was the politics that had me stumped. With no new novels on the horizon, I needed the work that Hearst—and perhaps Thalberg—could throw my direction. Otherwise, I would be going back to New York with a satchel full of debts and no way to pay them.

As I reached the road, I noticed a 1930 Packard parked at the foot of the castle's long driveway. Surprisingly, the gold star painted on the door showed it belonged to the county sheriff's department. What was it doing here? In the middle of the night?

I sat down to watch, huddled far enough from the road not to be noticed. The night was cold, but a sip of bourbon warmed me up. A burly man remained in the front seat, looking toward the hill. Most likely a deputy. He got out to stretch his legs, walking up toward the palace gate, and then back. I wanted another cigarette but didn't dare light one. After about fifteen minutes, a man on foot approached from the darkness.

"This has got to be done right," Knowles said, his voice carrying well. "Hearst is a cranky old son of a bitch. If he catches wind, it won't go down well."

"I can't do anything until you tell me who to arrest," a deep, gruff voice replied.

"Not sure yet. Could be the big gardener, or that black butler. You may even get to arrest Dashiell Hammett."

"Who?"

"A scribbler. Mysteries and stuff. So drunk most of the time he just stumbles around. He had McCann stashed in the kitchen."

"The kitchen? Is that where he was killed?"

"No. Got it on the grounds. Some kind of marble coffin fell on him."

"Are you making this up? You smell like my sister-in-law's sozzled brother."

"Ain't making nothing up, and that's not the point. If we want the goods, we need leverage on Hammett. Or Hearst, if he's already bought it."

"And you say this Blaze thing is worth $15,000?"

"At least."

"And you're cuttin' me in for ten percent?"

"Cash."

"You've got a deal, partner," the co-conspirator said, shaking hands. "But you better be playing straight with me."

"I've got to get back before they miss me. Be on time," Knowles said, returning up the road.

Unwilling to stretch my luck, I beat a hasty retreat to the general store, glad to see the lights still on. Tom met me at the door.

"What's wrong, Mr. Hammett? You looks a bit shook," he said.

"You could say that. Does Maybelle have a phone?"

It was four or five miles back up to the mansion, which took time driving on a dark, twisting road. I wasn't sure where Knowles was but doubted he was walking. He'd be back thirty or forty minutes before we were.

"You seem pretty intent there, Mr. Hammett. Went through three operators to place that call," Tom said.

"Hard to place a civilized call from the sticks. I'd be better off dispatching a carrier pigeon."

I was getting irritable. I'd been drinking most of the day and had little sleep. With sunrise a few hours away, I'd rather not stumble around like the drunk Knowles said I was.

"Goddamn it, what is it now?" I grumbled.

"Zebra," Tom said.

A herd of the striped donkeys were wandering on the road ahead of us. Tom reached to honk his horn, but I stopped him. I didn't know if the sound would be heard up the hill.

"Can you chase them off?" I asked.

"Sure 'nough," he said, climbing out of the cab.

What's next? I thought. *Elephants? Giraffe? Mike the lion?*

The zebra proved manageable, running for the pasture as Tom waved his arms. He came back, jumping into the driver's seat without any fuss. I watched the road carefully after that, wondering what new obstacle might appear. Tom glanced at my expression and appeared amused.

"I was worried there for a minute, Dash," Tom said. "Then I remembers, the gumshoe always looks doubtful just before they solve the crime. Builds up the suspense. That's what you're doing, isn't it? Building up the suspense?"

I dared to light a cigarette despite the modest wind, staring out into the darkness.

"Yeah," I said. "Working on the suspense."

We reached the shed below the Neptune Pool where Tom dropped me off before going to park the truck. I made my way up the marble steps in the dark, struggling not to trip. The tree branches seemed to drip like a Louisiana swamp, but I knew it was only an illusion of the fog.

I stumbled into my room, thinking just an hour of sleep would be a blessing. From the dim light coming through the door, I saw someone was already in my bed. I crept closer until able to make a quick conclusion. It didn't take a detective to see Saucy LaRue's luscious curves under my blanket.

"Miss LaRue, you can't stay here," I whispered. But she refused to respond.

For a moment, I considered looking for somewhere else to sleep. The cottage had a lot of bedrooms including one occupied by Bill, another by Johnny, and a third by Rocky. With Irving and Norma over in Casa del Mar, there were still several bedrooms to choose from.

But I didn't feel like shopping for new accommodations. Saucy had been given a room by Anna Lee. Why intrude on mine?

I turned on the desk lamp, keeping the green shade down, and approached the bed.

"Miss LaRue, wake up. You need to go downstairs," I quietly urged. For I didn't want her waking up suddenly and sticking a knife in me.

When she didn't stir, I gently rocked her shoulder. There was no reaction, which raised a concern. A terrible thought occurred to me. Was she dead?

I adjusted the lamp and pulled back the bedcover with trepidation. There were steaks of blood running from her nose and mouth. Her left arm was curled awkwardly across her chest. The knees were bent up, and there was no breathing. No, there was breathing. Shallow at first, and then stronger. Saucy was unconscious but alive.

This is just great, I thought. Nothing feeds the press more than a notorious thief and part-time prostitute found beaten-up in a mystery writer's bed. Good for sales, but hell on attorneys' fees.

I stepped back, wishing for a drink. But this was no time to get stupid. Was she badly injured or just bruised? Did I need to call a doctor?

Saucy moaned, then tried to turn over. I grabbed a towel, soaked it in water from the porcelain basin, and gently dabbed her swollen face.

"How you doing?" I whispered.

"Had worse," she answered, starting to move.

"Can you sit up?"

I propped her against the headboard, supported by several large pillows. Saucy was wearing a sleek blue evening dress, probably stolen. Red marks around the neck indicated attempted strangulation.

"Who did it?" I asked.

Saucy gave me a strange look. Did she know? Did she think I did it? Her eyes were clear. Focused. Not what I expected.

"That's not important now. We need to make this work," she said, spitting blood into the towel.

"We? Make what work?"

"You'll need to trust me on this, Mr. Hammett. As you writers like to say, the game is afoot."

"I don't get it."

"And I can't explain. Not now. Help me to Knowles's room. Put me in his bed, and then disappear. Bring the towel. The one with the blood on it."

She seemed very decided, issuing orders like someone accustomed to being obeyed. Perhaps it was a trick of her trade, but it worked. I grabbed the damp towel, lifted her from the bed, and carried her into hall, checking to see if we were being observed. The late hour worked to our benefit.

"What if Rocky's sleeping?" I asked.

"The big lug is off spooning with the maid," Saucy replied.

The carpeted floor allowed us to move in silence. I pushed the door open with my foot, peered inside, and set Saucy down in a big chair so I could pull back the bedcover. She crawled in on her own, took the towel, and smeared her face with blood. Then she handed the towel back to me.

"Take a powder," she said, lying back with another moan.

It wasn't faked. She was in a good deal of pain.

"Can't I at least get you something? A drink? Aspirin?" I asked.

"Yeah, you can help. Take a grip on my dress. Right here, at the shoulder," she said, guiding my hand. "Got it?"

"Got it," I said, my fingers wrapped through the strap.

Saucy took hold of her dress on the other side and gave it a strong tug, ripping the blouse open across the front. I glanced away for the sake of modesty.

"That should be enough, unless you think we need more drama," Saucy said.

It suddenly occurred to me that Saucy's New York accent had disappeared. She sounded more Philadelphia than Brooklyn.

"Enough drama for my tastes," I said.

"Fine. Now scram. And don't say anything about this."

I did as instructed.

———

The alarm rang at 6:30, theoretically after sunrise, though there was nothing but dense gray fog out the window. I planned to get up, for there was much to do, but rolled over instead, snuggling under the warm quilt. The next time I woke up, it was noon.

After a quick shower, I dressed for a cold day. I considered shaving, the white stubble on my chin making me look older, but didn't have the time.

The courtyard was silent as a tomb. Even the birds were keeping mum. I walked slowly through the gloom to avoid tripping on the Spanish tiles or falling into a planter. The great house was quiet, too. I passed through the Refectory and morning room, turning into the kitchen. The lights were on.

I smelled fresh bread. Saw butter on the counter, and slices of Swiss cheese. Julien and Sara were absent, possibly having lunch somewhere else. I made a ham sandwich to settle my stomach and moved on to the pantry.

"Got everybody?" I asked, entering Tom's small office.

Tom looked up with an expression of resignation.

"Theys right here," he said, holding up the index cards.

"*They* are right here," I corrected, sitting on a stool.

Tom had been working over our sketch of the crime scene, tagging spots where sets of footprints and fingerprints had been detected. It took me a moment to see Tom's concern.

"No mistakes?" I asked.

"Was extra careful."

Using a pencil as a pointer, Tom directed me to each set of clues in the area surrounding the sarcophagus.

"Yours, mine, and these others," Tom said.

"Mostly McCann's."

"He was there longest."

"Okay, let's take a look. Got everything?"

"Got everything we talked about."

We slipped out the side door, the theater to our right, the crime scene to the left. The visibility was still poor, but the fog was lifting.

It might even be a blue day at some point. We entered the secluded garden, the ground damp.

"Let's start with each suspect one at a time," I said, giving the map to Tom.

"Mr. Weissmuller," Tom began, pointing at the nearest bench.

I positioned myself according the prints, tracing what we could tell of Johnny's movements. He had stayed at the perimeter, always looking toward McCann.

"Carlos?" I asked.

Tom pointed to the far side of the coffin, where the iron bar had propped the lid open. I positioned my hands where his had been, judging the angle.

"We're sure this is the only place he touched?"

"The only place we've got prints," Tom confirmed.

Then we followed Thalberg's path through the scene, which was easy. There was the bench where he sat and the walking stick that he lost. Nothing indicated he had approached the sarcophagus.

Three sets of prints remained, all female. I moved around the small area to recreate their possible movements, squatted down to replicate their height, and tested my strength against the marble lid, wondering how difficult it was to move. Or attempt to move, assuming someone had tried. The photographs Tom had taken of the ground helped pinpoint who stood where.

"Is it as you thought, Mr. Dash?" Tom asked.

"I'm afraid so."

The fingerprint pattern didn't answer all the questions, but they did provide an obvious explanation.

"Others could have been here. Maybe didn't touch nothin'. Or maybe wore gloves," Tom suggested.

"It's conceivable. And not all of the shoeprints are distinctive."

"But you don't think so?"

"Let's follow Sherlock Holmes's theorem before making conclusions."

"When you have eliminated the impossible, whatever remains, however improbable, must be the truth," Tom quoted. "What about that note he was holdin'?"

"It was written by McCann to one of his targets," I said. "My guess is that notes were sent to Weissmuller, Shearer and Davies. And all of them showed. They don't tell us who killed him."

"So what are you not saying?"

"It's not about who sent the note, or who received the note. It's about who didn't want us to see the note."

"And that was?"

"That will be clear soon enough."

"You should take this to Miss Marion first," Tom said, handing me the diagrams with his observations in the margins.

Bringing Marion in on the investigation would be the right thing to do. It would also be illegal, for we had already trampled the very edge of the law. But there were serious ramifications to consider. A wrong decision could put me in Hearst's doghouse forever.

"We'll take this to Miss Davies when we need to," I said.

"You won't go to the sheriff first?"

"If the sheriff needs to be informed, it won't be by me."

———

My first thought was to find Hearst and tell him what I'd discovered, until realizing what a mistake that would be. McCann's death, as presented, could still result in the scandal he wanted to avoid. I needed to do more than solve the crime—I needed to solve the problem.

"Dash, you're getting a late start," Bill said, coming up in his tennis outfit. "Most of us are out on the court."

The fog had finally dissipated, providing a cool but pleasant April afternoon.

"Thalberg?" I asked.

"Not playing. He's up at the pool," Bill said.

"I'll be along in a few minutes," I promised.

I went toward the stairs, pausing to study the plaza while wondering what Rocky was doing. Several sarcastic comments occurred to me regarding his sleeping arrangements, which might tip him off, so I resolved to keep my mouth shut when next we met.

Thalberg was sitting on the sundeck in a folding chair, a stack of manuscripts on the table beside him. Kneeling next to the chair, much to my surprise, was Herr Münch. Münch was squatting awkwardly, his hands animated, his fine suit looking a bit wrinkled. They glanced in my direction.

"Good morning, Dash. Or is it now afternoon?" Thalberg said.

"Just a bit after, Irving," I responded, shaking his hand. When Münch rose to greet me, I nodded. "I don't mean to intrude."

"Ernst was explaining a situation to me. It seems Lieutenant Kemper is missing," Thalberg said.

Ernst? I thought. *Aren't we getting chummy.*

"I think I saw him last night. Outside Miss LaRue's room," I lied.

"That is not likely, sir. And I resent the implication," Münch said.

"And what implication would that be, sir?" I asked.

"That a loyal member of my personal staff would involve himself with a woman of such low character."

If he knew she had been beaten up, he was covering well. Thalberg seemed to have no clue.

181

"I'm sure the young man will turn up in good time," I said.

"You are playing the game well, Mr. Hammett," Münch said, peering at me through his monocle. "But we will still get what we want."

"And what is it you want?" I asked.

"You won't know that until it's too late," Münch said.

I looked for Thalberg's expression, wondering what he was thinking. I would not call him confident, but far from fretting.

"Irving, the next time you are in San Francisco, we should have lunch. The Tadish Grill?" Münch said.

"That sounds fine, Ernst," Thalberg agreed.

Münch nodded and left the pool area. For what devious reason, I could only guess. He wasn't dressed for tennis.

"You make strange friends," I remarked.

"I would not describe Herr Münch as a friend," Thalberg responded.

"What is it he wants?"

"He wants to know what I know."

"What do you know?"

"Enough."

"You haven't asked what *I* know," I said.

"I already know what you know."

I doubted that was true. Then again, I wasn't sure what we are talking about.

"None of this is happening for no reason."

"Ah, now you've finally gotten something right," Thalberg said, slowly rising from his chair.

I followed him around the immense swimming pool, passing the giant Greek temple to the edge of the hill. The ocean was a few miles away. Below us were roads, forests, and in the distance, several animal enclosures.

"Have you seen this?" Thalberg asked, taking a newspaper clipping from his pocket.

It was about Albert Einstein, the famous scientist. The year before, he had renounced his German citizenship and become a refugee in New York.

"I don't think Einstein stole the necklace," I said, handing the article back.

"Albert can't go back to Germany. They are burning his books. The German government has passed laws barring Jews from holding public offices. Lawyers, mayors, judges—all banned. Jews are not even allowed to teach at the universities. Those who have the money, and can get passports, are fleeing the country."

"What does this have to do with the Silver Blaze?"

"For all I know, probably nothing."

Thalberg returned to his chair, picked up a manuscript, and went back to work, looking for Hollywood's next big picture. I went up the stairs into the plaza.

———

I was halfway to the tennis courts when Knowles suddenly appeared from the lower road, running up the wide steps. I tried to duck behind a planter but he saw me.

"Not now. I have business," I said, raising a hand to put him off.

"Goddamnit, Hammett, I need your help," Knowles said.

He seemed in a bit of a panic. Not out of control, but anxious. His clothes were dirty. Disheveled. He hadn't shaved since yesterday.

"I'm not the Salvation Army," I said, turning to leave.

"You don't understand. Saucy got worked over. She's half-dead."

"Did you have a falling out over the spoils?"

"Goddamnit, I didn't do it. It was that stinkin' Kraut."

"Münch?"

"Kemper."

"How do you know that?"

"He confessed."

That gave me pause. Perhaps this would be easier than I thought.

"Start from the beginning," I said, sitting on a marble bench and taking out a cigarette. I offered one to Rocky, but he declined, standing nervously near a flower bed.

"I got back to my room just after dawn. Anna and I were watching the sunrise together," he said.

"There was no sunrise. Not with all this fog."

"We weren't paying that much attention. Anyway, when I got back, Saucy was in my bed. Choked. Hardly breathing. It didn't take a mystery writer to figure out who did it. We all know those Huns want the ice and thought Saucy could get it. So I went looking for the goddamn son of a bitch."

He paused, reached into his coat pocket for a flask, and took a swig. I motioned for him to be generous and he allowed me a taste.

"I saw Kemper on the road trying to make his getaway. He'd been asking Tom for a car but couldn't get one, so he started walkin'. I caught up, gave him a good smack, and dragged him down into the meadow. That's where he confessed."

"With a gun to his head?"

"That's not where I was pointing it, but he got the idea. He made up a cock and bull story about Saucy cutting a deal with Thalberg, and all he wanted was to make her a better offer, but things got out of hand."

"Strangling a partner in crime is rarely good business."

"She never partnered with those shits. She said the Krauts tried to grab her on the docks after she swiped the necklace, so she had to ditch it."

"With Skinny the Rat?"

"Don't make me laugh. She wouldn't give the Rat the time of day."

"Then who?"

"Never found out."

I didn't believe that, but for the moment, it didn't matter.

"And Kemper?"

"I demanded to know Münch's role in all this, but Kemper refused to say, so I shot him."

"You did what?!" I said, jumping up.

"I shot the son of a bitch."

"He's dead?"

"Don't know that I got that lucky. He started running, and the first shot likely hit him. After that, a flock of those goddamn zebras came running through. Almost trampled me. By the time I got back up, Kemper was in the woods."

"Rocky, you know this isn't good," I said.

"No one's gonna hang me for shooting a stinkin' Hun. Not one who beat up an innocent American girl."

Dumb as he seemed, Knowles knew something about the law. Or, at least, something about juries.

"I'll see if I can find Kemper. Lay low. Stay out of trouble," I said.

"No promises."

"What happened to Saucy? Is she still in your room?"

"Yeah. Got her a bag of ice and a bottle of Martin's."

"Go up to the big house and find Sara. She'll know what to do."

Knowles went off toward the mansion. He genuinely seemed concerned. I walked toward the tennis courts looking for Bill, meeting him on the way. He and Weissmuller were on their way back to the cottages, both sweaty from their game.

"Need a little help," I said, attempting to draw Bill aside.

"What is it now?" Bill asked.

I glanced at Johnny, hoping to get some privacy, but he insisted on listening.

"Rocky shot Lieutenant Kemper, who ran off into the forest. We need to find him."

"Shot him? Why?" Bill asked.

"That's a long story. Will you help me search?"

"I will," Johnny offered.

"I appreciate that, but you shouldn't get involved," I said.

"I'm already involved. How much do you know about tracking through a forest?" Johnny asked.

"Not a hell of a lot," I confessed.

"Meet me in the plaza in ten minutes. Bring a hat, water, and binoculars if you can find them," Johnny said. And then he ran off like he was chasing a lion.

"Can't say I'm much of a tracker either," Bill said.

"Are you welching on me?"

"No, just warning."

"Get into some real clothes," I said, pointing Bill to his room. "And better find that hat Johnny was talking about."

Bill saluted and left, looking doubtful. I couldn't blame him. I really had no idea how to search for a wounded man in such a wilderness but figured someone had to.

Tom appeared from a side door of the house, looking frustrated.

"What's this about Miss LaRue?" Tom asked.

"Appears she had a falling out with the Germans, and now Kemper may be shot."

"We better find out before Mr. Hearst does," Tom said.

"I'm forming a search party. Mr. Powell and Mr. Weissmuller are waiting for me."

"We can go down to the stables. Get you some horses," Tom said. But when he noticed my expression, he thought better of the idea.

"You do better walkin'. I'll have Mr. Brand lend a hand."

"Got any binoculars?" I asked.

"I'll set them outside the front door. Get you a hat and a proper coat, too."

Tom went back into the house. I returned to the bungalows, found a pair of boots, and snuck a peek in Rocky's room. LaRue was propped up against the headboard, wrapped in quilt and reading a newspaper. The bottle of Martin's sat nearby. Though I wouldn't claim to be fond of her, I had to admit, she had spunk.

The three of us gathered in the plaza. When Maureen saw us, she asked what we were doing. Bill made up a story about going fishing, which she didn't believe for a minute. I suppose the lack of fishing poles was a clue. Bill really was one of those actors who needed a script.

With Maureen joining us, we followed the trail that Rocky had described, noticing the zebra herd in the foothills. The trees weren't so thick that we couldn't see where to go, though footprints or blood splatters would have been helpful. Off in the distance, I noticed Mr. Brand on horseback, riding slowly along the ridge.

"Must seem like old times, eh, Johnny?" Bill said.

"How so?" Johnny asked.

"Roaming through the jungle searching for prey? Might be quicker if you swung from the trees," Bill prodded.

"Four of us came into the forest, Bill. It doesn't mean all four of us need to come back out," Johnny said.

"What do you think, Maureen?" I asked.

"I think Bill would look silly riding a rhinoceros," she answered.

There was a rumble, the leaves suddenly shaking. Tree branches dipped. I held out my hands to keep balance. Was it one of those famous California earthquakes?

"Elk!" Bill shouted, running for a patch of trees.

Johnny was already rushing past him, Maureen scooped up in his arms. I looked back, seeing nothing but a brown blur, and ducked behind an oak. Seconds later, the giant deer came running by with pounding hooves, five, ten, twenty of them, the antlers on the male swinging back and forth. And just like that, they were gone.

"That was close," Bill said, brushing leaves off his jacket.

"Try paying attention. Next time it might be the lion," Johnny said.

"The lion?" Bill asked.

"They let him out during the day," Maureen said.

"He was back that way a few minutes ago," Johnny said, squinting toward the meadow. "Can't see him now."

Bill looked in every direction, staying close to the tree. Then Maureen laughed. And I laughed. Johnny grinned. It took Bill a moment to realize he was being played.

We'd only gone a few hundred more yards when I heard moaning. And there he was, sitting under an oak, cradling his arm.

"Stay back! I have a gun!" Kemper shouted, the accent more Minnesota than German.

"It's me. Hammett. Are you hurt bad?" I called out.

"Come closer," he said.

We approached cautiously. Kemper had the gun in his lap. The cuff of his jacket was stained, but I didn't see any gushes of blood. It looked like a flesh wound.

I knelt down to take a closer look, and then realized I hadn't brought a first aid kit. Johnny pushed me aside and opened his pack, pulling out a roll of bandages.

"We will get you back to the house. Sara can take care of this until we find a hospital," Johnny said.

"No hospital. No one must hear of this," Kemper said through labored breaths.

"It could get infected," Johnny warned.

"I will have it treated when Herr Münch and I return to the Consulate," Kemper replied.

Johnny shrugged. He didn't know why Kemper wanted it hushed up, nor did he seem to care. None of my search party knew about Saucy, and it was better that they didn't.

Chapter Ten

NEW YORKERS

I walked Kemper back to the house, watching the trail for trouble. I did not want Knowles to shoot him again or have him trampled by zebras. Not that I cared what happened to the young idiot, as long as it didn't happen on the Ranch. Maureen disappeared with Bill, wandering off toward the stables. As I anticipated, Knowles appeared on the marble steps just as we were approaching the mansion.

"Let me have him," Rocky said, punching a fist into his palm.

"Not today," I answered, pulling Kemper by the elbow.

I felt capable of handling Knowles, though it helped to know Weissmuller was only a step behind me.

"He tried to kill Saucy and frame me for her murder. He's got to pay for that," Rocky said.

"I did not frame anyone. And I did not try to kill her," Kemper said. "It was a fair fight."

Kemper pulled up his shirt, revealing a bloody bandage wrapped around his ribs.

"She stuck me with this," Kemper said, taking a tiger stripe switchblade from his side pocket. The same one Saucy had held to my throat. The sly vixen had apparently gotten it back by picking my pocket.

"I'll take that," I said, wrapping the weapon in my handkerchief.

"Hell, a little nick like that ain't no excuse for chokin' a woman," Rocky said.

"Mr. Knowles, seems I remember you getting into quite a spat with her just yesterday," I recalled. "Or was that a lover's quarrel?"

"I ain't never been her lover," Rocky said with a frown.

"Business partner?" I asked.

Knowles spun around and headed back toward the cottages. He'd had enough.

"Thank you, Mr. Hammett," Kemper said.

"Don't thank me. If we were down on the highway, I'd let the son of a bitch teach you better manners."

Johnny led Kemper into the big house, looking for Sara. Hearst's cook was getting a lot of patients this weekend.

With the plaza suddenly quiet, I considered getting some lunch. But the kitchen was probably crowded with Kemper, Sara, Julien, and no doubt Hearst coming down to see what the latest trouble was. Perhaps a cigarette and a snort would suffice until everything calmed down. And then Alice emerged from the front doors.

The mid-afternoon sun reflected nicely off her long reddish hair, bringing out the pinkish color of her face. She saw me, hesitated for a moment, and then smiled.

"Dash, are you all right?" she asked.

I took her hand, led her around the side of the mansion, and into the small garden near the sarcophagus.

"Smoke?" I asked, taking out my Camels. She shook her head.

"This is where it happened?" Alice asked.

"Yes. There, in that stone box," I replied, pointing toward the death scene. She refused to look.

"Good riddance," Alice said, taking a seat on the bench facing the other direction.

"Not a fan?"

"Sharkey wasn't good at making friends."

"Who killed him?"

"It wasn't Marion."

I sat on the bench next to her, finished my cigarette, and patted my jacket, hoping for a flask. I stupidly hadn't brought one.

"Why would I think Marion did it?"

"You know about the photos."

"Yes, I know."

I could tell her devotion to Marion was more than employer and employee. Marion was her rescuer. Her hero.

"Don't worry. Everything is going to be okay," I said. "Think I can get some food without going to the kitchen?"

Half an hour later, I was up at the tennis courts. Maureen, Johnny, Norma and Bill were playing doubles. The afternoon was growing cool and cloudy. Alice brought me a tuna sandwich before going back to work.

Though getting a tennis outfit would have been no trouble, I declined to get on the court. Marion appeared, taking a seat next to me.

"Pops is getting impatient," she stated.

"Everything is under control," I said.

"How can that be?"

"This case is not so complicated. It would be less complicated if you tell Mr. Hearst the truth about you and Norma."

"Me and Norma? You said...?"

"That you and Norma are not lovers. According to some, you're not even very close friends. But that's not what the notes were about, were they? Even Sharkey's photos are only a loose connection. Something you didn't want to explain if W.R. started asking questions."

"Perhaps you should explain yourself, Mr. Hammett," Marion said.

I watched as Bill hit a splendid serve that skipped by Maureen. She looked stunning in shorts. I took several notes out of my pocket.

"This note was from Sharkey to Weissmuller. It hints that gossip about his marriage can get worse if he doesn't play ball. Weissmuller didn't take kindly to the threat."

"Johnny killed McCann?" Marion asked.

"No, of course not. Maybe mussed his hair a little, but it left Sharkey on edge. This second note was given to Norma, hinting about the photos. Sharkey wanted Norma to put pressure on you to pay him off, but Norma went to Thalberg instead. Thalberg shut the blackmail down, but not before you received a summons. Irving was already gone when you showed up."

I showed Marion the final scrap of paper. It read, *Miss Davies, we need to talk.*

She looked at me with a mystified expression.

"This isn't the real note. It was destroyed," Marion said.

"Yes, I guessed that. This is a copy."

"Where did you get it?"

"I made it to see how you'd react."

"Did I act appropriately?"

"Well enough. Are you ready to explain now?"

"Sharkey wanted money. Not a lot. He wouldn't explain why," Marion said, slipping the fake note in her pocket.

"I know why, and it had nothing to do with the photos. Sharkey had a partner who needed to be paid off without knowing the true nature of this weekend's business. Did Sharkey know why you'd really find the photos embarrassing?"

"You do a lot of guessing."

"Not so much. W.R. wants you in the Wimpole movie, but you don't want to do it. You're wonderful in comedies. Not so much these costume flicks. To avoid a falling out between Hearst and Thalberg, you've been meeting with Norma. Passing her information. Sharkey's photos of your meetings were going to raise uncomfortable questions. How am I doing?"

"Now I know why your books are so good."

"If it helps, I have no intention of revealing any of this to W.R. That's between you and him. Just so long as it doesn't complicate the bigger picture."

"I appreciate that, Dash. More than you know. Pops would be so hurt if he learned I don't want to do these historical dramas."

She put a reassuring hand on my knee. Marion could be a good friend, and until I started writing again, I needed good friends.

––––––––––

Sunday night marked the end of the weekend for Hearst's guests. After a nice meal in the Refectory and a final gathering in the

Assembly Room, they would be driven down the hill. Those who drove themselves had their cars. The rest would be taken to the train station in San Luis Obispo.

Hearst arrived from his private door just after seven, shaking hands. Münch had been invited to dinner. Kemper and Knowles had not. I noticed the German lingering close to the great man and paused to observe.

"Mr. Hearst, we must talk privately," Münch said, drawing him aside.

"I don't see the necessity," Hearst said.

"I assure you, there is something you must know," Münch pressed.

Hearst huffed with impatience, then waved me over. He knew I was within earshot the whole time.

"Dash, you will come with us," Hearst ordered.

Münch wasn't happy about my inclusion, but I sensed Hearst wanted a witness that he could influence should it become necessary. We went up a flight of wooden stairs to his library on the second floor, the big room cluttered as ever. Hearst took his usual chair behind the large desk. I selected a stool, sitting off to one side. Münch pulled a bench around, realized he'd have the lowest seat in the room, and decided to stand instead.

"At times, I speak for the German government," Münch began. "But now I speak privately, to you. We have an unpleasant situation. The Silver Blaze is stolen. A man is dead. My aide is shot. If these events are discovered by your competitors, it will result in scandal."

"That is possible," Hearst agreed, watchful. I noticed his breath was short. He rubbed his hands together, leaning forward in the chair.

"It is more than possible," Münch said. "But it does not need to be so."

"How is that?" Hearst asked.

"You have friends, Mr. Hearst. Friends who would say nothing about the necklace and make these problems go away," Münch said.

I wondered if he was a magician but held my counsel until asked.

"Such friends are good to have, Herr Münch. What friendship would I need to show in exchange?"

"Nothing you have not shown already. You have been fair to my country's new leadership. You appreciate strength. As the Reich struggles to achieve order, we would like to know our friends in America support us," Münch explained.

"I will need to visit Germany again soon and see this new order for myself," Hearst said. "In the meantime, I will consider what you've said."

"Of course, sir. Of course," Münch said. He reached across the desk to shake hands, but it was wide enough to let Hearst decline without being rude.

"Herr Münch, if I may be so bold, how will Mr. Hearst's friends help him with the problems we've had this weekend?" I asked.

"All will be fine," Münch said. "Shall we speak again after dinner?"

"After dinner," Hearst agreed.

Münch gave me a snide smile and slithered from the library.

"I think that's been his game all along," I said, sliding off the stool to kneel at Hearst's side. "The necklace wasn't given to me for safekeeping. It was planted so Münch could follow me here and create an international incident."

"Yes. And you fell for it," Hearst agreed.

"The game's not over."

"What are you suggesting?"

"Fight fire with fire."

Hearst stood up, wandered to the big fireplace where a stack of logs was burning, and looked up at an oil painting. It was a portrait of his father, George Hearst, a rags-to-riches miner who became a U.S. Senator.

"My father was a grand old guy. Lots of friends. But he had sharp elbows when he needed them," Hearst fondly recalled. "Dug for gold. Silver. Copper. Even diamonds. And anyone who cheated him soon found out what that meant."

"What do you want me to do, Chief?" I asked.

Hearst glanced back, gave me an inscrutable look, and waved me away.

I returned to the Assembly Room, checking to see what everyone was doing. While most of the guests were gathered around the piano, Thalberg was sitting alone on a couch near the fire. I noticed he had a fancy walking stick but hadn't been using it. I quietly strolled over to take a seat next to him.

"It's time to come clean," I said.

"Come clean about what?" Thalberg asked, looking better than he had all weekend.

His eyes seemed brighter. The posture straighter.

Before we got down to brass tacks, Marion arrived with a pewter tray holding a bottle of Gordon's Dry Gin and martini glasses. There was also vermouth, lemon twists, and green olives.

"Would you gentlemen prefer your cocktails shaken or stirred?" she asked.

"Give mine a good shake," Irving said.

"Good for me, too," I said.

Marion mixed the drinks in a fancy silver shaker, pouring them with a flair, and then added the olives.

"May I get you anything else?" she asked.

There was an interested twinkle in her blue eyes. Not mere curiosity. She was seeking information, perhaps by reading our expressions.

"Leave the tray, dear. Mr. Hammett has something to get off his chest," Thalberg said.

"May I help?" she asked.

"We're doing fine, Marion. Thank you," he assured her.

Marion reluctantly set the tray on a marble end table and returned to her guests. Thalberg tucked his scarf tighter. Even near the fireplace, the room was drafty.

"That confirms a suspicion," I remarked.

"Miss Davies is a very insightful woman, and it shows in her acting. Sad W.R. won't let her play the roles she's good at."

"She's not going to get the Wimpole movie, is she?"

"No.

"Or Marie Antoinette?"

"Certainly not."

"Both parts to Norma?"

"Probably."

"And Hearst will go on the warpath. Pull funding. Direct his newspapers to ignore MGM films. Maybe move Cosmopolitan over to Warner Brothers?"

"That is all possible, but I think we'll still be friends. It's just business."

"What sort of business brings Germans to the Enchanted Hill?"

"Where is that coming from?"

"Are you going to tell me what this is all about, or should I guess?"

"I don't know what you mean."

But Thalberg wasn't the actor his wife was. He leaned back in his chair, looking a little less smug. He reached for the Gordon's, poured a splash in his half-empty glass, and offered the shaker to me. I declined.

"What are you implying?" he finally asked.

"I'm implying that it was you who stole the Silver Blaze. Not you personally. You hired LaRue to perform the theft."

"I don't crash boats in New York Harbor, Mr. Hammett. As much as that would make for an exciting screenplay. I did put out an inquiry for a talented professional who might make the attempt."

"Which didn't make LaRue happy when she wasn't given her cut."

"I didn't realize she'd been cheated until last night."

"Is that why you provoked Münch? To get her out of the way?"

That tossed him, but just for the barest moment. His lips showed the tiniest trace of a smile.

"You must have your fun, mustn't you?" he said.

"Tell me your version."

"I agreed to give her a finder's fee, but only if she kept quiet until the game played itself out. She seems pleased with the arrangement."

"How pleased was Mr. Knowles with the arrangement?"

"We haven't had the opportunity to discuss it. Apparently, Sharkey misled Knowles about the true nature of our business here. I saw no point in giving him information he didn't already have."

"Fair enough. But it has had unfortunate consequences."

"Even I didn't suspect how far Münch would go to embarrass W.R."

"How far were you prepared to go?"

Thalberg set aside his glass, groaned as he stood from the chair, and walked to the north window. The forest was shrouded in fog. He carried the cane without leaning on it.

"Dash, your political sympathies aren't particularly popular in Hollywood at the moment," he remarked without looking in my direction. There was no judgment in his tone. No accusation. Merely a simple statement of fact. "But I'm sure you've followed the rise of fascism in Germany with as much trepidation as I have. What they're doing... what Hitler is doing... isn't politics as usual. Not like we've seen in Italy. This is something different. Something the world hasn't seen before."

"What does that have to do with stealing diamonds?" I asked.

"A little. Perhaps."

"I've got a hunch about this."

"Tell Hearst, don't tell him. That's up to you. But telling him isn't going to make you any friends."

I sipped my martini thoughtfully and let the olive swirl in the glass. Thalberg knew all along I'd figure out his plan. And he knew what I would do.

"Mr. Hearst asked me to keep a scandal away from his palace. The rest of it is none of my business," I said.

Thalberg turned, sized me up, and reached to shake my hand. It was a strong grip for a sick man.

"I've always thought highly of you," he said.

"That's reassuring," I replied.

Tom appeared, announcing it was time for dinner. I pointed to Thalberg's cane.

"There may be fireworks later. Keep that stick close."

"Wouldn't the gun hidden in your waistband be more effective?" Thalberg said.

"I've never shot anybody, and I don't want to start tonight."

"It would make a dramatic end to the story."

"Drama can be overrated."

———————

It was another splendid meal. Succulent garlic salmon with cheese covered broccoli, au gratin potatoes, lemon slices, and all the trimmings. I noticed Hearst kept the wine bottle at the other end of the table, out of my reach. Movies were the primary topic of conversation, and Herr Münch made a point of saying how popular American films were in Germany.

Toward the end of the main course, there was a tap on my shoulder.

"Excuse me, Mr. Hammett. You needed up front," Tom whispered.

I folded my napkin and quietly followed him to the door.

"What's up?" I asked.

"Got some troublemakers."

"My friends from New York?"

"No, ain't seen them yet," Tom replied.

Tom and I entered the Assembly Room to find Knowles and a deputy sheriff waiting for us. The same deputy I'd seen on the road the night before. Bill entered a moment later, standing just behind me.

"Rocky, I thought you'd left us," I said.

"We still got business, Hammett. And since you don't want to play ball, we'll just have to do this the hard way," Knowles replied.

"What are you talking about?" I said, glancing over at the deputy.

The man was middle-aged. Turning gray. Gaining weight. His faded brown uniform was tattered at the cuffs and pantlegs. Stubble showed he hadn't shaved in several days, and rings under the brown eyes indicated he didn't sleep well. Probably money trouble, compounded by few chances for advancement. A ripe mark for opportunists.

"I know Sharkey McCann was murdered," Knowles stated. "Either by you, or that Mexican gardener. Or maybe he was killed by your butler friend. On your orders."

"Now why would I want Sharkey McCann dead?" I asked.

"So you could sell the dingus to Hearst and not share the reward," Knowles said.

The deputy stepped back at hearing Hearst's name mentioned. I wondered if he'd considered what Knowles was asking of him.

"Sir, I don't believe we've been introduced. Dashiell Hammett, mystery writer," I said, going to shake the deputy's hand.

"Deputy Sheriff Frank Walters," he answered, giving me a cautious look. "Mr. Knowles came to me with some serious allegations."

"And you've not reported them to headquarters yet. You would like to investigate on your own first. Maybe find an accommodation to avoid anyone being embarrassed?" I suggested.

"Something like that," he answered, a nervous flutter in his throat.

"I hope you haven't been misinformed, Deputy Walters," I said. "As far as I know, McCann isn't dead. He was running around the ranch Friday night in meetings with Miss Davies and Miss Shearer. And the last time anyone saw McCann, he was in the garden with Knowles."

"That's a lie! You've got him stashed in the pantry," Knowles said.

I looked at Tom as if Knowles must be insane. Bill appeared jittery.

"Easy enough to solve. Let's take a look," Deputy Walters said.

"No problem, sur. No's problem," Tom said, bowing deeply.

We followed Tom out the front door, around the side of the building, and through the side door, being quiet to avoid disturbing the dinner party. Only Julien was in the kitchen, glancing up from making desert. He went back to work without comment.

Tom went down the stairs first, opened the door to the cold storage room, and turned on the light. Then he stepped back against the wall. The only table in the room had ingredients on it for making a cake.

"He's supposed to be here, covered by a sheet," Knowles said, searching around. But the room was too small to hide anything as large as a body.

"Don't knows what ya means, sur. Who was here?" Tom said.

"It's a damn trick," Knowles complained.

The deputy looked in, seeing nothing. Bill sighed with relief. I took a half-step up.

"If we wish to find Mr. McCann, maybe we should start with where he and Knowles were last seen together?" I said.

It didn't take any imagination for Knowles to realize what that would mean.

"They put him back," Knowles said.

"Back where?" I asked.

Knowles charged out the door, everyone rushing to keep up. We went around the front of the house, along the path to the garden, and straight to the sarcophagus. The area had been raked that morning.

"He's in there," Knowles said, pointing a finger.

"How would you know that?" I asked.

"You told me," Knowles said.

"First you said he was hiding in the pantry, and now you say he's in a marble box. But if I did kill McCann, why in the world would I tell you where the body is?" I asked.

Deputy Walters seemed to wonder about that, too.

"Maybe he's not in there," Knowles conceded. "Whether he is or isn't, that ain't the point. You've got McCann's diamonds. They belong to me. Time to fess up."

The night was cold, the area secluded. Not a place for a confrontation with two armed men.

"Let's talk this out over drinks," I said, leading the way back to the Assembly Room. I let Knowles and Walters go through the doors first, followed by Bill. I stopped Tom on the porch.

"Are they here yet?" I asked, looking at the road. Tom glanced at his watch.

"Coming along now, sir. Be here in a few minutes."

I gave Tom a nod and went inside, joining Bill near the grand fireplace. Knowles and Walters stood in the middle of the room. Tom remained near the big doors. The fire felt good.

"What is it you're really seeking, Mr. Walters?" I asked, finding the tray of martinis that Marion had left on the table.

"Rocky says there's a reward for some sort of necklace," Walters replied.

"There isn't any reward. And suggesting that Mr. Hearst is buying black market diamonds might not help your career," I said.

"Maybe we should call your headquarters for further instructions?" Bill added.

"Maybe we've had enough of your crap," Knowles said, suddenly pulling a pistol from his waistband.

It was a nice gun. A Smith and Wesson .38. Popular in detective novels. He nudged Walters, who reluctantly drew his service revolver from the leather holster.

"Shooting someone in Hearst's living room might be hard to

explain, don't you think?" I said. And then I pulled a gun from under my coat, careful to point it at Knowles and not the officer.

"You're bluffing, Hammett," Knowles said.

"Maybe," I replied.

Suddenly, I heard Tom speak up. Somebody was coming in. "Please, stop," I heard Tom say.

Alice walked through the front door, dressed in a conservative business suit. She had several files in her arms, probably from doing evening research for Marion. Knowles grabbed her around the waist, holding the pistol up.

"This changes everything, don't it, Hammett? I've got your girl," Knowles said.

"She's not my girl."

"I know you like her."

"Not that much."

"I'm not his girl, and he does like me that much. Now get your paws off me," Alice said, wiggling free. I doubted Knowles had any intention of shooting her.

"Can't a girl get any sleep around here?" a woman suddenly said.

We all turned toward the long couch near the south window. Saucy had popped up out of nowhere, her vivid green eyes wide open. She was holding a hideaway. Small caliber by appearance. I guessed it was a Derringer but couldn't be sure.

"Who the hell is she?" Walters asked.

"Hammett's partner," Knowles said.

"He's lying. She's Knowles's partner," I countered.

As Saucy wasn't pointing her gun at anyone in particular, it was hard to know whose side she was on.

"You're outnumbered, Rocky," Bill said, now at my side. And he was also holding a pistol.

"Where'd you get that?" I whispered.

"It's a prop from my last movie," he whispered back.

His hand was steady. The expression determined. I really hadn't given Bill that much credit as an actor.

"You're not going to shoot," Knowles said.

"I might," I replied.

"I might, too," Bill said.

Bold words coming from a man with a rubber gun. I gently pushed Bill's arm down so he wouldn't be a target.

"Thank you, Mr. Powell, but I think we should all take a breath," I said. "What do you think, Deputy? Is this really what you signed on for?"

Walters glanced at Knowles, less sure than he'd been before. I knew enough cops, even shady ones, to know they'd only go so far.

"Give the stolen property back to Mr. Knowles and we'll call it even," Walters finally said.

"You haven't had your drink yet," I said, offering the glass.

Walters backed away, wondering what he should do. I looked up at the ornate clock on the wall.

"Tom?" I asked.

Tom peeked out into the plaza, and then he stepped back, holding the door open.

"We's got company, Mr. Hammett," Tom announced.

We heard footsteps on the stone pavement coming in our direction. Everyone turned, wondering what it meant. A bit of tension lingered in the air. Then two men casually strolled into the room. Both wore heavy overcoats, their wide-brim fedoras pulled down. The taller of the two took his hat off.

"Jesus Christ," Knowles said, lowering his gun.

"Jesus Christ who?" Walters said, pointing his weapon toward the newcomer. Knowles desperately shoved it aside.

"Don't even think it, Frank. Not for a second," Knowles said, his breath short.

The visitors lingered at the door, then handed their hats to Tom, who bowed and backed away. I crossed the room to shake hands, putting the .45 back in my waistband.

"Welcome, my friend. You're right on time," I said.

"Who the hell is it?" Walters asked.

"Bugsy Siegel," Knowles said.

Siegel frowned, a hand hidden under his coat.

"I'm sorry, Mr. Siegel. I didn't mean to say that," Knowles quickly apologized.

After taking in the situation, Siegel decided not to make an issue of the *faux pas*. He and his companion removed their coats, looking at the vast museum half-hidden in the nighttime shadows.

"You have some explaining to do, Mr. Hammett," Siegel said, returning my handshake without enthusiasm.

"Would you care for a drink?" I asked.

Siegel gave me a cold stare before following me to the piano.

"Chunky?" Bill asked, belatedly recognizing the second visitor.

"I don't believe we've met," I said.

"Pat DiCicco," the gentleman said, shaking my hand. "I represent certain interests here in Hollywood."

I knew the name. Married to the actress Thelma Todd, DiCicco was tall, handsome, and exuded a touch of class. One of his clients was said to be Lucky Luciano.

Bugsy gazed around the cluttered museum before spotting Saucy half-hidden behind the couch. He walked over, made her straighten up, and examined her swollen face.

"Who did this to you? Was it Knowles?" Bugsy asked.

207

Saucy glanced over, knowing Rocky's fate was in her hands. I detected the briefest sense of satisfaction.

"It was the German," Saucy replied. "He wanted the Blaze."

"Do you have it?" Siegel asked.

"No. Hammett does," Saucy said.

"Where is this German now?" Bugsy pressed.

"He'll be along soon," I interrupted. "And he will be dealt with."

Bugsy gave me a look. We didn't know each other well. A casual meeting every now and then on the street or in a café. I couldn't tell what he was thinking.

"The Blaze?" he asked.

Before I could answer, William Randolph Hearst burst into the room.

"What the hell is going here?" he demanded.

MARION DAVIES

Chapter Eleven

The Silver Blaze

The dinner party had broken up with Thalberg, Norma, Maureen and Johnny following Hearst into the room. I thought it best we not discuss too many details.

"Mr. Hearst, this is Mr. Benjamin Siegel of New York," I introduced. "And I believe you already know Mr. DiCicco."

"Yes, hello Pat. How is Thelma?" Hearst said, shaking DiCicco's hand. He looked Bugsy over, then stepped back with only a nod.

"Welcome, Pat. And Mr. Siegel," Marion said. "May we get you anything? Are you hungry?"

"No thank you, ma'am," Siegel answered.

"Appreciated, Marion. Maybe later," DiCicco said.

"What brings you gentlemen all the way up here?" Marion asked.

"Business with Mr. Hammett," DiCicco replied, causing Hearst to give me an angry stare.

"It's just a misunderstanding," I said.

"Seems to be lots of those going around," Johnny complained.

"Let's all relax. Tom, get everyone another round of drinks," I said. "Maybe it's time for a few explanations."

"Past time," Hearst grunted. He looked unhappy to have his one-drink rule so terribly abused, but that didn't stop me from abusing it. I wanted everyone relaxed before getting down to business.

Thalberg sat on the couch near the fireplace with Norma standing behind him. Marion, Maureen and Johnny were at the piano. Bill took Alice off to the side, making sure she was okay. Siegel took a seat in a large leather chair where Tom handed him a martini. DiCicco joined Norma, smiling and making small talk. Making their appearance, Münch and Kemper stood next to an ornate table. Knowles and Walters lingered near the door for a moment, and then the deputy decided to make a quick getaway. Good move on his part.

I looked for Saucy, who had disappeared, but she suddenly popped up again in a chair next to Siegel.

"Where did she come from?" Hearst asked, pointing his finger.

"New York Port Authority. Investigating a customs violation," Saucy said, flashing a gold badge. And it looked real, too.

As Tom was pouring drinks, I drew Hearst aside, leading him toward a far corner.

"How did your discussion with Herr Münch go?" I asked.

We were being watched but not listened to.

"Says all he wants is my friendship."

"What are you going to do?"

"What are *you* going to do?"

"My plan is to resolve the dilemma with as little fuss as possible. But we might need to bend a few rules."

"What sort of rules?"

I gave the great man a pat on the shoulder and returned to the fireplace. Tom handed me a squat glass of Scotch on ice. He looked for my cue and I nodded, allowing him to scamper off. Then I strolled toward Knowles.

"A little midnight cheer?" I asked, holding out the glass.

"Got my own," he said, drawing a pint of Martin's from his coat pocket.

"I might need some of that before the evening is done," I said.

"Earn it," Knowles replied.

I sipped my scotch, wandering over to the piano where the light was better.

"Are you prepared to return our property now, Mr. Hammett?" Münch asked.

"I am prepared to make the Silver Blaze available to its proper owner, Herr Münch. Though I doubt that will be to Hermann Göring's stooge."

That got a rise out of Münch, and instant outrage from Kemper. Even Hearst was caught off-guard. As Kemper stepped toward me with fists clenched, I faced him calmly. A punch in the face can be painful, but redeeming as well. It would have suited my purposes, but Münch called off his dog.

I glanced to Knowles for his reaction. He seemed pleased.

Tom appeared with a bowl of soapy water, placing it on the ornate table in the middle of the room. I calmly walked toward the darkest corner of the hall near the bay windows, paused before the tapestry with a penknife, and returned with a white encrusted object, dipping it in the water bowl.

"Did you just cut a piece off that wall hanging?" Bill asked.

"No, Bill. This has been pinned to the queen's neck since Friday afternoon, pretending to be her broach," I replied.

I gave the object a good swirl in the bowl, and then Tom came up with a dish towel, letting me dry it. With the flour washed off, the dull white string of stones suddenly came alive.

"Ladies and gentlemen, the Silver Blaze," I announced, letting the glittering necklace dangle in the lamp light.

Münch made a grab for it, but I was too quick, giving him an evil smile. When Kemper moved toward me, Rocky suddenly rushed forward, too.

"It's mine," Rocky said.

"It belongs to the Fatherland," Kemper disagreed.

"It doesn't belong to either of you," I said, retreating to the fireplace.

"What's on your mind, Dash?" Bill asked.

"To return the Blaze to its legitimate owner," I replied. "And that being said, I think it's a good time for us to call it a day."

"Without telling us what this was all about?" Johnny asked.

"Without telling *me* what is was all about?" Hearst said.

"Are you sure want to know, Mr. Hearst? Are you sure you want your guests to know?"

Hearst looked around the room. It was a large crowd for keeping secrets, but oddly enough, filled with loyal people. Or, at least, ones with a vested interest in avoiding bad publicity.

"What do you think, Mr. Siegel? Is this something we can talk about?" I asked.

"That is really up to Mr. Thalberg. If he doesn't mind, I don't either," Bugsy replied.

All eyes turned to Thalberg, most in surprise.

"You may as well tell the whole story, Dash. If you know it," Thalberg said.

"Most of it, I think," I said, going to the piano for a refill. Norma topped off my glass, smiling the whole time.

"I must admit, a few elements of this case had me mystified," I continued. "Until I realized this was never about the Silver Blaze at all. Was it, Irving?"

I paused for his reaction, but he just nodded with a mild grin. I began to stroll around the room.

"Like any conspiracy, there was some planning, some surprise opportunities, and a few curves. It began in New York Harbor, with the help of Mr. Siegel's contacts on the docks. He and Miss Saucy LaRue planned to steal the Silver Blaze from Hamar Schacht, and it proved successful."

"We don't consider it stealing," Saucy defended.

I glanced at Bugsy for his reaction. But then, he was a criminal. I doubt he considered stealing a moral failing.

"You said it wasn't about the necklace," Hearst said, growing impatient.

"It wasn't, and it still isn't," I said. "You see, the Silver Blaze was once the property of the Austrian Crown Prince. A symbol of Austria's former glory. It comes with a degree of pride, and prestige. When it was acquired by Franz Rosenthal after the war, some in Germany took offense. For you see, Franz Rosenthal is a Jew. And when Germany passed new laws against Jews last year, Rosenthal decided it was time to leave the country. That is when Herr Göring saw his opportunity. Rosenthal could leave Germany, but not with the Silver Blaze. He was forced to sell to Schacht at a fraction of its true value. Isn't that right, Herr Münch?"

"The Silver Blaze is a priceless relic of the Reich," Münch said. "Herr Göring's attempt to acquire it is patriotic."

I could have said something about that, but his admission was enough for my purposes.

"Göring couldn't demand the necklace directly, not without looking like a gangster, so Schacht got temporary custody, and his wife insisted on wearing it to New York. When Mr. Thalberg heard the Blaze was headed to America, he saw his opportunity. What better way to strike back at the Germans than steal their new acquisition?"

"Irving? Is that true?" Hearst asked.

"No reason to let a damn Nazi have it, W.R.," Thalberg said.

"But Thalberg needed help. Mr. DiCicco there is not just an aspiring movie producer. He's an old friend of Mr. Charlie Luciano in New York. Luciano could care less about what's going on in Germany, but he knows Mr. Siegel does."

"Enough to break up their rallies in New York," Siegel said.

"The Friends just wish to show respect for the Fatherland," Münch said.

"*My* friends will show you all the respect you deserve," Siegel promised.

Herr Münch sloughed off the threat.

"As has been rumored, certain elements have influence on the New York docks," I said. "Mr. Siegel hired a pro for the job, arranged a diversion, and recovered the necklace from the men who stole it from Rosenthal."

"Hey! Watch what you say," Kemper protested, taking a step forward.

"Calm down, Lieutenant," Münch said, grabbing his arm. "Let Mr. Hammett play his game."

"Don't worry, Mr. Kemper. You're going to like this," I said. "Miss LaRue, would you like to chip in?"

Saucy looked at Thalberg, then Siegel, finding no objections.

"It was a piece of cake," Saucy said. "I went aboard the Deutschland disguised as a customs agent. White suit, black hat. Awful shoes. When I asked Mrs. Schacht to declare her jewelry, she was completely taken in. Nice stuff, too. When the ships collided, I snatched the Blaze and disappeared in the confusion. I wanted to take the whole box, but Mr. Thalberg forbade it. From there I gave the necklace to McCann and waited for my fee. Which wasn't paid."

"My fee was overlooked, too," Bugsy said. "And all I wanted was reimbursement for the longshoremen."

"All will be taken care of. I promise," Thalberg said.

"Sharkey got the stolen necklace? And brought it here?" Johnny asked.

"Not exactly. Sharkey got on a plane, flown by Rocky, and arrived in Los Angeles. All without telling his old army buddy what it was really about. Sharkey promised you proceeds from a blackmail scheme, didn't he?"

"Wasn't the first time," Knowles acknowledged. "But he was usually more subtle. It never got him killed before."

"Bad luck, I'm sure," I said.

"So who killed him? Someone stealing the necklace?" Bill asked.

"We'll get around to that," I answered. "Now I don't know exactly when the next part of the puzzle emerged, but at some point, Irving saw a new opportunity. He knew the Germans would do anything to get the Blaze back, and likely in an ill-mannered fashion."

"I will show you ill-manners," Kemper said, suddenly charging toward me with fists clenched.

"Lieutenant, stand down!" Münch shouted.

I put up my arms in defense, but Knowles got to him first, tackling him halfway across the room. Kemper rolled over, swinging a fist, but Rocky pounded him in the face with several powerful punches. Kemper was a strong kid, struggling to fight Knowles off, but Rocky had a saloon brawler's edge.

"This is for Saucy, you goddamn son of a bitch," Knowles growled, breaking his victim's nose. "And this is for sticking her in my bed."

Rocky's next blow left Kemper lying flat, unable to defend himself. Rocky pulled Kemper into a sitting position and considered knocking out his teeth. But he paused. Most rough and tumble men live by a code, even bad-tempered ones like Rocky.

"My turn," LaRue said, appearing out of nowhere to smash a vase over Kemper's head. "That's for the black eye, you stinking piece of garbage."

I have no idea if it was an antique vase. It probably was. When LaRue looked around for another one, Bill grabbed her by the shoulders.

"Take it easy, honey," Bill said.

As Saucy calmed down, Bill and I assisted her to a chair.

"Don't worry, Miss LaRue. His reward is coming," I softly whispered.

"This is better than the movies," Alice said, watching from the sidelines.

It looked like Knowles wasn't through with Kemper yet, but Hearst stepped forward with a frown. Knowles backed off.

Kemper was laid out on the floor, groaning. I doubt there were serious injuries, having seen my fair share of bar fights. Münch pulled Kemper to the nearest couch, helped by Tom. Which struck me as particularly odd. A black man helping a member of the master race? Tom saw me staring and smiled, sharing my thought.

"Where was I? Oh, yes. Thalberg. This is where you come in, Mr. Hearst."

"Me? What do I have to do with any of this lunacy?" Hearst said.

"When McCann delivered the Blaze to Irving, he decided to show you the true nature of the new Germany. Knowing I was on my way up here, he had McCann give the necklace to a slippery fellow named Skinny the Rat, an old acquaintance of mine from the Bowery. As ordered, the Rat passed it to me at the Cocoanut Grove with a woeful tale of a wronged waitress. Then McCann secretly tipped off Herr Münch where the necklace could be found."

"You set this up?" Hearst said, frowning at Thalberg. Everyone else was curious, too. Thalberg rose to the occasion.

"W.R., times have been hard for many influential men. They fear communism. They fear mob rule. Some see fascism as the answer. Even you, my good friend, have flirted with their ideology."

"That's not true," Hearst said.

"I truly hope it isn't, but I needed you to see them for what they really are. Up close. I knew if Münch came to the Ranch looking for the diamonds—"

"That he'd try to strong-arm Hearst?" I said.

"Yes. And W.R. isn't someone who likes being pushed around," Thalberg said. "I also know him to be a fair man with no love for dictators."

"Why would you give the necklace to Dash?" Maureen asked.

"I knew Dash would not be sympathetic to the agents sent to retrieve it, so the necklace would be safe. And I was right," Thalberg said with satisfaction.

"I must take offense. We are not thugs. Bugs Siegel is the thug,"

217

Münch objected. Kemper moaned from the couch but said nothing.

"You have my apology, sir," I replied, giving Münch a nod.

I looked toward Bugsy, but the mobster was cool, sitting upright with a martini in one hand and the other under his coat.

"Having gotten the Silver Blaze to the Ranch under clandestine circumstances, Irving arrived with McCann to await Herr Münch's arrival, but Sharkey had a complication."

I picked up the bottle of scotch off the piano and strolled over to Rocky. He was still out of breath from the fight.

"How do you fair, my friend?" I asked.

"Fair enough," Knowles said. I refilled his glass and continued my speech.

"You see, Sharkey had told Rocky that blackmail was the reason for all the cloak and dagger. It was the cover story, so he decided to play it according to the script."

"It wasn't my script," Thalberg insisted. "McCann was improvising without my knowledge."

"Be that as it may, it resulted in a series of late-night meetings and a terrible accident that threw Irving's plan into turmoil," I said.

"Accident?" Marion asked.

"Perhaps an accident of his own making," I added. "For others were on Sharkey's trail. Rocky apparently showed up the next day, but he might have gotten here the night before and had a falling out with his partner."

"I did no such thing!" Rocky shouted, starting to get up.

"Relax, Rocky. Saucy is a good suspect, too," I said.

"You flatter me, Mr. Hammett. But I have an alibi. Don't I, Mr. Siegel?" she said.

"We both do," Bugsy said, enjoying my performance.

"And then there is Herr Münch and his lackey, desperate to

please their masters. And only hours behind their prey," I said.

"We were not here. And even if we were, we have diplomatic immunity," Münch said.

"Odd that you would need diplomatic immunity if you weren't here," I remarked. "What do you think, Mr. Hearst? Does an innocent man need diplomatic immunity?"

"I would not think so," Hearst said.

"That is not what I meant, Mr. Hearst. Your second-rate novelist will not frame me."

"Maybe I can frame your lackey?" I said. "Someone needs to take the fall."

All eyes turned toward Kemper as he struggled to sit up. He didn't seem to grasp the implications.

"Irving? Is this true? Were all these people after the necklace?" Marion asked.

"Several players knew Dash had the item. The killer could be any of them," Thalberg replied. "Too bad, too. It was all going according to plan until Sharkey got greedy."

"I think it went a bit better than planned," I said.

"How so?" Bill asked, leaning forward. As they all were. I thought it unfortunate no one had brought a camera.

"Having convinced himself that I did indeed have the Blaze, Herr Münch went to Mr. Hearst and demanded its return. Just as Thalberg planned. But Herr Münch saw a bigger play. He would offer to keep the scandal secret in exchange for friendly press notices. That was a miscalculation. Tell me, sir, was secrecy your only offer? Or would you have allowed Mr. Hearst to keep the Silver Blaze as a bribe?"

"I deny all of this," Münch answered. "I came only to inquire about stolen property. Property you have confessed to obtaining illegally."

219

"That's one way of looking at it," I said. "Though if it were known that you attempted to blackmail Mr. Hearst, right here in his own home, that might not look so good in tomorrow's newspaper."

"No accusations have been made," Münch insisted.

I looked for Hearst's reaction. An accusation had been made, in the Billiard Room, and in my presence. Hearst could not have been happy about the German's deceit.

"Attempting to murder Miss LaRue won't look good in tomorrow's newspapers, either," Bill added. "A nice wholesome American girl strangled and beaten."

"I had nothing to do with that. Kemper..." Münch sputtered before stopping himself.

"Kemper confronted LaRue, hoping she knew where the necklace was, but it got out of control. Didn't it?" I suggested.

"She drew a knife. Stuck it in my ribs," Kemper said. "I acted in self-defense."

"And then you stashed her in my room," I mentioned.

"I was afraid. I panicked," Kemper admitted.

"Your room?" Knowles asked, staring in my direction. "How did Saucy end up in *my* room?"

"I confess, my friend, it was me," I said. "I know how you like a good joke."

Rocky scowled. I couldn't help smiling. Nor did I mention it was Saucy's idea to provoke trouble between Knowles and Kemper. A plan that worked brilliantly. I gave Saucy a quick wink.

"So what do you think, Herr Münch? Are you still threatening to accuse Mr. Hearst of soliciting stolen property?" I asked.

"Yes, Herr Münch. Is that your intention?" Hearst questioned.

"No. No, of course not. Such an idea never occurred to me," Münch replied.

"See that it doesn't. I will need to visit your country soon. Your new leader and I will have a talk," Hearst said.

"So, Lieutenant Kemper, do you admit to killing McCann?" I said, kneeling next to the couch. "It was an accident, wasn't it? Perhaps he got angry. Became aggressive. You pushed him backward, and the marble fell on him. Isn't that what happened?"

Kemper looked at the crowd staring at him, ready to denounce my accusation.

"If it was self-defense, I'm sure there will be no repercussions," I pressed. "And as a gesture of friendship, I believe Mr. Hearst will ignore this whole unfortunate incident. No shame will come to Herr Münch, or Germany, for this sordid business. What do you think, Mr. Hearst?"

Though Hearst appeared displeased, he was not anxious for a scandal. He reluctantly nodded.

"Herr Münch?" I asked.

Münch rubbed his chin thoughtfully, raised his monocle to study his assistant, and looked at me with a grudging respect. Kemper was holding his breath, waiting for his master's response.

"It was an accident," Münch conceded. "Lieutenant Kemper did everything he could for the poor man, but it was too late."

Kemper stared at Münch in disbelief. And resignation. I knelt down next to Münch and returned the monocle I'd won at the pool game. Fingerprints and all.

"I'll need something back for this," I warned.

"My pleasure, Dash," Münch said, tucking the trophy into his pocket.

"Did I play the game well, Herr Münch?"

"I wish you were German," he replied.

I returned to the fireplace, standing next to Bill.

"Well, ladies and gentlemen, I believe that concludes our business," I announced with relief.

"It doesn't conclude all of our business. What's going to happen to the necklace?" Johnny asked.

"That's a fair question," I said, letting the Silver Blaze hang in front of the fireplace, where the flames reflected its brilliance.

"It's beautiful," Maureen said, reaching out.

I let her hold it, thinking how gorgeous it would look around her slender neck. Then I let Norma and Marion have a glimpse. Norma admired the workmanship. Marion was less impressed, finding it gaudy.

Last but not least, I held the necklace up to Alice's throat, imagining her wearing it. The dance of the light from the fireplace matched the dance in her eyes.

"Thank you, Dash," she said, looking down.

"What do you think, Mr. Hearst?" I asked.

"The sooner it's off my ranch, the better," he replied.

I went to the other side of the room where Saucy was sitting next to Rocky, holding the Blaze up for a brief moment. She had seen it before.

"Here it is, Rocky. The dingus. The goods. The ice. The real thing," I said, holding it before him.

"I don't care about the damn rocks, Hammett. I want the reward," Rocky said.

I laughed and stepped to the big easy chair where Thalberg was sitting, pausing with the necklace held in both palms.

"Thank you, Dash. You've done a great job," Thalberg said, reaching to take it from me. But I drew the necklace back.

"I don't think so, Mr. Thalberg," I said, less than happy with the way he had manipulated me.

Siegel had moved from his big chair, standing next to Saucy. He smiled as I approached.

"Benny, I believe this belongs to the Rosenthal family," I said. "Perhaps you can return it to them?"

"It will be my pleasure," Bugsy said, shaking my hand.

Surprisingly, I woke up in time for breakfast. I packed my belongings and looked out the window, seeing a sunny day. The fog was gone. It would make driving back to Los Angeles easier.

Leaving my bag on the bed, I passed through the plaza on my way to the big house. The groundskeepers were back, trimming trees and weeding the flower beds. I noticed Carlos and tipped my fedora. He grudgingly smiled. Off to the side, I saw where the county coroner was removing McCann's body from the sarcophagus. He only had one assistant. They both looked bored.

Just inside the heavy doors, I encountered Tom on his way out. His suit was more casual. Without guests to cater to, he didn't need the butler outfit.

"Good to see you, Mr. Hammett," he said with a bow.

I glanced around to see if anyone was watching us, but no one was there.

"Mr. Wheatley, that should be, it's good to see you, Dash. And thank you. A good morning to you, too."

"Thank you, Dash. And thanks for letting me help."

"Your service was invaluable. Are you prepared to keep the secret?"

"I won't be telling anybody."

"It's better that way. Nothing good can come of it."

"I kin give you and Mr. Powell a ride down to your car after breakfast, if that's okay?"

"That will be fine," I said. "Where is Mr. Powell this morning?"

"He and Miss O'Sullivan are playing one last round of tennis. They be along soon."

I reached to shake his hand. He gave me a big grin and a firm grip.

Passing through the wide doors into the Assembly Room, I started down the hall toward the breakfast room. Just a few steps short of the kitchen, I was stopped by William Randolph Hearst. He was wearing his purple silk robe, thick bedroom slippers, and a wool scarf. I didn't know if he was wandering through the mansion or waiting for me.

"I hear you're leaving this morning," Hearst said.

By the tone, I could tell he thought it wasn't a moment too soon.

"Have appointments this afternoon. Mr. Thalberg wants to discuss a sequel to The Thin Man."

"Another Thin Man?"

"Who knows? Maybe there'll be a whole series of them," I hoped.

"You owe me scripts for Agent X-9. Don't make me find someone else."

"What's happening with McCann?"

"No questions so far. That may change after the autopsy."

"This may help," I said, taking a letter out of my coat pocket.

Hearst opened the envelope and took a moment to look it over.

"It's an affidavit. Signed by Ernst Münch," he concluded.

"Yes. It says his private secretary, Lt. Kemper, was drinking with Ambrose McCann when he fell into the planter and was fatally injured. The letter says that if the police have more questions, they can contact them at the German Embassy in Washington."

"How did you get this?"

"I traded a monocle for it. And a promise not to put any German villains in my next book," I answered, trying not to smile.

"This is not what I wanted, Mr. Hammett," Hearst said.

"It's the best I could do with what I had, sir. You and Miss Davies had nothing to do with Thomas Ince's death ten years ago, yet you've been suspected of murdering him ever since. This incident was much closer to home. No amount of explanations was going to avoid the worst kind of suspicions."

Hearst paused to think that over. He knew I was right.

"No laws have been broken, so far as I know. Keep it that way," he ordered.

"Yes, sir. No broken laws," I agreed.

Hearst gave a stern look, adjusted his robe, and turned toward a staircase leading up to the second floor. I would only see him one more time, two years later at the Vanderbilt Theater in New York. When he got up and walked out on one of Lillian Hellman's plays.

I glanced in the kitchen on my way back to the breakfast room, waving to Sara and whispering a thank you. I didn't see Julien. A moment later, I was entering the breakfast room, now flooded with morning light.

"Good morning, Dash. Sleep well?" Marion asked, sitting at the table with Alice.

With the fog having lifted early, they were prepared for a warm April day. Marion wore a frilly white dress and light make-up. Alice had a brown wool suit with a tight skirt going just below her knees. The room was otherwise empty, breakfast sitting in colorful platters. I noticed scrambled eggs, bacon, ham and cornbread. The coffee was steaming. I was hungry.

"Thank you, Miss Davies," I said, taking a seat. "Good morning, Alice."

"You look well. No hangover?" Alice inquired.

"No more than usual," I replied, helping myself to a full plate.

"I suppose you'll be leaving soon?" Marion said.

"Yes. Tom is giving Bill and I a ride down the hill."

"Did you enjoy your visit?" Marion asked.

"Very much. Thank you for providing a mystery. It made the weekend more memorable than most."

"Thank you for being discreet about the photos," she said.

"That's what we detectives do. We ferret out secrets. Solve crimes. Protect our clients," I said, giving her a strong look.

"Did Marion need so much protection?" Alice inquired.

"I had to fudge a bit when reporting to Mr. Hearst."

"How did Pops take the news?" Marion asked.

"Well enough, considering it's all a lie," I said.

"A lie?" Alice said.

"Please, ladies. We all know Kemper wasn't even on the hill Friday night," I said.

"I don't understand," Alice said.

I sipped my coffee before crunching on a slice of bacon. Excellent, as always. I was no stranger to the good life, though perhaps not this good. I doubted Hearst would ever extend me another invitation to his castle.

"Would you care to explain?" Marion asked.

"Are you sure you want me to?"

"I think it's best we all know where we stand," Marion answered.

She was one smart lady. Smarter than most I'd met in Hollywood.

"I thought you might say that, so I've written the name of the real killer on this piece of paper," I said, holding up a folded note. It was written on the same type of stationery all the other notes had been written on. A bit of irony there.

The women looked at each other with a trace of apprehension but betrayed little of their thoughts.

"I'm sorry, Marion, but if Kemper's confession doesn't fly, I may have to turn you in."

"No!" Alice said.

"If not Kemper, the police might pin it on someone else. Carlos or Tom. Or me. I can't let that happen, can I?"

"It wasn't Marion. I did it," Alice confessed.

"Alice, don't say that. You don't need to," Marion warned.

"I won't let you get in trouble," Alice insisted.

Marion looked at me. I pointed at the folded note. Marion read it, frowned, and then showed the paper to Alice. It read, *Alice.*

"You already knew?" Alice asked.

"It wasn't hard. Between the footprints, the fingerprints, the comings and goings during the movie, and you whacking me over the head with a shoe, there weren't really any other suspects."

"What do you think happened, Mr. Hammett?" Marion asked.

"After you met with Sharkey and refused to give him any money, Alice went to confront him. She was mad, anxious to protect you. Sharkey decided to take advantage, offering to lower his price in exchange for... shall we say, certain favors? Alice mentioned once that Sharkey was heavy with the claws."

Alice nodded, not realizing that while she had been probing me for information, she had divulged plenty of her own.

"At some point, he started moving toward Alice. She resisted. He grabbed her. Alice pushed him, and he stumbled backward into the marble box. When he started to climb out, probably making threats, she picked up Thalberg's forgotten cane and swung, hitting the support bar."

"I didn't mean to kill him. It was dark. I only swung to keep him back," Alice said.

"And then you went to Marion for help," I said. "The two of you tried to lift the lid, but it was too heavy. And it was obviously too late. One of you wiped the prints off Thalberg's cane and threw it in the bushes, then returned to the movie, hoping no one would discover your absence."

"Hard to prove, Mr. Hammett," Marion said with bent eyebrows.

"I have no intention of proving anything. Mr. Hearst asked me to find out what happened, and I did. My job is done."

"What does that mean?" Alice asked.

"It means you can do whatever you want with the information."

Both ladies visibly relaxed. For a moment.

"Does anyone else know?" Marion asked.

"Everyone has a different version of events, some more truthful than others," I answered. "Only you know about this note."

"And what do you want in exchange?" Marion asked.

"I've had trouble writing lately. I'd like to keep busy until my focus returns. But you're under no obligations. I wouldn't do that."

"That sounds fair," Marion agreed. "Alice, I think you should disappear for a while. Have time to recover. We have an office in New York that reviews Broadway plays."

"I like New York, but I'm going to miss you," Alice said.

"As I will miss you," Marion said. "So, is everything settled?"

I nodded and took another sip of my coffee. The eggs were good.

Marion gracefully left the room, looking satisfied with the results. I turned to Alice.

"I find myself in New York a lot these days," I said. "Maybe we can get together for drinks?"

Postscript

Irving Thalberg continued producing movies including *A Night at the Opera* and *Mutiny on the Bounty* until dying in 1936. He was 37 years old.

Norma Shearer retired in 1942. Known for playing strong independent women, she was nominated for six Academy Awards.

Johnny Weissmuller made ten more Tarzan movies before starring as Jungle Jim in 1948, forever typecast as a jungle-man.

Maureen O'Sullivan left Hollywood in 1942 to raise a family. She made five dozen movies in her career but remained best known for playing Jane.

William Powell was engaged to Jean Harlow until her sudden death in 1937. He appeared in five more *Thin Man* movies.

Benjamin "Bugsy" Siegel built the Flamingo Hotel in Las Vegas. In 1947, he was murdered in the home of actress Virginia Hill. He was 41.

William Randolph Hearst was close to bankruptcy near the end of the 1930s. Marion Davies wrote him a check for one million dollars.

Marion Davies retired in 1937 and remained with Hearst until his death in 1951. Out of respect for Hearst's widow, Marion did not attend the funeral.

Dashiell Hammett worked in Hollywood before joining the army during World War II. Blacklisted during the McCarthy Era, he died broke in 1961. After writing *The Thin Man*, he never published another novel.

Selected works of Dashiell Hammett

<u>NOVELS</u>
The Dain Curse (New York & London: Knopf 1930)
Red Harvest (New York & London: Knopf 1929)
The Maltese Falcon (New York & London: Knopf, 1930)
The Glass Key (New York & London: Knopf April 24, 1931)
The Thin Man (New York & London: Knopf 1934)

<u>*SECRET AGENT X-9*</u>
Secret Agent X-9 Book 1. David McKay, 1934. Written by Dashiell Hammett. Illustrated by Alex Raymond

Secret Agent X-9 Book 2. David McKay, 1934. Written by Dashiell Hammett. Illustrated by Alex Raymond

SELECTED SHORT STORIES BY DASHIELL HAMMETT
"A Man Called Spade" (July, 1932, The American Magazine)
"Too Many Have Lived" (October, 1932, The American Magazine
"They Can Only Hang You Once" (November 19, 1932, Colliers)
"Bodies Piled Up" (*Black Mask*, December 1, 1923)
"The Tenth Clew" ("The Tenth Clue") (*Black Mask*, Jan., 1924)
"One Hour" (*Black Mask*, April 1924)
"The Girl with Silver Eyes" (*Black Mask*, June 1924)
"Dead Yellow Women" (*Black Mask*, November 1925)
"The Gutting of Couffignal" (*Black Mask*, December 1925)
"Creeping Siamese" (*Black Mask*, March 1926)
"The Big Knock-Over" (*Black Mask*, February 1927)
"$106,000 Blood Money" (*Black Mask*, May 1927)
"The Main Death" (*Black Mask*, June 1927)
"The Cleansing of Poisonville" (*Black Mask*, November 1927)

Novels by Gregory Urbach

Dashiell Hammett and the Hearst Castle Mystery
When a body is discovered on the Hearst estate, America's
foremost mystery writer is given 48 hours to solve the crime

Rachel From the Edge
A brilliant young woman is hounded by a merciless press,
though not so merciless as her dead boyfriend's ex-wife

Magistrate of the Dark Land
A cowardly lawyer seeks two kidnapped
girls in a war-torn medieval land

Custer at the Alamo
Sent 40 years in the past by a spell of Sitting Bull, General Custer
and the 7th Cavalry join Davy Crockett to defend the Alamo

Custer and Crockett: After the Alamo
Stranded in time, General George Custer and
Davy Crockett set out to win independence for Texas

Diminished Capacity
Accused of shooting the president, a troubled war veteran
seeks redemption for his crime. But is he guilty?

Diminished Capacity 2: Second Chances
Jack Lawrence and the slain president's daughter seek to
build a new life in the glare of a relentless media

Waters of the Moon
Born on the moon and raised by computers, young Grey Waters struggled to survive in a world ruled by machines. But when travelers to his long-abandoned moonbase were threatened, he turned against his mentors to save the woman he loved

Tranquility's Child
Tranquility's End
Tranquility's Heirs
Tranquility Besieged
Tranquility in Darkness
Tranquility Down
Tranquility Divided
Tranquility Under the Eagles
Tranquility's Last Stand

Slave of Akrona
A mysterious castaway finds new love while challenging his overseers on a conquered alien planet

Rebels of Akrona
A soldier from another world struggles to free a conquered alien planet

About the Author

An avid student of history, Gregory Urbach has been writing adventure stories for nearly 30 years. From his days working for a campus newspaper, he has also pursued an interest in politics and popular culture. His degree in Urban Studies proved useful when writing the nine book Tranquility moonbase series. In 2013, he published his first fantasy novel, *Magistrate of the Dark Land*, followed by *Custer at the Alamo*, *Custer and Crockett*, and *Slave of Akrona*. In 2018, the crime thrillers *Diminished Capacity* and *Diminished Capacity 2* were released. All of the author's books reflect worlds where the concepts of good and evil are challenged by complicated realities.